Ashes
of the
Cinderbark

Andrew Towton

Towton Publishing

Ashes
OF THE
Cinderbark

ANDREW TOWTON

Ashes of the Cinderbark

For my mother, who encouraged me every step of the way.

ACKNOWLEDGEMENTS

Special thanks to Brian and Mike, whose feedback I greatly appreciate. And to Craig (aka Robotron), who taught me to love history.

Thanks to Cameron Slusar for my cover photo and to Wendy Dewar Hughes for editing and book design.

CHAPTER ONE

With the honed skills of a practiced skulker, Ivo wormed his way through the narrow cracks in the crowd. Like honey poured over a crusty loaf, he oozed deeper into the packed masses. Most of the people had donned their best outfits: coloured hoods and split tunics, along with long, form-fitting hose and calfskin boots. Ivo's heart jumped. The only time the crowd got this fancied up was when there was a burning. Or a beheading. In a land where soot blocked the sun, the people still found ways to entertain themselves. Staring down at his ragged red tunic, Ivo couldn't help feeling underdressed. Nor could he deny a nagging sense of isolation: groups of people chatted amongst themselves, laughing and cursing, and enjoying their day out. Husbands held wives close, and friends shared skins of cheap wine.

Who knows? Today might be my lucky day. Maybe there was a woman in the crowd willing to stoop to Ivo's level. Or failing that, someone to keep him from drinking alone.

Halfway into the teeming mass, the speaker's voice became clear. It was a dry, old voice, one that belonged to a man with enough money to have lived far too long.

"... and our fair Rendsheim will be the first to find this great gift, and once again make this city one of the wonders of the world!"

Oh great, Ivo thought, *he's trying to sell us on something.* No doubt this was one of Rudolph's lackeys, giving a speech in an attempt to make the Duke appear more amiable. It was bound to be a long, drawn out affair. Despite this prospect, Ivo decided to stay, even if there wasn't going to be an execution. Better than counting the rats in his cellar or watching rainbows in the creosote-choked waterways. Besides, it gave him time to ogle potential mates.

The unseen speaker continued, growing ever more passionate. His voice bounced off the close-packed houses that pressed in on the great square. "This tool of the gods will let us fill the world with the wonders of the ancients! The mighty wyverns and sturdy Wollok will again be known to these lands. And, greatest of all, we shall once again see Cinderbark flourish as it did in the time of our fathers! Once more, the forges will burn with this noble tree, and once more Rendsheim will be the centre of the world!"

Another roar rose from the crowd.

Burn it all to cinder, these idiots will cheer for anything, Ivo mused.

"But," the speaker continued once the cheers had died down, "such a venture requires great sacrifice. Duke Rudolph, in his most benevolent wisdom, has surmised that no doubt others would seek the same prize as we do. Even as we speak, the lecherous, conniving Borig of Stahlsheim is mustering a force to march to this fabled temple! The wretch would see the yoke of the old monarchy placed upon Rendsheim once again! And place his putrid lineage on the throne!" Ivo chuckled uneasily, a thin smile crossing his gaunt features. The way they described Borig just about sums up every noble he had ever heard of.

After much booing and hissing directed toward Borig's name, the speaker added, "…which is why his Royal Sir, Duke Rudolph, has imposed a city wide conscription." The crowd went silent, and the faint sound of armoured boots on paving stones echoed from the side streets.

"Starting in this very square, all able-bodied men between seventeen and fifty winters are required to serve a maximum of two years military service. Any attempting to resist will be punished to the fullest extent of our just and fair courts."

Ivo froze, eyes stuck open and mouth agape. For a moment, it seemed as if he had simply died as he stood. The thought of conscription terrified Ivo more than eating the food from the merchants by the sewers. He was a pacifist—a coward, to the layman. His toughest opponent to date was a plank of pine that was more knot than tree, and though he managed to make a passable bench he was left weeping over his blistered hands.

Ivo knew he had to escape. With uncharacteristic grace, he spun on his heels, only to be greeted by the dull sheen of a regiment of soldiers blocking his planned escape. Ivo's head twisted around as he realized that during the orator's rousing speech over a hundred armed and armoured thugs had encircled the town square. Wide-brimmed helmets covered their heads, each blackened from the heat of the forge and left unpolished. Great chainmail coats shielded most of the infantry, the rusting rings layered under thick, padded tunics, as stained as their helmets. Worst of all were their weapons; gnarled, hooked things that were one part axe and one part pick. These monstrous tools came from the tools charcoal workers used, with hooks to pull lighter logs and cutting edges to trim larger ones. Ivo didn't want to picture their effect against unguarded flesh.

Frantic, Ivo searched for an exit. In his rush to find a safe way home, he bowled over the old, the sick, and anyone smaller and weaker than he. In his haste, Ivo failed to notice the soldier until he buried his face in copious chest hair. The infantryman had done away with his mail jacket, and instead wore a greasy aketon. The padding reeked of old broth, onion, and sweat.

Vainly spitting chest hairs, Ivo felt a meaty fist clamp his slim shoulder. The soldier bent close enough that the quaking carpenter nearly retched at the man's fetid breath.

"Going somewhere?" the soldier rumbled, cocking an eyebrow.

Ivo shrank from the hulking bruiser, eyes on his feet. He struggled to say something, anything, to get out of this mess. "I don't... not... don't qualify..."

The soldier's porcine features took on a quizzical quality, as if the brain behind the face wasn't quite as small as his appearance suggested. "Well, you do look scrawny for a lad of seventeen," the man said, mocking sympathy. He brought his other filthy paw to Ivo's face. It stank of dung and blood.

The soldier grabbed Ivo's pointed chin, and ran a thumb across the light dusting of stubble. "But this little patch o' scrub makes me think you ain't seventeen. So either you's be one of the ugliest women I've ever seen, or you's been lying to me." He leaned in even closer. In a raspy whisper, he added, "An' you wouldn't be lyin' to me, would you, bud?"

Ivo just kept his eyes down. "Good. Then step into line, you little shit!" The soldier shoved Ivo into the murmuring crowd, where he was caught up in the flow of moving flesh. Hundreds of people edged along, poor bastards like him, looking for an escape from the prospect of a miserable existence of drills, rations, and bodily harm.

His dark eyes darted from side to side as he walked on his toes, casting about for some alley or ditch to throw himself down. Such opportunities presented themselves in the urban sprawl of Rendsheim, but now Ivo saw that a number of crossbow toting goons had joined their polarm-bearing brethren, bolts loaded and ready to fire. Though his scrawny frame made a small target, Ivo decided not to test the accuracy of the city's defense force.

Ivo knew he was trapped like a rat stuck in the tar pits by the sewers. He looked skyward, eyes watering as he watched the plumes of smoke rise from crumbling chimneys. Self-loathing and defeatism flooded his being. *Why did I leave the bloody house?*

The winding, pitted streets of Rendsheim took the unwilling crowd past the vast walls of the city, the road inclining at a manageable angle. Shutters closed as the procession passed run-down homes. Squads of soldiers bashed down doors and hauled men out by their collars anyway. All were thrown into the throng, prodded by wicked billhooks and cruel swords. Their final destination was clear.

Cinder Gap.

Ivo knew the place too well. The thugs from the market square herded the crowd of press-ganged sods towards the expansive bridge that crossed the dale between Rendsheim and the Charred Hill, upon which sat the city's barracks. The Hill itself had long been built over, with nothing left of the original mound. Now, the ramparts were a sheer face of sun-bleached stone, set in a perfect circle over two hundred feet away from the walls of Rendsheim. A squat, rotund bastion found perch at the far end of the circle, with training grounds set around the perimeter. Smoke poured from unseen pipes and vents that honeycombed the Hill; the furnaces and refineries nestled deep within the structure worked nonstop.

The gap between the city and the hill dropped fifty feet into a rocky gorge with nothing but dead grass and cinder to break one's fall. Considering how narrow the bridge was, it was a wonder more people didn't make the trip down. Surprisingly ornate for military stonework, the bridge was divided into twenty-foot sections, with each section being marked by a wider platform that sat upon great stone pillars. The side railing, uniformly rising and dipping in crenellations, offered little protection from a slip.

Pressed forward from behind, Ivo found himself looking over the edge as he migrated to the far left side. Ash swirled past as it blew from the city's charcoal pits, grey clumps sticking to his chopped auburn hair as he peered into the chasm below. It was hardly the first time he had stared down the gap. He could count on both hands how many times he'd found himself looking down upon the merciful rocks, contemplating whether or not to make the jump. The only difference now was someone might try to stop him. *Just my luck.*

The carpenter inhaled deeply. He was screwed, no two ways about it. Mustering what little willpower he had, he steeled himself. *Really*, Ivo pondered, *how bad could a few months in the army be? Food, rooming, medical expenses...*

A cry came up from Charred Hill, sharp and shrill. The call for a medic soon followed. An injury on the training grounds.

Ivo's pupils narrowed as his eyes went wide. *Laceration, disembowelment, amputation...* so much for making the best of a bad situation. By the time he had crossed the bridge, he was quivering like a mound of tar.

Absorbed in self-pity, Ivo failed to notice one of the guards creeping up on him. A harsh, raspy, "Don't worry," was spat in his ear. Ivo jumped, wheeled, and searched for something nearby with which to defend himself. All he saw was the gap riddled grin of a soldier, clad in the standard issue chainmail coat.

"No need to be so jumpy, little fella," the man grunted. "You won't have to go through the training grounds."

Ivo drew in a quick breath.

"Naw, they'll be too busy scraping you out of the bloodworks once Brutus is done with you." Ivo's heart dropped and he clutched his gut. He had heard legends about old Brutus from his half cousin, who had served as a guard for twenty years. She said he was as old as the Charred Hill, and about half the weight. More scar than man, he was the one who evaluated, assigned, and broke new recruits. If you walked away with a few bruises and cuts, you were a shoe in for the Duke's guard or the elite divisions. The remaining recruits usually had to be stitched up and carried to their units.

The grinning soldier gave Ivo a hefty shove and continued to shadow the wild-eyed conscript. Ivo looked around to take stock. Herded like cattle, the entire group from the town square was being funnelled into the bastion's mighty ironclad doors. As the bastion grew closer, its scale became apparent. Hardly squat, the tower loomed over the training area, immense enough to house an army.

It's gonna need to house an army, Ivo thought as he and the last of the conscripts were prodded inside.

In the pressed huddle of the pack, and at his slight height, all Ivo could see were the hooded heads of those around him. If he didn't know better, he would have thought he was in some packed, poorly lit tavern. The sounds, however, told a much more sinister story.

It started as a faint tapping of metal on metal, barely audible. A frenzied collection of clangs, grunts, and eventually screaming followed. The time between these sounds varied, from a few seconds to a minute at the longest, but always in the same order. A few times, the crunch of bone or the plop of meat on stone replaced the scream, echoed by a heavy thud as something dropped to the ground. Then, a deep bass, "Next," reverberated through the room, and the mob grew smaller by one person.

It wasn't long before Ivo was able to take in the main spectacle. At the centre of the room, illuminated by creosote-burning lamps, stood the most gargantuan man Ivo had ever seen.

A thumb-like head thrust up between a pair of inhumanly broad shoulders, which strained at a worn red arming jacket. A wide, almost comical moustache dramatically shot horizontally across his face, crooked and stained dark with grease and sweat. One cold black eye glared into the crowd from under its shaggy brow, the other completely absent from its shadowed socket. To say his gut ballooned would be doing the man's paunch a disservice. Ivo was unable to find the words to describe this monumentally grotesque individual.

Then, Ivo caught the shimmer of something he had never seen in his lifetime. Across the man's sprawling girth was a scarred and pitted breastplate, not like the coats of plates the guards wore, but made from two colossal slabs of steel. *It has to be a relic*, he thought. There wasn't a forge left on the continent hot enough to make plates that size. It was forged using pyroquettes, charcoal made from the extinct Cinderbark.

This must be Brutus. None but the duke's most trusted soldiers would have been given a set of such rare armour.

Still glowering at the crowd with his one good eye, Brutus thundered, "Next", shaking the flagstones of the tower. When no one stepped up, the trainer took matters into his own hands. He stomped towards the gathered crowd, grabbed the nearest victim and hurled him into the light. The middle-aged man in a tan tunic landed heavily in a dark crimson pool. Blood.

A sword joined him, thrown by a guard lurking in the shadows. Brutus had assumed his position at the other end of the makeshift arena, hefting a solid steel sledgehammer. At least Ivo thought it was a sledgehammer; it could have been a steel cart axel capped with a small anvil.

The poor bastard across from Brutus got to his feet, blood dripping from his sleeves. The blade now found an unsteady place in his right hand. It was by no means a small sword, but compared to Brutus' hammer, it looked like a woodworkers knife.

Nonchalantly waving at the conscript, Brutus began the evaluation.

With all the confidence of a press-ganged peasant, the man froze, refusing to take the fight to Brutus. The mammoth trainer rolled his one good eye, and muttered under his breath. It was clear to Ivo he took no delight in his job.

In three earthshaking steps, Brutus cleared the distance between him and his cowering combatant. The man barely had time to bring his sword up before the massive trainer swung his hammer into the conscript's knees. The poor sod crumpled to the ground, squealing as he clutched the bloody mess of his ruined legs.

Even before the man hit the ground, Brutus barked to a nearby guard bearing a long, ragged piece of parchment. "Slow reaction time, no attempt to defend himself. Take him to the engineers, let them sort out this mess."

Without a word, another guard descended on the crippled peasant, hauling him screaming into the darkness at the far side of the room. Once his echoing cries could no longer be heard, Brutus turned to the crowd and once again bellowed, "Next."

Before he could find a corner to slink into, Ivo found himself flung forward by the same gap-toothed guard who had hounded him at the bridge. "Have fun with this one, Brutus!" he called before finding a good spot to stand and watch.

Ivo pushed himself up from his hands and knees, and stared up at the mountain of fat and muscle before him. He felt like a mouse under the gaze of a cat. Had he not voided himself earlier, surely he would be doing so now.

Ivo gaped wide-eyed at the monumental warrior standing across from him. Brutus gave the young carpenter one good look up and down, before shouting over his shoulder, "Shield!" then brought his steely gaze back to Ivo and nodded to his left.

What does that nod mean? Ivo failed to notice the linen-covered training shield twirling his way.

With a crack, the four foot long shield caught the lad square in the ribs, bottom point first. Ivo's vision went fuzzy, and flashes of light filled his eyes as agony shot through him. For a moment, he stood firm; the shield rattled against the cobblestone floor. He gritted his teeth as he stared down Brutus. Then a low moan escaped from him before he dropped like a bag of charcoal, hard and sudden.

Brutus would have none of it. He glowered at the chuckling soldier who had lobbed the shield. "My quarters. After training."

"On your feet or in the morgue, new meat!" Brutus barked at Ivo who hauled himself up, using the tall shield as a support.

His vision still blurry, he fiddled with the straps of the shield, binding it to his left arm. The shield itself wasn't fancy, no doubt made in the barracks out of leftover timber. It was heavy, unbalanced, and uglier than the rear end of a Wollok, but felt surprisingly reassuring nonetheless.

Ivo turned back to the instructor. It was clear there was no avoiding this. If he kept his head down and his limbs un-smashed and he might survive long enough to see his hovel again. Mentally steeling himself, Ivo readied for combat.

Wait. No one had given him a sword.

Apparently, Brutus wasn't concerned with Ivo's lack of weapon. The brute was barging towards Ivo, hammer raised, aimed at his skull. Ivo hugged the shield to his chest. The hammer smashed into its timbers with a groan and splinter. The impact of the hit threw him off balance swinging him to the left. Brutus changed his footing, and brought the hammer back in the opposite direction. Ivo managed to swing the shield in front of him again, deflecting the meteoric impact to the side.

There was no time to congratulate himself. He was far too busy trying not to die. The third swing came too fast for him, whistling as it swept under the shield where it caught him in the legs. The young carpenter clenched his teeth and awaited the sickening crack of his knee shattering.

But the only crack that came was his skull on the floor. Mercifully, Brutus had elected to hook Ivo's leg with the head of his hammer, pulling it from under him and sending the conscript sprawling. Ivo landed heavily on his back, the shield nearly twisting his arm from its socket. Dazed, Ivo could just make out the shape of a hammer, flying towards his unprotected face.

With a thud and a spray of dust, Brutus' hammer landed inches from Ivo's right ear. The instructor had let Ivo go without a broken bone, but it appeared he still had to show the whelp his place. And it had worked; Ivo lay on the ground for a good twenty seconds before he dared breathe again. Brutus just snorted before shouting over his shoulder, "Basic defensive ability. Strong survival instinct. Put him with the pavisiers."

Ivo tried to sit up. His right ear was deaf from the ringing of the hammer. The shield, still strapped to his arm, tilted at an awkward angle. *Better than the infantry or engineer battalions*, he thought, shaking his head. The engineers were too labor intensive and the infantry offered too high a risk of bodily harm.

Too bad he had no idea what a pavisier was.

CHAPTER TWO

Ivo soon learned that each barracks was a self-contained affair of about five hundred square feet, and fit everything a unit of fifty needed. After being shoved down corridor after corridor by vicious guards, he stood near the entrance and looked around. The low walls were a collection of timber and iron fittings, and large lamps set in regular intervals. Above him the bustle of the next floor could be heard, footsteps and muffled voices emanating from the thick planks.

The far wall was stacked three high with rugged, stained bunks, interspersed with a few aged tables and benches. These cramped, dim quarters continued for half the length of the hall, the rest being taken up by various tools of the crossbowman's trade.

The last fifty feet of the hall were lined with weapon stands and armour racks. Small wooden plaques carved with names and initials denoted the owners of different pieces of kit. Ivo was sure most of the people in the hall couldn't read the scribbling—hell, he couldn't read it himself—but this seemed like a place with draconian punishments for theft.

Ivo noticed a squat counter to his right, along with a podgy hog in an apron and stained green tunic. It seemed anyone who was anyone in this place had a potbelly like a prize-winning pig's. *The quartermaster, I hope.* Inhaling the thick, rank air, Ivo moved towards the counter.

Scrounging up enough courage to look up from his feet, Ivo was greeted with the back of the quartermaster's head. A long mane of greasy red hair covered his non-existent neck. He was tapping away at boot nails, unaware of the gaunt, bug-eyed scrub standing behind him.

Ivo coughed into his hand. When there was no response, he inhaled deeper and coughed louder. Still no response. Ivo inhaled all his scrawny frame would allow and heaved into his hand. The quartermaster shot around faster than Ivo expected from a man of his bulk.

"Scorch your bones, Hugo, go down to the healer's quarters or I'll send you there myself..." he cried, his voice thick with accent. Then his eyes widened. "Oh," he said, "new blood. Sorry. Thought you were someone else."

The quartermaster's thick, frizzy beard hung to his chest, uniformly flat, and clearly burned by the heat of a furnace. The man's grey eyes peered out of his thick skull, lined black with soot.

"Well, I guess you'll be needin' your kit then." He began to rummage through a pile of discarded gear on the floor. "Now what was your assignment?" he called over his shoulder.

"Pavisier...I think," Ivo returned. The quartermaster nodded, and continued to dig.

"You know, lucky we're getting a few more of your lot. Been long on gear and short on manpower since last winter."

"What happened last winter?"

The quartermaster shuddered. "The unit was nearly wiped out, that's what bloody happened. Duke Lug sent us out to "pacify" some backwards-arse hamlet a day's march from Rendsheim. Middle of the winter no less! Nearly lost my bollocks in the frost." He flung a cracked helmet to the side. "Well, the folk at the hamlet weren't workin' alone. No sooner do we start shooting at 'em that we see Duke Borig's boys coming in from the side. They charged us—most of 'em were on horses. Been short on manpower ever since."

Ivo's lips drew tight as his brow furrowed. The quartermaster raised an eyebrow. "You a conscript?"

"Yes, as of today," Ivo mumbled, slumping forwards.

"Shite, you don't even get paid for this." The burly man shook his head as he looked another helmet over. "I tell you, Duke Lug has somethin' in mind, and it's never good..."

Finally, the quartermaster got up. In his calloused hands he gripped a broad-brimmed helmet, like those the other soldiers wore, and a stitched up aketon with a high collar. "Well, lucky you then," the quartermaster continued. "You got the easy bit. We work in twos here—one pavisier and one crossbowman. The crossbows do all the hard work, loadin' and shootin' and the like, and all you got to do is lug around the pavise for 'em."

Ivo cocked his head. "Pavise?"

The quartermaster nodded. "Fancy foreign word for a big bloody shield. You plonk 'er down, and you and your crossbow buddy are safe from any unwanted attention. Well, at least from the front..." The quartermaster set Ivo's gear on the table. "Don't worry, we'll get you yours at basic training. For now, here's your armour, belts, and a few pouches."

Ivo picked the gear up and found it surprisingly heavy for such a small amount of iron.

"It may be just padding," the quartermaster commented, "but that jacket can stop a crossbow bolt at fifty paces. Just don't try it, doesn't work all the time. Last guy wearing this figured that out right quick." The quartermaster tapped on a large seam stitched over the chest, stained darker than the rest of the aketon.

The quartermaster then pointed to the weapon and armour stands at the other end of the hall. "Find an empty spot, mark it, and leave your gear there. Then go circulate. Probably a good idea to meet your partner, seein' as you'll be workin' together." The quartermaster swept his arm to a circle of grunting soldiers playing dice around a table. "She's hard to miss. Got a scar that'd make a medical cadaver blush."

Ivo deposited his kit on an unclaimed stand, eyeing his peers' equipment. Coats of chainmail reinforced with hardened leather and small, overlapping plates hung on nearby pegs. A few even incorporated sections of pyroquette steel. Ivo noted they were a marked improvement from his blood- and sweat-drenched aketon. As he stepped away from the racks, he swore the stink of the jacket would never leave his nostrils.

His hands now free, Ivo did his best to pick out his assigned partner from the gambling soldiers. He could make out many, many scars by the light of the candle at their table. Each looked deeper than the last, criss-crossing faces like the old roads on maps. Ivo would have to get closer to find his quarry.

Ivo crept toward the table. Sitting between two rows of bunks, it was a snug affair, each soldier sitting shoulder to shoulder with his or her comrades. It would be a tight squeeze for Ivo to get closer, so he chose to stand at the edge of the group and peered over shoulders. Of the twelve soldiers assembled, three were women. *That narrows it down.*

Puffing out his chest, Ivo squeaked, "Excuse me..."

In an instant all eyes at the table were on him. The conscript's pupils narrowed. *I'm gonna die, I'm gonna die, I'm gonna die...*

Ivo's best impression of a statue lasted a minute before one of the soldiers stood up to confront him. She was a foot taller than he, and towered over him even from the other side of the table. Broad shouldered, she still wore her pale aketon, which was surprisingly well maintained. And the woman certainly filled it out; she was sturdily built with powerful arms and a strong core. Her medium-sized bust and wide hips betrayed a feminine shape, reminiscent of the tribes of old. Not lingering at her chest too long in fear of reprisal, Ivo moved his gaze to her face.

With her sharp, narrow chin and a long, narrow nose, it seemed to Ivo every feature on this woman was sharp—her grey eyes in particular—sharper than a woodsman's axe and the same colour as fresh ash. Her black hair was cut short, and shaved along either side. A jagged, pale scar ran from just under her missing earlobe to the bottom of her chin. *At least I found my partner.*

The whole time Ivo was taking in the soldier, she was sizing him up. "You gonna stand there lock jawed or are you going to piss off?" she barked, a sentiment echoed by the rest of the table.

"I...I..."

She reached for her belt, hand at the hilt of her dagger.

Like an unclogged drain, Ivo began to spew. "I'm your new replacement shield bearer guy and I don't know why I'm here. PLEASE DON'T KILL ME!" His arms shot up to cover his face. The woman raised an eyebrow, disgust crossing her face.

"You're my new pavisier? Really. Roland is either having a laugh or he really wants me dead."

From the other side of the room, the quartermaster retorted, "Be nice to the scrub, Helena. He just got conscripted, and he doesn't even want to be here. Give him a chance."

Ivo nodded dumbly from behind his concealing hands, and parroted, "Yeah, please be nice to the scrub."

Helena shook her head. "They'll be replacing you in a week, toothpick. How you got past Brutus is beyond me, but here you got to earn respect."

Ivo nodded.

"What's your name, scrub?" Helena asked, sitting back down.

"I-Ivo."

Helena leaned back, thought furrowing her brow. "Hmm, I knew an Ivo once, panhandler who worked up and down the streets of Blacklung Road. Found him dead in a ditch, head caved in." She leaned forward. "Odds are you'll end up like him."

Ivo remained silent. Helena stared down her new shield bearer. "Tell you what scrub. Either grow a pair and say something back, or piss off and play with yourself in the corner."

Ivo chose the latter. He left the jeering cluster behind, and head down, he moped his way to the farthest corner of the room he could find, slid into an unused bunk, and wept. He was too tired to cry, but internally he bawled.

I'm stuck. Stuck with her, here. He tried to invoke every god he had ever heard of, his sniffling prayers mumbled into his pillow.

It was a gentle, steady tap that pulled Ivo from his gloom. He rolled in his louse-infested bunk, wiping his nose on his sleeve. *What does she want?* he wondered, assuming his new partner had come to mock him further. But it wasn't Helena's razor sharp mug. Rather it was the great, stinking beard of the unit's quartermaster. The hefty fellow was bent over as he peered into Ivo's sanctuary of straw and sheets.

Ivo looked his visitor up and down. A small pouch dangled daintily between Roland's sausage-like fingers. To Ivo it appeared to be full of many small, round items. *Embers. Gotta be! Maybe I could bribe my way out...*

"Look," Roland began, rubbing his thick neck, "don't let Helena get to ya. She's seen more shield bearers die than you've had bad meals. She never has a partner for more than a month, they either drop dead or are too buggered up to serve."

Ivo's brow furrowed. The quartermaster continued. "You can't see that much death and be all right in the head, especially when its people you work with closely. But give 'er time, she'll warm to you. I hope." The quartermaster handed over the dainty bag. "Anyhoo, I brought ya these."

Ivo recoiled. The strong smell of oil and soot burned his nose. Roland brought his meaty fist back, and opened the pouch. "Don't worry, it's not goin' ta hurt ya! Just a little somethin' to lighten the mood."

Roland handed Ivo the open pouch. Trepidation gave way to curiosity. Ivo nudged away from the safety of the bunk to take a peek. Within the leather pouch was a dozen or so small, round cookies, the kind served on holidays.

Ivo looked up at Roland's beaming face, plastering on a false smile of his own. It may not have been what he wanted, but it was better than nothing. "Picked these up on my trip into town," Roland said, a grinning. Even though a few teeth short and as yellow as timber, the man's smile made Ivo brighten.

The quartermaster gently placed the pouch next to Ivo. "Was gonna eat them myself," he stated, "but you looked like you needed 'em more than me." The timber creaked as he planted himself next to the Ivo on the bunk. "Look, I'm sorry you got roped into this. It ain't an easy life, soldiery, and frankly it's an outrage paupers like yourself are getting press-ganged into service."

"Actually, I'm a carpenter. Guild certified."

Roland raised an eyebrow as he looked over Ivo's bargain-bin tunic. He shook his head. "At any rate, I feel bad for ya. Torn away from your friends and family, your warm bed and your roaring fire."

Do I tell him I have none of those?

"It takes a special kind of person to be a soldier. And I know it'll be a harsh few weeks for ya. Just gotta keep lookin' forward." With a mighty thump on Ivo's back, Roland got up and plodded back to his counter. He gave Ivo one last nod before returning to sort the units supplies.

Ivo watched the quartermaster as he worked, not entirely sure about what had just transpired. He couldn't remember the last pep talk he got, but he was certain there was no exchange of baked goods. Gingerly, Ivo reached into the open pouch and grabbed one of the small cookies. He held it like a precious gem, and brought it up to his gaze, taking in the glorious, uneven edges and the small chunks of dried fruit. The crust felt soft and crumbly, like the finest charcoal in the world. He popped the little cookie into his mouth, slowly chewing the tender, luscious tidbit. It almost melted on his tongue, the buttery treat eliciting memories of a childhood Ivo had only dreamed of. He thought of friends he'd never met at ponds where he'd never been, and lovers he had never loved in places still unseen. Ivo didn't care if his memories were real or not. Right now it was he and these cookies.

"Taste better than Embers," he mumbled to himself.

CHAPTER THREE

Ivo lay awake in the long hours of the early morning dark. His unit's schedule had them in bed at sundown, the candles blown out and the soldiers to their bunks. The execution was precise, each soldier having been drilled to prepare for bed in near unison. What they had failed to do, however, was train the soldiers not to snore.

There are watermills quieter than these louts! A rumbling, rolling ruckus rocked the room without rest! *Must be all the broken noses,* Ivo mused. Whatever it was, it made sleeping nigh on impossible. He tried to stuff his ears with cloth and cover his head with a straw pillow, but nothing would keep out the noise. Three hours in, Ivo had given up, content to rest his eyes while thoughts blew through his mind like soot through the fields. Images of blackened steel, honed by hand, clattering against his boney frame haunted him. Shivers shot down his crooked spine. His mind raced and he could find no way to calm himself.

Really, he thought, *how much fighting do crossbowmen do? They spend the whole time lobbing bolts over the unlucky ones. Maybe all those scars are from poor shaving.* He paused for a moment, realizing how flawed his logic was. Most of the women in the unit were also cut up like a rat served for lunch, and Ivo was sure not all of them grew facial hair.

He blew out one last, prolonged sigh before sleep finally hit him like a sack of charcoal.

Morning came far too soon. As a carpenter, he got most of his work done after lunch, and it had been a year since he had seen the sunrise stain the ashen clouds over the city red. So when the unit commander gave the wake up call, Ivo didn't respond. Three hours of sleep and a day filled with worry and work had left him about as fit for training as a corpse.

Ivo heard rattling intrude on his sleep, the sound like a giant bag of coins tossed down a flight of stairs. A tap on his shoulder elicited a soft groan, but sleep still held him.

In an instant, Ivo felt himself yanked out of bed with enough force to send him flying into the bunk across the hall. Crashing down onto the hard timbers of the floor, he shot awake and ready to scurry to the nearest hidey-hole he could spy.

All he saw were the cold, blue eyes of a seasoned soldier. She was much like Helena; obviously female, but built like a workhorse. Her head had been cleanly shaven, and she kept herself well groomed. But her broad chin and protruding cheekbones made it clear she was by no means a woman of wealthy breeding. Ivo surmised she was a farmer's daughter who had made a name for herself in the military.

"On your feet," she commanded, the sternness brought Ivo scrambling up. Looking over her new soldier, she bluntly stated, "I didn't think we press-ganged beggars into service these days."

A flash assessment told Ivo her torso was completely covered in a coat of heat-blackened mail, with a solid, arching plate worn over the belly. Interlaced within the rings were small, heat-treated plates, not pyroquette quality, but still sturdier than what they had given Ivo.

"Actually, miss..."

"Sir," she cut him off, her gaze darkening at his insubordination.

"Sorry mi- sir!" Ivo mewed.

"Sorry doesn't fix gashes or grow back limbs. Now I recommend you get your shit together, and form up with the rest of the unit. Training yard in twenty minutes."

Putting her armoured hands behind her back, she wheeled on the spot and marched towards the doors. "By the by," she called back, "breakfast was an hour ago. Good luck making it to lunch."

Outside on the west side of the Charred Hill, the clouds of soot had thinned enough the sun could be picked out from the haze. Picnic weather anywhere else, but for Ivo it only provided a marginally pleasant backdrop to his suffering. Starved, tired, and anxious, he wished he had taken the chance to jump down Cinder Gap.

The whole unit had gathered in the far left field of the massive fortification, flanked by specialized grounds that Ivo assumed were for riding practice. They were outfitted in full combat gear. This meant his stinking jacket and a helmet that hinted at the smell of boiled cabbages. *Maybe the last guy used it as a cooking pot,* Ivo considered.

Nervously glancing from under the brim of his helmet, Ivo surveyed the field. It was plain and empty, save for two stands. One contained thirty crossbows, left unstrung and propped up on their stocks. The other was stacked with a similar number of shields. At least Ivo thought they were shields; to him they had as much in common with a shield as a mountain did with an anthill.

Rectangular monstrosities, curved slightly and rounded at the top, each shield was at least an inch thick and covered in a heavy linen coat painted with the small ember. Standing at over five feet tall and half as wide, they would cover the carrier and anyone standing behind him or her.

Ivo knew he wasn't getting a crossbow, and that meant he'd be forced to lug the shield about. His shoulders sank even lower. Looking around, he saw a few other fresh faces, conscripts like him at odds with the tough-as-nails regulars. *At least I'm not suffering alone,* he thought.

The two groups were divided, veterans on one side and fresh meat on the other. The ratio was two conscripts for every veteran. Ivo assumed this was in case the unit lost a couple greenhorns to training.

The commander, who had been speaking to Roland, now marched towards her unit. The clanking of armour heralded her arrival, and the regulars went silent, standing at the ready. The conscripts huddled a little closer at her approach. Ivo found himself surrounded.

The commander wasted no time. "Today we cover basic training, for both crossbowmen and pavisiers. For the regulars, you know the drill, but for the conscripts, this will introduce you to your charge. A pavisier is harmless without the crossbow, and a crossbowman is dead without his shield bearer. Any questions?"

She scanned the two groups of soldiers. "Grab your gear from the quartermaster. Two lines." The regulars marched off, conscripts trailing behind.

Moving as one cluster, the greenhorns shuffled toward the shields, and the warm, greasy face of the quartermaster.

"That's the saddest line I've seen in thirteen years. Shape up," the commander hollered. Bumping into one another, the conscripts formed sloppy line.

From the far side of the fields came the thunk of firing crossbows as the regulars took shots at straw targets arrayed at the other end of the field. The conscript in front of Ivo fumbled with the arm straps on the shield, buckled the shoulder harness to the wrist buckle, and pulled his head down in the mess of straps. It took Roland a good five minutes to sort the lad out. With a slap on the shoulder, he sent him to whatever abuse awaited him.

Then it was Ivo's turn. Roland, who was wearing the same green tunic as yesterday, brightened. "Hope you slept well, Mr...uh..."

"Ivo." He was too tired for niceties.

"Right," Roland nodded. "Well, we'll get ya set right up,

Mr. Ivo." The quartermaster bent over, grunting, and browsed his selection of shields. "The 1st Arbalesters always get the good stuff..." he mumbled.

He hefted a pavise from its slot in the rack, and waddled toward Ivo. What made this shield better than the others, Ivo couldn't tell, but he wasn't about to argue with a quartermaster.

"Righty ho, then," Roland said, handing Ivo the shield. Taking it in both hands, he nearly toppled once all the weight was on him. The shield made contact with the ground, and then with a thunk, Ivo's brow connected with the hard edge of the shield.

Roland laughed heartily, and even a few of the nervous conscripts chuckled at Ivo's misfortune. He rubbed his head, scowling at his comrades.

"Don't worry 'bout the smack," Roland said, patting Ivo on the shoulder. "Happens more often than ya'd think. Now this is how you carry it."

Roland helped Ivo get the shoulder harness over his head and around the warped curve of his back, before latching his arm into the straps near the upper portion of the shield. It would be near impossible to get himself out of all the straps should the need to suddenly flee arise.

"So why aren't any of the regulars over here?" Ivo said, looking around.

"Well..." Roland began, "to be blunt, you don't usually live long enough to be a regular in this job." Ivo's eyes widened, and his knees knocked. Roland tried to reassure him. "Now it's not like you're going to be doin' this long. Most of the time when the Duke calls for conscription it's for a short campaign, usually just a show of force at the borders."

Ivo exhaled. He may not be here long, but it only took one bolt to the chest to ruin his chance at making it home. He pondered his odds as Roland tightened the shoulder harness, bringing much of the shield's weight onto Ivo's torso. "There we go, all set."

Ivo tested out the heft of the shield. It was still bloody heavy, but more in line with the bundles of lumber he worked with. "Now run off and play," Roland chuckled. "Helena's probably waiting for you."

Ivo made a face.

"Oh come now, lad," Roland scolded. "She's not that bad once you get to know her. Bad, but not that bad. Besides, hold up the line and Rook'll be on your arse like soot on a sheep."

"Rook?"

"Oop..." Roland clasped his meaty paw to his mouth. Pulling it away, he whispered, "It's Commander Rook. If you want to keep your arse intact, I would just call her Commander. Not fond of informalities, that one. Now get going."

Ivo turned towards the regulars. His eyes wandered towards the bridge over Cinder Gap, but his dreams of escape fizzled at the sight of several armed guards defending the bridgehead. It would be suicide to run now. And for all his moping, Ivo found it difficult to force himself to run to his death. He sighed and shuffled toward Helena.

His partner wore a long mail coat studded with plates. Instead of a gut plate like Rook wore, Helena had on a thick, padded jacket fitted over her torso, leaving arms free for ease of movement. Her helmet, like Ivo's, was round and wide-brimmed.

Taking up a position several feet behind her, Ivo was content to casually watch his partner wind up her crossbow and unleash bolt after bolt at the target. She took no notice of Ivo, more focused on her shooting than the sad soldier behind her. Unable to sit because of his hulking pavise, he was forced to stand as one after another the other novices was given a shield.

A half hour later all the conscripts had received shields and lined up behind their partners. The remaining pavisiers were told to stand at the far end of the field. *Probably some other strenuous activity to build "character,"* Ivo suspected. Rook, who had kept her eye on the conscripts, once again stepped forward to address the crowd. The regulars promptly ceased firing and turned to their commander.

"Now we begin training." Rook held up a crossbow bolt, which bore a strange, soft looking ball on its tip. "These are the bolts you will be using. The head is coated in tree sap and fired until it's nice and bouncy. It won't kill you, but you'll be flat on your ass." She lowered the bolt, and added, "So don't get hit."

"Now, the basics of the exercise: This is a trust building exercise, for the conscripts to know their role in the partnership." She pointed to the centre of the field, were Roland was marking two lines with powdered chalk. "Two teams stand behind these two lines, across from each other." She began to pace as she addressed her unit. "The main goal; knock out all the crossbowmen from the other team. The pavisiers job is to hold up the shields and defend the crossbows. Any questions?"

The regulars knew the drill, and the initiates seemed too frightened to speak. "Good, now get to it." In their pairings, the soldiers made for either side of the gap. Ivo, not grasping the rules of the game, was brought out of thought by a sharp slap on the back of the head.

"Don't bugger this up, scrub," Helena threatened. "I'd rather not split my lip on the training field because your twiggy little arms snap when you lift that thing."

She shouldered past him and marched towards the line facing the edge of the hill. Taking a quick look around, Ivo made sure no one was watching him. Then, as discretely as possible, he made a rude gesture towards the back of Helena's head before he scurried off after her.

The two crudely laid lines sat fifty feet apart, with enough room for half the unit to comfortably spread out on either side. The other conscripts sat back like kids working the pits, waiting for the more experienced to call them in. The regulars, eyeing each other up, chose their places along the line, and waved for their shield bearers.

Helena, rather than taking her time in selecting her spot, shoved another regular out of the way and told him to sod off. The one eyed veteran gave way, spitting before he made for a new spot. Helena turned to Ivo, who began jogging towards her as soon as her eyes were on him.

"The mutt can follow orders," she mused as Ivo planted himself between her and the other line. "Now to see if you're gonna be a guard dog or a bitch."

Charming, Ivo thought.

Another smack to the back of his head got his attention. "Now look, bitch..."

Ivo seethed, mentally prepared a tirade that would make a seasoned soldier blush. He leaned back, and inhaled deeply, then made eye contact with Helena. Like piss on a campfire, Ivo's rage sputtered before those terrifying grey eyes. His gaze dropped in an instant.

Helena rapped the top of Ivo's helmet, the clang resonating through the protective lining. "Got something on your chest, meat?"

"I...Ivo."

"I, what now?"

"My name is...yeah," was all he could get out.

"Not here, it's not," she snorted. "Until you grow a pair, I'm calling you bitch. Got that?"

Ivo nodded.

"Good, now plop that little shield of yours down and don't stick your head out until this is over."

Ivo obediently turned around and planted his pavise even with the line. Vainly, he tried to find a way to sit and still hold the pavise, but was forced to settle with kneeling. His view was the back of the shield.

The regulars crouched behind their pavisiers, steadied their crossbows and took aim. The clatter of rolling metal rang out as the bolts were set lose, the locks spinning free in their sockets. Then, each of the regulars set their crossbow down and looped a small hook that hung from their belts around the string. With much grunting, they spanned their crossbows, pulled another training bolt from their belt quivers, and readied themselves all over again.

It sounded like quite the spectacle. But all Ivo could see was linen and leather straps, only the occasional thunk of bolt against shield breaking the monotony of his position. He began to wonder why he had been so worried in the first place; this was less dangerous than his old job. If it weren't for the company he was forced to keep and the niggling pain in his knees, this might be relatively pleasant.

Lack of sleep and dull surroundings finally took their toll on Ivo. He leaned farther and farther to his right, until finally the warm embrace of sleep took him and he fell.

It was a pleasant, seven-second sleep, interrupted by an obscenely powerful crack to Ivo's eyebrow. His eyes sprang open as his head shot back, the shot hitting its target. Momentum carried him and his shield sheltered him as he curled into a ball.

The call came out to pause the training, and Ivo could see Rook and Roland marching towards him. Helena, who had narrowly dodged a second bolt, took matters into her own hands. Finding an exposed section of Ivo's back, she gave him a sharp kick with steel-capped boots. "What kind of moron sticks their head out into a firing range?" she muttered, and wound up for another kick.

"Easy, Helena!" Roland called as he waddled towards Ivo. "Rook'll take care of this."

"What did we talk about Roland?" Rook said, not turning her head to face the quartermaster.

"Er, sorry sir. Force o' habit."

The commander, stopped over the crumpled heap that was Ivo and attempted to pry the shield off of him. Unwilling to let his cover go, Ivo clung to the shield like a turtle to its shell.

"Come on, fella," Roland said softly as he bent over. "Let's get this off of ya and see what the damage is like."

Reluctantly, Ivo released his grip. Immediately, his head roiled with pain, the dull light of the sun searing his eyes.

"Oh, that's a good 'un," Roland chuckled as he looked Ivo over.

Ivo had been hit square over the right eye. The force was enough to split the brow clean open and blood oozed down his face.

"Roland, take him off the training field, get him fixed up. He can hit the showers with the rest of the unit once we're done here." Rook then turned to Helena. "Congratulations, you just earned the afternoon off."

Roland hauled the crumpled conscript to his feet, nearly launching the scrawny Ivo into the air. Now adding shoulder pain to his growing list of complaints, Ivo brought his hand to his brow. Feeling the warm wetness, he examined his hand. Ivo nearly toppled over.

Roland steadied his queasy acquaintance, the wrapped a limb around Ivo's shoulder. "This way fella," Roland comforted him. "I'll get you patched up right good."

Ivo groggily nodded. "You're a doctor?"

"Nope," Roland stated, "but since we didn't get assigned a medic, I'm the best the unit's got. Took a few years apprenticing under a butcher, really the same principle."

Ivo was about to object, but a whiff of Roland's underarm forced his mouth shut. At least his head had stopped ringing, although the blood flowing from his brow obstructed his vision.

At a small area where the training field met the pathways of the training grounds a few medical essentials were set out on a handful of tables; spirits, bandages, and a rusty saw that made the prospect of gangrene favourable. *No, not rust*, Ivo thought. *Blood.*

"Don't worry, nothing' major," Roland told Ivo as he dumped him onto one of the benches. "Just a bit of a bump on the noggin. I remember last week a fellow caught the stave off a ballista during engineer training, looking over the edge of the hill. Spring steel sliced him clean in half. Hoo... Took us over an hour to find were his other half landed."

Ivo doubled over and wretched onto the brown grass of the field, in part due to Roland's colourful storytelling, and also due to his concussion.

"Oop, weak stomach on ya. Here," Roland grabbed a small water skin from his belt. His sausage-like fingers fumbled with the cork for a moment, before he popped it free. "Take a swig o' that."

Reluctantly, Ivo took the flask from Roland. He brought it to his nose, sniffing the contents. Immediately his eyes started to water as new aromas ravaged his nostrils. Recoiling, he shoved the skin back into Roland's hands. The quartermaster had a hearty laugh, and said, "Boy can't take his medicine? Come on lad, this stuff is packed with spices and herbs and all that healer stuff. Take away that headache right quick."

Ivo brought the bottle back to his face. On the bright side, he realized if this drink killed him he wouldn't have to continue his tour of duty. Plugging his nose, he knocked back a mighty swig of the drink. Even before the liquid touched his tongue he could feel the burn; a combination of strong spirits and grated roots. But it was too late to stop now. He downed the caustic beverage.

As soon as the liquid cleared Ivo's throat his nostrils flared open, ash-encrusted snot oozed forth as his body rejected the drink. A dry hacking cough rose up as his throat closed. It took him another minute to calm down. Roland chortled. "Puts some char on your bones, don't it? How's the head?"

"Actually," he said in surprise. "It's almost gone."

"Told ya!" Roland beamed. Then the smile vanished and he leaned in close. "Just keep it between you and me, would ya kindly?" Ivo raised an eyebrow until the searing pain of his wound forced him to stop.

"That stuff ain't cheap," Roland whispered. "And if word gets out, everyone in the unit will want a swig. Then there'd be none left for Roland, now would there?" Ivo nodded, and blood drenched his face.

"Shite!" Roland cursed. "I'll get right on that." With surprising speed, Roland grabbed the nearest bundle of rags and began to bandage up Ivo's head.

Roland seemed like the kind of guy that Ivo could call plenty of favours from. "So, Mr. Roland, sir..." Ivo began hile Roland wrapped up his wound.

"Just Roland," the quartermaster interjected. "I ain't an officer."

"Right, Roland..." Ivo stumbled. "If that brew is so expensive, then why share it with me?"

Roland stopped bandaging for a moment, before letting out a sigh and continuing his work. "Well, honestly, you remind me of my brother. Quiet type, never really bothered anyone, bit on the lean side."

Probably because you ate all the food, Ivo mused.

"He also in the military?"

"Nope. By now he's probably scattered across Osseus Reach, downwind from the funeral pyres. He's been dead for a while now."

Ivo unskilled in social nuances, pried further. "Died in action?"

"No, don't know what got him," Roland replied, his tone softening. "Started coughin' one day. Didn't stop till he died." The quartermaster continued his work in silence.

Ivo, not used to these kinds of situations, mustered up the best apology he could.

"Don't worry about it," Roland remarked, "it's not like hushin' up about it'll bring him back."

With one final knot, Roland tied up Ivo's head bandage. Ivo touched it. Already the blood was starting to soak through. "You know, for a Rendsheimer, you bleed like a Brenerburger," Roland joked, grinning.

A Brenerburger? Ivo turned away. On the training field, the unit had moved on to formation drilling.

"Meant nothin' by it, lad," Roland said, giving Ivo a hearty slap on the back. "Go on, watch from the sidelines until your unit hits the showers."

CHAPTER FOUR

The sickly sun hung low in the sky as the 4th Arbalesters completed their day's training. With a bark from Rook, they trudged toward Charred Hill's showers. Rook had worked them like logging mules, punctuating the painful trust training with lengthy jogs, equipment and all. The conscripts got the worst of the intensive regime; more than a few had split lips and black eyes. The open-faced helmets, while comfortable and unrestrictive, did little to stop the tar tipped bolts the regulars lobbed.

Dirty looks were thrown at Ivo as he rejoined the unit. Helena spat a gob of soot-speckled snot at Ivo's feet as she passed. Hardly the first insult she gave him, but that didn't make it sting any less. Hanging his head, Ivo joined in the march.

Rook took the unit along the central road that led to the bastion. Lights flickered from the squat tower, and the training fields were clear. The other units had turned in for the day, giving Ivo's unit free reign with the Charred Hill's legendary showers.

Nearly as famous as The Pits that churned out charcoal by the boatload, the showers were a marvel of engineering. Running flush with the north wall of the bastion, this intricate systems of gears and ropes pulled buckets of boiling hot spring water from the furnaces below, heated with the venting gases of the forges. The water was then dumped into wooden vats suspended above the stone courtyard, before burbling into a series of troughs that direct the water into many smaller streams.

Ivo welcomed the thought of standing under warm water. Not only was his head throbbing, but now the chill of the coming night sapped the heat from his bones. With such little sunlight, there was no radiant heat around Rendsheim, save for what blew off of the pits.

Ivo looked around as his unit entered the fenced courtyard. Waist high paddocks were neatly set in rows, the boards joined with dovetailing. As a carpenter, Ivo marvelled at the construction of the rigging. Intricate joints and grooves took the place of nails, and every section was built to last.

The regulars of the unit began to undress. Pairing off, they assisted one another with hard to reach straps and heavy mail coats. Gear clattered against flagstone as one by one they stripped, before moving to their favoured paddocks. To Ivo's surprise this was a unisex shower. In town, bathhouses often had two heated pools, separated by a wall. It was hardly a case of piety; worship of the old gods had fallen out centuries ago. Rather a social courtesy held over from a bygone era.

But Ivo supposed a soldier was a soldier. In truth, he was more intimidated than morally concerned. It was one thing to be naked together with a woman in courtship. It was a whole different story to be stripped bare in front of women in peak physical condition, all trained to kill. Ivo knew he wouldn't measure up, and this time not just in the trousers department.

Keeping his eyes on the floor, he reluctantly shed his uniform. The wound on his head had clotted, and Ivo unwound the bandage. He found hooks along the bastion wall, and stashed the crusty bandage there.

Hesitant to remove his loose undergarments and raising his eyes just enough to locate an empty stall, Ivo shuffled down the courtyard. The boiling water was already flowing down the troughs, and the regulars had begun bathing. Rags were provided at each stall, although Ivo questioned their sanitary value.

From his chosen stall, Ivo could see the rolling, stump riddled hills of his homeland. He'd been lucky; this stall didn't back on to another. Testing the water, he removed his undergarments, and gently laid them over the edge of the stall. That's where he caught a glimpse of Helena.

From a hundred stalls and he had chosen the one next to her. Immediately he turned red, and his hands shot for his crotch. His gaze jumped up, then immediately down. Helena was stark bleedin' naked. She laughed at Ivo's discomfort. "Yeah, I'd be pretty embarrassed if I was packin' a twig like that."

Ivo dared not glance to his right. Helena kept up the verbal abuse. "Come off it, have you never seen a woman naked before? Honestly, wouldn't surprise me." He shuffled farther to his left, trying to hide his shame as water poured over his back.

Helena sighed. She reached over the stall and gave Ivo a pat on the back. "Look scrub, you're a soldier now, like it or not. As much as it scares me, my life might depend on you, and vice-versa. You may have flunked basic training, and you may have the backbone of an earthworm, but the least you can do is look me in the eye and stand up for yourself."

Was this a ruse, an attempt to humiliate him further, or was she genuinely trying to help him? Gingerly, he tilted his head up to her piercing gaze. He opened his mouth and all that came out was a wet, burbling stream of nonsense. He was standing under the spout, his head tilted up, and his mouth was filled with water.

Helena laughed again, crossing her arms over her modest bust. "At least it's a start. Still gonna call you bitch though, at least until you can go through a day of training without losing a pint of blood." She returned to her bathing. "Just a little warning," Helena added. "If I catch you staring at my tits, I'll force-feed you your own twig with a side of spring greens."

"Noted," was the only reply Ivo could muster.

CHAPTER FIVE

A familiar, searing agony coursed through the lungs of Rudolph Lug. The duke threw his head back, bellowed, and toppled the wooden table before him as he rose from his seat. His eyes darkened, the ebon mists enveloping his vision until all was blackness. Blindly, he swung his right hand back, making contact with the servant who stood beside him. She thudded to the floor, the sound barely registering on Lug in his altered state.

Crumpling to his knees, the duke let out a dirge, singing songs so old the words had lost all meaning to the tides of time. Blood streaked tears rolled down his cheeks, staining the white of his satin robe. Finally, Lug fell forward, onto a down pillow placed by another of his servants.

His singing had stopped, and his lungs cooled. Now Lug could feel a creeping clarity fall over his ailing mind, and once again his thoughts were his own. *Transcendence*, he thought.

Rudolph's bloodshot eyes cracked open, the haze having lifted in his slumber. He didn't know how long he had been out; perhaps an hour, perhaps a day. The drug was by no means predictable.

Slowly turning over, bones aching, he saw that he was in his study. It was a modest room, set in the highest level of the bastion on the Charred Hill. The soot stained timbers of his bookshelves greeted him, and the familiar smell of aged paper clung to him. The table he had toppled still lay on its side, and a small brass tube had rolled toward the doorway.

Lug had been fortunate; he had only been out for an hour. The servants hadn't had the opportunity to rectify the mess the duke had caused. Incanflagarat was a harsh substance, and on more than one occasion Rudolph had physically assaulted his furniture.

A combination of Cinderbark ash, wyvern bile, and mirrorleaf, it seared the mind, body, and soul, leaving steely muscle and a sharp intelligence. Lug had used the drug for years now, refining his physique and mind in equal measure—a far cry from the inbred, dull-eyed child from which he had ascended. He mused on his misspent youth, the time before the drug had made him who he was. Wild parties, orgiastic feasting, and other, darker vices all played in the twilight of his mind. And that damnable dealer who had sold Lug the burning powder. He recalled the first trip, the horrifying depths he plunged to, the terrors of the old world tearing at him, until being pulled into the glorious light of clarity and charisma. He recalled his own inadequacy burning away, making him the clear heir to Rendsheim's throne. It was nearly perfect.

But now in his forties, Rudolph felt himself slowing down. The plain, leather-covered box holding his incanflagarat was empty, and his hidden stash was running low. He had another two, maybe three years before he ran out. Years of abuse had left him ruined. While his physique was enviable, inside he was a mess of charred organs and black blood. He knew that if he stopped his habit, he would be dead in a manner of weeks, so dependent was he on the narcotic.

Sprawled on the floor, bleeding from his nose, Rudolph began to appreciate his own mortality. A rare moment of self-pity threatened to grasp him, only to be washed aside by an indomitable will. *Bah*, he thought, *there's time for that later. I have work to do.*

Bringing himself up to a sitting position, Rudolph was greeted by a cyclopean, moustachioed face. "Ah, Brutus!" Lug said warmly. The trainer bowed. He wore his gut plate, coated in a layer of dried blood. "Good to see your still enjoying your job. I do apologize for the delay, I was predisposed."

Brutus said nothing.

"All business as usual," Rudolph remarked, holding out his hand.

Brutus hoisted the duke back to his feet. Rudolph's white robe had been wrinkled in his daze; crimson streaks ran the length of the front. His short grey hair, usually well kept, lay matted against his skull.

"Ah, I am a mess," he stated. Clapping, he called out, "Elis, be a dear and fetch me a new outfit. Something sporting, I'm inspecting the troops today."

Elis came through the door, her left eye swollen shut. "Elis, my dear, I do apologize," Lug cried, clasping his hands together and holding them to his chest. "Please, make your way to the maids' quarters. I'll have a hot bath drawn for you. You have the rest of the day off."

Elis cracked a smile, and profusely thanked her lord. She bowed, and was about to turn for the stairs when Rudolph interrupted her. "Upupup. Aren't we forgetting something?" He shook his finger. "After you grab me my clothes. Thank you."

The servant bowed again before departing for Lug's bedchamber. "Now, let's talk, Brutus," Lug said as he wiped his lip. Black blood stained the hem of his sleeve, but he did not care. "How many soldiers have we press ganged?"

"Two hundred yesterday," Brutus grumbled, "and at least as many today. That preacher is working wonders."

"Good to hear. In a week we'll have the numbers I need." Rudolph grinned. "Borig won't know what hit him. Come, friend, let's look at the rosters. I want to know the quality of my new soldiers."

CHAPTER SIX

Ivo's jaw cracked as the sandbag smashed into the side of his head. He tripped over the iron stand of the training dummy and planted shoulder first into unyielding wood. Day two of training wasn't any easier on Ivo than the previous day had been.

"Someone make sure the bitch is still breathing!" Rook called from the sidelines.

"Great," Ivo grumbled to himself, "now she's picked it up." Ivo rolled onto his back, staring up at the grey skies above. The unit underwent melee training two fields northeast from their previous site, and Ivo could truly say the grass wasn't any greener. If anything, the dried blood gave it more of a russet tone.

But this wasn't the time to contemplate the hue of grass. He had to get back on his feet or Rook would have him run a lap around the hill. For Ivo, an individual whose running was reserved solely for emergency trips to the outhouse, another lap would kill him. Grunting, he pushed himself into a sitting position then back onto his feet.

These fields were more intricate than those from the previous day. No open ground and target ranges. Only large, wooden structures crisscrossed with walkways and dotted with swinging sandbags. And, for good measure, a healthy sprinkling of training dummies, simple T-shaped stands on a rotating base, the left arm bearing a round shield and the right a weighted sack on a rope. When a trainee hit the shield, the bag swung at his head, forcing him to react.

Roland had been grumbling about the poor quality of these

dummies. While Ivo was getting his gear, the quartermaster told him Rook had repurposed the dummies from mounted lance training. Useless for any nuanced sword work, they were good enough for carpenters and merchants to get the gist of scrapping.

After brushing himself off, Ivo brought his axe up to make sure the haft was still intact. It looked more like a lumber axe than a weapon; a broad, tapering blade on a short and splintered haft. But Ivo was no military expert, and it certainly wasn't the worst weapon on the rack. The poor bastard behind him got a broken sword, two feet of chipped blade ending in a jagged edge, the cross guard held onto it with string.

Ivo turned back to the dummy, the clatter of other such dummies echoing around him. He whipped his axe around and smashed into the shield of the dummy. With equal force, the sandbag wheeled about, this time narrowly clipping his helmet. The wide brim rotated left from the impact, and spun Ivo's head with it. Quickly, he recovered and brought his axe up to catch the shield as it swung towards him on its return trip. The impact ran down the haft and into Ivo's unprotected hands. Cringing, he dropped his makeshift weapon, which stuck fast in the wood bellow.

Rook, who had been watching Ivo's failings, called to Roland, "Get him some leather bindings, at least until he grows callouses." Nodding, Roland turned around, pulling a thin strip of leather from his workstation. Ivo, still shaking his hand, made his way to the quartermaster.

"Never designed for wet-work, that axe," Roland mumbled as he grabbed the weapon from Ivo. He wrapped the makeshift binding around the bottom of the haft before securing it in place with a few shoe nails.

Taking the axe from Roland, Ivo asked, "What's with the repurposed farm tools?"

The quartermaster shook his head then leaned in to

whisper, "The whole armoury is empty, every last spear and glaive. Duke's been recruitin' faster than we can manufacture. Been a logistical nightmare for a week now."

Ivo raised an eyebrow. Though he didn't understand what logistical meant, he was unaware of how drained the armoury was. "Seems the only people who get any decent kit are the regulars," Roland continued, "and even then they have to make do with second hand quality."

"Any idea what's going on? I mean, he's pulling people off the street and marching them to this hellhole."

"Ask him yourself," Roland retorted, already working on another project. "The duke is givin' a speech later today."

Ivo shrugged, then turned back to the training fields. *Royal prick*, Ivo thought. *Thinks he could order me around just because he has money and power. And soldiers.* Actually, Ivo thought, those things did allow duke Rudolph order him around. That didn't make Ivo any happier though. For now, he would have to content himself with plotting his escape. Or failing that, find a way to procure a better weapon.

Ivo's moping was interrupted by the brassy tones of a horn echoing from the peak of Charred Hill's bastion. In harsh, curt blasts the horn jabbed Ivo's ears and rattled his eyes. *Burn it all, who died?* he wondered.

"In line, scrubs!" Rook called from her vantage point. The usually stoic commander was fuming, attempting to round up the conscripts into a single group. She hopped from her platform, prodding the slow and the dumb into a rough rectangle.

"If you plan on makin' it to tomorrow," Roland said behind Ivo, "you'd best be gettin' yourself over there." Not wasting time to thank the quartermaster, Ivo jogged towards the group. Already, the regulars had appeared from their private field, lined up in four perfect rows. Each had a crossbow slung over his or here shoulder, and their melee weapons hung at their sides.

"Training, my ass," Ivo grumbled as he edged into line with the rest of the conscripts. The regulars were all spick and span, with not a drop of blood or sweat on them. *No one comes out of training that well dressed.* Even Ivo knew that.

"All right scrubs," Rook calmly called out, once again on her platform. "Duke Rudolph Lug has graciously taken the time to come down here and look over his new recruits. For the regulars, this is business as usual. But for the scrubs, here's the basics."

Rook held up her left hand and raised her fingers with each command. "One, no talking. Two, keep in formation. Three, do not drop any of your gear. And four, don't embarrass yourself." She then brought her right hand up. "Anyone breaks any of these rules..." she swept her right hand over her left, retracting her fingers, "... will lose a finger. I hope I'm being clear."

Murmured concern rose from the conscripts. "That counts as talking," Rook shouted, her hand at the small knife at her side. The murmuring stopped. "Now grab your shields and get in line behind the regulars."

It wasn't just Ivo's unit getting ready for parade. The whole army was out on display. Ivo looked around at the collected masses, at least five thousand strong. He could pick out other units of crossbows, with their own miserable looking pavisiers. On the far south fields, mail-clad serjeants sat atop mighty war horses, their spears held high and proud.

And around the base of the bastion gathered the most formidable looking group of men Ivo had ever seen. Fewer than fifty in total, these were Rudolph's guards, the soldiers of the Scorched Banner. Each was clad head to toe in pyroquette-forged plate, with sharp, arching curves, and trimmed with brass. In perfect unison, they marched through the bastion's gate, before parting and standing to either side of the entrance.

What kind of fop makes an entrance like that? Ivo wondered.

CHAPTER SEVEN

Rudolph Lug adjusted his armoured collar for the fourth time. "Honestly Brutus, I feel like a damn tin can," he griped to the nearby Cyclops.

"Not my fault you refuse to get it adjusted," Brutus grumbled. "Besides, it shows respect to the soldiers."

"Respect? Half of them can't even bloody well read! What kind of respect could I possibly show them?"

Brutus aside, Rudolph was flanked by two of his guard. Standing just out of sight of the doorway, the duke made his final preparations. His armour was light, with a mail coat under a brigandine made from small iron plates riveted between red velvet. Over that, his neck and shoulders were covered in a fine, brass rimmed chainmail collar. But for all its splendour, Rudolph hated this armour. He enjoyed the martial sports, fencing and the like, but he always preferred his robes. Incanflagarat abuse left his nerves sensitive, and anything beyond soft fabrics made his skin burn.

Satisfied he was presentable, Rudolph made for the door. The grey sky stung his eyes, and his pallid skin itched as the ash-flecked breeze blew past him. But the duke showed little sign of discomfort; he had learned to maintain an aura of noble indifference. With great confidence, he strode down the central road leading to the bastion, flanked by his guards. "No fanfare?" Lug murmured to Brutus, having expected at least a brass section.

"There's some…resentment towards you, sir," Brutus stated.

Rudolph raised an eyebrow. "On the bright side," he snorted, "we didn't give crossbows to the conscripts."

Rudolph and his retinue had reached the first crossroad, where the first encircling path intersected the road to the bastion. Here, a tall platform had been erected and elaborately decorated. Voluminous banners weakly flapped in the dying breeze, each emblazoned with a stylized ember. "Not quite as flashy as I would of liked..." Lug murmured. Leaning to Brutus, he added, "Remind me to get the names of the crew who put this up."

Brutus grunted affirmatively.

Taking one last breath of the rancid air, Lug ascended the wooden platform. Upon reaching the pinnacle, he was greeted with a glorious sight. Rank after rank of troops stood at the ready. Heavy cavalry, skirmishers, pavise crossbows, all at his command.

Holding his arms out before him, Lug awaited his applause. The regulars clashed their weapons and fists against their shields and armour, creating a symphony of steel on steel. The conscripts, taken off guard by the sudden cacophony, remained silent, cautiously eyeing up their veteran counterparts.

Lug heard the wrathful bellow as one of the commanders told his unit to follow suit. Untrained and unmotivated—not the soldiers Lug was looking for. *Well, perhaps a few words of encouragement would put the proverbial fire under them. Or failing that, a literal one.*

Lug gestured for silence. In unison, the regulars ceased their clanging, while the conscripts carried on for several more seconds. It took another bellow to silence them. Lug cleared his throat, and began his speech in a booming voice fit for the theatre.

"Dear soldiers of Rendheim, guardians of the ember, I have come here today to salute you." He flourished his hands, and bent in an elaborate bow. *Lost on these simpletons,* he thought. Slowly, he brought himself back up, his overburdened organs aching at this sudden shift in position. He gritted his teeth through the agony, and continued, "I salute you, for it is by your blood and sweat that this city is kept free. But it is a burden you can no longer bear alone.

"There is a threat out there, one that may well tear our beautiful city apart brick by brick. Duke Borig of Stahlsheim, Duke Utwic of Brennerberg, Duke Petyr of the Black Sands, these are all names I'm sure you know."

A hiss came up from the crowd.

"Yes, these are the names of the men who would do away with our glorious city, who would see our homes burned and our charcoal ripped from us." The hissing intensified, and insults were slung towards the leaders in question. Holding up his hand, Lug waited for quiet.

Satisfied, he continued, "Yes, it seems their treachery knows no bounds. Like attracts like, and scum attracts scum. These "nobles" have been dealing with one another in back rooms and dark alleys. They envy us; hate us. They would do anything to see us burn, even if it means working together."

The shouting from the crowd grew louder than before, and it took the work of several commanders to keep the mass in line.

"My dear soldiers," Rudolph continued, shifting his tone to one more somber, "our enemies are searching for any and every way to dominate us. They know that should they challenge us in fair and just combat their losses would be so great as to render their victory pyrrhic, should victory be won at all. So they seek a tool to defeat us, a weapon of a bygone age so terrible the old gods shut it away."

Murmuring spread through the ranks. Long ago, the old gods had been replaced with new ones, namely coin and commerce. Lug was told that they abandoned this world, fleeing the felled forests and soot-choked skies.

"Yes, a tool, used in the shaping of this world—one with the power to create, and destroy. This entente, this league formed against us wishes to use this tool to take from us what they do not have."

"This is why I must spread the burden, handing it in part to our soldiers, and in part to our people. For the life of every man, woman, and child in this fair city will depend on our victory. This is why I must ask you, noble conscripts and citizen soldiers, to help me bear this burden. With unity in mind and spirit, we will triumph over Borig, Petyr and Utwic, cast them down, and take this artifact for ourselves. For I, your beloved lord, shall use this gift to once against make this duchy the shining jewel of the world! Go! Prepare, for the time is near at hand!"

The assembled forces broke out it roaring applause, and the cry went out. "For the Ember, for Rudolph!"

Lug grinned as his name was chanted, and he took one last bow before descending the pedestal. Brutus awaited the Duke at the bottom, sitting on the first step. Standing, he greeted Lug.

"Sounds like they bought it," Lug chuckled, and patted his friend on the shoulder. "Couldn't believe it either. Old gods, magic tools, feh. The only gods left are self-made ones."

"Like yourself, sir?" Brutus chimed in.

"Indeed," Lug replied smugly. "Now tell me, Brutus, any word from our spies?"

Brutus nodded. "Borig has brought his brother in, along with five hundred hill dwellers. They'll be ready to move in a month. Utwic is still trying to bring his sons under control, and his forces are spread throughout his duchy. And Petyr..."

"Yes? What about him?" Rudolph inquired.

"Well, been no sign of him or his armies. We think he's either been replaced in a coup, or he's got a trick up his sleeve."

Rudolph hummed. "No matter, just have these hayseeds in marching in order with the regulars before the week is over. I don't want any disappointments."

Brutus nodded, and made his way into the crowds. Lug headed straight for the bastion; he had other business to attend to.

CHAPTER EIGHT

A week into training Ivo found himself pining for his drafty townhouse. Free food and bedding meant little to him when the latter and often the former were infested with lice. To make matters worse, Brutus had personally taken to overseeing training, and Rook was on her toes at all times. She drove the conscripts like dogs, drilling them hour after hour, day after day. Lunch was taken during a lengthy jog, and dinner in between sparring matches. Even the regulars, for all their experience, began to show signs of fatigue.

For all that, Ivo still preferred the gruelling, tortuous days to the sleepless nights. The snoring no longer fazed him, but it was his unquiet mind that kept him awake into the wee hours of the morning. Slowly, as his body went limp and his breath shallowed, a creeping paranoia rustled at the edges of his brain. Terrors would seep from the dark places of his mind, creeping into his thoughts unbidden. Images of blood and death, vistas of unimaginable battles in which he was but a pawn appeared. He had seen himself die time and time again, by both bolt and blade.

It had been such a night, and Ivo felt himself drift back into the waking world. Reeking of fear, he no longer wondered why the bunks adjacent to his were empty. Throwing off his soaked covers, Ivo got up, and sat at the edge of his bed. It was the dawn of the eighth day of Ivo's imprisonment here, and already his peers were up and about.

No one acknowledged Ivo's waking; his quiet nature made him an outcast in the barracks. The only contact he had was with Roland. The portly quartermaster had an eye on Ivo at all times, either on the training field and in the barracks. On several occasions, he had requisitioned Ivo to help with some of his workload, and in return, he smuggled in bits of dried meat or baked goods. It was a nice supplement to wilted cabbage and sprouting onions, and the work kept Ivo's mind busy.

Today, Ivo was set to help the quartermaster haul in a number of crates containing field supplies for the unit. The work would take the two of them well into the afternoon, and while that got Ivo out of the morning jog, he still groaned at the prospect of hauling hundreds of boxes through the twisting guts of the Charred Hill.

Ivo rubbed the crust from his eyes, and was about to get to his feet when a familiar voice assaulted his ear. "Didn't know this was a unit of delivery boys."

Ivo turned his head. Helena was standing next to his bunk, arms crossed. She hadn't armoured up for the day's training, and was still in her form-fitting tunic. "Damn shame I couldn't live up to your standards there, Ivan." Ivo raised a finger, preparing to correct her. "No no," Helena held her hand up, "you need not speak. I've fought in the greatest battles of our age, but nothing compares to buffing the scuffs out of boots."

"Come off it now, Helena," Roland called as he made his way to the bunk. "He's doin' the work so you don't have to. Now get to training, there's a couple dangerous targets that need puttin' down."

Helena turned to Roland, and barked back, "You're not the one who has to stand behind this broom handle. If he can't hold up his end of the bargain, my blood'll be on your hands." With that, she wheeled and stomped off.

Roland shook his head, and leaned on Ivo's bunk, the aged timbers creaking. "You really got to stand up to her you know." Roland said as he watched Helena work her way to the armour stands. "She's all bark. Stand up to her and she'll start treatin' ya like an equal."

"Her only equals are the she-bears that drag people screaming from their homes," Ivo grumbled.

"Not a bad analogy." Roland leaned in and whispered, "Just don't run it by her."

Deep in the labyrinthine innards of Charred Hill, Ivo toiled. While solid in appearance, the hill was wormed through with corridors, side rooms, and shafts. Running from below the training grounds to beneath the base of the hill, great storerooms and housing units were stacked above one another. Built over a once verdant spring, the bubbling water now served a more industrious master. Smiths clanged away with water driven hammers, acrid smoke and steam pouring into vents to turn cogs and wheels in the floors above.

It reminded Ivo of the stories he was told in his youth, about an afterlife reserved for the damned. Little light, baking heat, and sour air seemed as close a fit to the underworld as Ivo would find in this life. To make matters worse, his discomfort was enhanced further by the great weight of his cargo. On the sixth level, Ivo was tasked with taking crates of whetstones to one of many service elevators, and from there to his units barracks. *Who thought stones would be so bloody heavy?*

Moving one of the last crates, Ivo heard a rumbling from the far end of the corridor. The stained timbers of the floor began to bounce, and Ivo dove for the nearest doorway. No sooner did he clear himself from the hall that a group of soldiers, four in total, turned the corner, hauling a prodigious chest. Whatever was locked within must have been of great importance, and by the stink coming off of it, perishable.

Without slowing, the soldiers ran past Ivo's hiding place, and turned another corner at the far end of the hall. Ivo was just about to return to his duties when he felt another rumbling, much similar to the first. Ducking back in, he waited for another group of soldiers. Instead, he spotted Roland stomping past him.

"You bleedin' morons!" he yelled as he tried his best to keep pace. "Everything through my level has to be recorded!" Stopping, Roland's shoulders dropped. Shaking his head, he turned around, were he saw a confused Ivo poking his head out the door. "Oh, hello there," Roland brightened up a bit. "Sorry 'bout leavin' you to do the liftin' yourself. I was busy trying to get the proper paperwork for that chest." Roland exhaled, and rubbed his eyes as he said, "Basic procedure. Flaunted, just like that."

"Any idea what it was? Seems important," Ivo said as he stepped out into the hall.

"No idea. Wasn't from my stash, or any of the other quartermaster's. I didn't see any stamp or seal on it. But if it goes through my level, I have to jot down the serial number and contents of the box. Otherwise shit just ends up disappearing. All I know is its heading for the elevators down."

CHAPTER NINE

Rudolph threw the lid of the unmarked chest back with enough force to crack its rim on the cold, hard ground. Inhaling deeply, he savoured the pungent aroma that wafted forth.

"Ah, just lovely," he mused before looking up, nodding at the four soldiers responsible for bringing him the chest. "Thank you, gentlemen. I do appreciate your haste in the matter."

Standing, Lug turned away and moved towards one of the many tables in his laboratory. Deep beneath the hill these halls were the oldest structures in all of Rendsheim. Gothic arches held up a stone ceiling, carved from the very bones of the earth. Torches barely lit the full scope of the hall, grimly illuminating the gruesome visages of gargoyles and demons chiseled into the stonework. This was where the nobles of old were buried, a long line of Lugs resting beneath the chiseled lids of coffins. And more recently, the site of Rudolph's experimentation.

Stepping towards his cluttered table, Rudolph gestured towards the soldiers, and called over his shoulder, "Of course, when I say leave it at the door, I mean it. Shame you had to waltz right in."

Snapping his fingers, the whistle of crossbow bolts filled the air. The four soldiers dropped dead, each cleanly felled with a shot to the head or neck. Unseen in the dark, Rudolph's personal guards reloaded their weapons.

"Damn shame, those boys had some urgency," Brutus commented from the other side of the table.

"Four decent soldiers is hardly worth jeopardizing our work, now is it?" Rudolph commented. He called over his shoulder, "Gentlemen, please dispose of our guests." Soft footsteps could be heard behind the duke as his fanatical guards quickly moved the bodies into the concealing darkness. Turning back to his work, he continued, "Now where were we."

"The bottles in the chest," Brutus grunted back.

"Oh, silly me." Lug spun on his heels and returned to the chest. Within were a number of intricate glass bottles, each brimming with a foul-looking liquid.

"Is it supposed to look like week old piss?" Rudolph called over his shoulder.

"I'm no alchemist," Brutus replied.

Selecting a bottle at random, Rudolph returned to the table, on which he had placed his alchemy equipment. It was an old set, the glass beakers stained black with soot. But it served Rudolph's purposes.

"Apparently they extract this from deep sea leviathans in the far north," he commented as he pondered over the bottle. The liquid was bright yellow and viscous. "If I am correct, this is the perfect substitute for wyvern bile."

Gingerly, Rudolph poured the liquid into a beaker he already had simmering over the heat. Within the beaker he had combined ground quartz and Wollok droppings. He surmised each was imbued with the same power as the component parts of incanflagarat, albeit at much lower levels.

The vile liquid hissed as it hit the other ingredients, creating a thick, pale smoke that wafted out of the beaker. "Strange," Rudolph murmured, "incanflagarat is supposed to combust upon mixing."

"Shit in, shit out," Brutus grunted.

Looking up with a sneer, Rudolp replied, "Thank you, Brutus." Pulling the flask from its stand, Lug swirled around the now crystalline contents. "Hmm...looks the part," he murmured. "Just to be safe..." Rudolph turned, and called out, "Elis! Be a dear and come over here."

The young maid emerged from the shadows. Along with Brutus and the guards, she was the only one allowed in the laboratory, and even then, she remained sequestered behind the door to one of the many side rooms. She smoothed her cream-coloured dress as she approached the table.

"Ah, Elis, there you are," Rudolph smiled as he turned around. In his hands was a small, silver serving tray, upon which a line of grey dust was placed. "Now, if you would be so kind as to take a whiff of this powder. I've been working on a new bathing salt, and I would like an opinion on the aroma."

Rudolph extended the tray towards Elis with his left hand. Cautiously, the serving girl leaned in to take a small sniff.

"Come now, girl, take a deep breath," Rudolph's eyes twitched. Leaning in, Elis took another sniff, this one slightly deeper.

"Oh, for fuck's sake!" Rudolph bellowed. With trained speed, his right hand shot out and grabbed the back of the maid's head, slamming her face into the tray. She started to flail, and her breath deepened.

In a few moments, she went limp. Rudolph, satisfied that she had inhaled enough of the powder, let her go. Rather than retreating, Elis remained there, bent over.

"Bravo! Worked flawlessly," Brutus commented from behind Rudolph.

"Shut up and give it a bloody minute," Rudolph barked back.

Just as he finished that retort, Elis doubled over, scratching at her throat. Flopping to her knees, she violently began to wretch, first bile, then blood. Wet, heaving breaths were taken between outbursts. It wasn't long before the vomiting stopped, and she rolled to her side, eyes wide open. If not for her quaking Rudolph would have assumed her dead.

"Damn it," Rudolph muttered. Pacing, he mumbled to himself. Lifting his head back up, Rudolph barked, "Someone get her out of her, see if any of the medics can treat her. I don't think she'll remember this little incident."

"Don't think she'll be able to remember anything ever again," Brutus said.

"These ingredients were not pure enough," Rudolph stated through clenched teeth. In a fit of rage, he swung his arms across the table, glass and metal crashing to the floor. "Burn it all to cinder!" he cried out. Slamming his fists on the table, he vibrated, then went limp. There he lay for a second, head down in his arms, before he stood back up.

"We can't synthesize it. We can't get the mix right," Lug mumbled to himself. Looking at Brutus, he said, "We need to get to that temple before Borig or Petyr. There's incanflagarat there, and I'll be damned if I let those lunatics get a hold of it." Standing to his full height, Rudolph continued, "We march tomorrow. Meet me in the war room."

Brutus nodded, and marched off towards the door.

His military advisor gone, Rudolph reached into his robes. From one of many discreet pockets he produced a small silver locket on a long chain. Adorning this small locket was an ember, embossed on either side. Like a coin, he rolled the locket through his fingers, before flicking it in the air with his thumb. With practiced speed he snatched it before looking it over again.

Rudolph glanced over his shoulder to confirm that Brutus was gone. He caught the last gleaming light bouncing off the cyclops' bald head before the heavy door closed shut. Rudolph smirked, before turning back to his locket. Reaching up with his other hand, he opened the clasp.

The gilded confines once housed a small, hand painted portrait of Rudolph's departed mother, but the duke had since repurposed the relic. Now, Rudolph used it to stash a small amount of blood red powder. A throwback from his misbegotten youth, this powder was purely recreational.

Kilnmaster's Lung was the common name for it; made from a combination of powdered pottery and the leaves of crimson ferns that dotted the charcoal pits.

Leaning in, Rudolph inhaled deeply. The shards of ceramic ripped open the lining of his nose, flooding his blood with the powerful sedative contained within the leaves. Despite years of abuse, the drug never failed to leave the duke with a serene calm. Shaking his head, Rudolph returned the locket to his robe. He wiped the blood from his lip with the hem of his robe, and pinched the bridge of his nose. Once the bleeding had subsided, he turned to the door.

Many, many storeys above the tomb-turned-laboratory, Rudolph emerged into the dull light of the ashen sky. Upon the roof of the squat bastion sat the war room. A construct of wood and black iron, it was as if a smaller keep was placed on the leviathan bulk of the fortress below. Broad, soot-stained beams were bolted together with heavy steel reinforcements. Over a hundred feet wide and long, it served as the last line of defense should a foe fight through the labyrinth of the tower.

The guards patrolling the battlements of the war room stiffened when they saw their lord approaching. They shouldered their weapons and stood at attention. Rudolph had no time for such formalities. "Open the damned doors!" he roared as he made his way to the entrance. Within moments, the rattle of massive locks could be heard on the other side of the hardwood doors. Slowly, the gate pulled inward, the immense weight of each door hindering the guards.

Rudolph rolled his eyes, and without breaking stride, placed a hand on each of the doors. Gritting his teeth, the duke heaved, creating an opening wide enough to fit his svelte physique. With haste, he passed the two dumbfounded soldiers at the gate who tried their best to apologize to the duke. Rudolph ignored their feeble mumbling, and waved for the doors to be shut as he passed.

Within the timber and iron confines of the palisade was a covered courtyard, the flagstone of the bastion below still exposed at his feet. A thick, oil-cured tarp was strung over the space, anchored at each corner of the small fortification. The sun weakly probed the room through the gap along the edge of the fabric, and along with several smouldering torches, made the war room bright enough to make out the details on maps.

Taking up the lion's share of the space was a long, worn out table, upon which moth eaten maps were strewn. And at the far end stood Brutus, who was busy marking down points on the various charts. Rudolph quickly moved to join him.

Not looking up, Brutus commented, "Got to oil the hinges on the gate."

Rudolph shook his head, and replied, "What we "got to" do, dear friend, is be more discerning when we pick my guards."

Brutus shrugged, and pulled a fresh chart towards him. It was a map of Rendsheim, Rudolph's duchy, and many of the nearby duchies. To the west, near the coast, was the Black Sands, a stretch of fishing villages and boatyards. To the northeast, nestled in the mountains and surrounded by rivers, was Stahlsheim.

"Borig," he began, tapping on the crude sketching of the mountain city, "is ready to march." Running his fingers over the rough surface of the parchment, he moved to a bridge crossing a wide river. "We have demolition teams at Fisherman's Choke. The bridge is already coming down. Borig will be forced to take the southern crossings should he decide to go on the offensive."

Rudolph nodded. "Has Utwic got his sons under control?"

Brutus shook his head. "Full blown civil war," he grunted. "Brennerberg is gone. Naught but ash now. Utwic is hanging from a gibbet."

Rudolph raised his eyebrows. "Which son did the deed?"

"Otis," Brutus replied.

"Send an envoy along with two thousand pounds of charcoal. Never know when you could use an ally like that."

Brutus grunted in agreement.

"And Petyr?"

"Still no idea," Brutus replied, moving his hand to the banks of the emerald sea. "If he's making a move, he's doing it by sea. Travelling north, like us. Bypass the rough terrain."

Rudolph gritted his teeth. "Anything we can do to slow him down?" he asked. "Hire mercenaries, sabotage his ships?"

"Tried it," Brutus replied. "Problem is we can't find his main fleet."

"So he's already under way..." Rudolph chewed his lip. "We can still beat him if we move first. Send a force to attack his port at Dalwik, see if we can't draw him back. The rest march with us for the Stahlsheim. From there you and I make for the temple."

Chapter Ten

The grounds were in a commotion when Ivo made it back to the surface. Hours of dim light had left him troglodytic, and his eyes burned in the pale sunlight. But the echoing call of orders and the clatter of nailed boots betrayed the hectic nature of the field.

Once his eyes had adjusted, he could make out vast columns of troops, the entire garrison of Charred Hill, falling into tight ranks. Alongside each unit was a train of carts, packed high with barrels, bags, and crates.

Immediately Ivo assumed the worst. "We're under attack!" he cried, turning to dive back into the depths of the hill. There he would find a safe nook, if it weren't for the firm hold of a hand on his collar.

"C'mon bitch, the order's gone out," came the harsh, degrading voice of Helena. Choking, Ivo fell on his rear, sharp pain shooting up his back. Looking up, he could see his partner, already armoured and hauling her steel spanned crossbow.

"Order? What order?" Ivo asked, wondering if he could still make a break for it.

Helena rolled her eyes. "You deaf? The order to muster! We got to be ready to march in an hour. Duke himself said so."

Ivo cocked his head. Helena sighed. "What, you breathe in too much mould down there? Get your ass armoured up, and get your shield on the cart!" Hauling Ivo to his feet with her free hand, Helena pointed to where their unit was. There Rook barked orders, the unit's conscripts as orderly as a band of drunkards.

Ivo turned back to Helena, only to find she had already taken off. This left Ivo alone, and mortified. "Shitshitshitshit...." he stammered as he ran for the safety of the barracks. *Perhaps if I hid under one of the beds....*

His train of thought was interrupted by a booming call, echoing from the roof of the bastion. It was Brutus. "Make haste, we move in forty minutes! I will personally see to the execution of any and all deserters or layabouts! You have been warned!"

Ivo spun on his heels, and ran towards his unit. His mind was racing as he hurried. *Go to war or have my head smashed in by a cyclops*, he considered. *Maybe if I play dead. Can't execute a dead man...*

Ivo's scheming was interrupted by the heavy plodding coming from behind him. Slowing, he turned his head. It was Roland. The quartermaster had time to change his clothes, switching from a stained red tunic to a less stained green one. His apron was covered in tools, and under his right arm was a small anvil. "Oh, Ivo!" he called, heaving for breath. "C'mon, I need you to help me get the forge packed!"

Ivo groaned, then slowed to match Roland's pace. Without warning, the quartermaster tossed Ivo the anvil. The weight pulled the weedy conscript to his left, nearly throwing him over. Stumbling, Ivo managed to catch his footing just in time to encounter one of the carts, face first. The impact forced Ivo to drop the anvil, which stuck firm in the dry soil. Bringing his hands up to his face, Ivo cried out.

He pulled his hands away and saw blood. The gash over his right eye had reopened from the impact, and oozed blood. "Damn it, bitch! There's time to bleed when there's fighting to be done!" It was Rook, who had taken position on one of the carts in the centre of the wagon train. "Pick the damn anvil up and get over here!"

Still woozy, Ivo bent down and hefted the anvil. Grunting with exertion, he was able to bring it up to waist level, and began the long waddle to his cart. Rook gave him one last look of disgust before returning to her duties. Roland, who had deposited his tools at his own personal cart, was already running back to the bastion. As the two passed, he called to Ivo, "Careful with that! Was my grandfather's. Try not to break it now!"

With much groaning and cursing, Ivo lifted the anvil the last few inches onto the back of the cart. The wooden frame dipped slightly, the hefty slab of iron forcing the wheels deeper into the dirt of the field. Relieved of his unwanted burden, Ivo leaned back on the cart, taking a moment to collect his thoughts and breath.

His rest was cut short by the berating call of Rook. "Off your ass!"

Ivo jumped, and made his way for the doors into the guts of the bastion. *Maybe if I slipped in as everyone else was leaving...*

"Hold up, bitch!" she called after him. He stopped mid stride, and cautiously turned. "You're going with Roland. I wouldn't want for you to get lost and miss the march."

"But..." Ivo wracked his brain, "I have to go back...to the barracks...to get..." His eyes darted about as he tried to come up with an excuse. From cart to cart he narrowed down the list, until he finally caught a glimpse of the weapons cart.

"My gear!" Confidence surged through Ivo. Puffing out his chest, he continued, "Yes! A soldier needs gear to...soldier. A shield to shield himself and an axe to...axe others."

Rook sneered. "Right. Well, good thing you're not much of a soldier. Besides, your gear was already loaded on the quartermaster's cart. Helena had to pick up your slack. Trust me, she has some choice words for you." The wind knocked out of his sails, Ivo deflated.

"Time to mope at your funeral," Rook barked before turning back to her work. "Now get moving."

Ivo found Roland emerging once again from the tenebrous passages of the bastion's inner workings. The stocky quartermaster had with him two hulking crates, each rattling with bits and pieces used in the maintenance of military hardware. "Ah, if I didn't know better, I'd say you were trying to sneak away on me!" Roland said with a chuckle.

Ivo was surprised the quartermaster didn't know better.

"Anyhoo, if you would be so kind as to take one of these crates."

Ivo looked the crates up and down, before moving in to grab the top one. To his pleasant surprise it was relatively light.

"Oof, thank ya kindly," Roland said, hefting the remaining crate. With a nod, Roland made his way to the unit's wagon train, with a disheartened Ivo in tow.

"Any word on what's going on?" Ivo inquired. "Are we going to anywhere that involves, say, fighting?"

Roland shook his head. "No, you got lucky Ivan." Ivo grimaced, but let the mistake slide. "We're going to Dalwik, on the Black Sands. The army's been split in two, and the 4th Arbalasters are stuck doing siege work."

"And the other half?" Ivo asked.

Roland shrugged. "Don't know. Didn't say anything on the report."

The two continued for some way in silence, before Ivo inquired, "Is it dangerous? Being in a siege."

Roland chuckled. "Really depends on which side you're on, doesn't it?" When Ivo didn't laugh with him, Roland continued, "In all honesty, its mostly sitting around waiting for the poor bastards holed up to starve to death. Doubt there'll be much fighting at all." Ivo sighed, relieved. "Dysentery, that's a whole other matter..."

Roland was just about finished his horror story when they reached the carts. "...we found the poor bastard dead in a puddle of his own mess. My advice; if it ain't brewed, don't drink it." Already queasy, Ivo did all he could to stop himself from heaving. Roland, seeing his assistant's unease, added,

"Better you hear it from me than go through it yourself."

Placing the crates on the overburdened wagons, Roland turned to Rook, who was looking over the soldiers gathered nearby.

"We're all packed up here, sir!" Roland called.

Rook turned to them, and nodded. "Good, we're about to make way." She then pointed to Ivo. "New meat! Enough playing shopkeeper. Get in line with the rest of the troops."

Roland patted Ivo on the back. "I'll see you at dinner I suppose. Assuming we don't pull an all nighter..." Stepping away, Roland moved to the front of the cart, which had been harnessed to two decrepit nags. After struggling to haul himself up, the quartermaster plopped himself into the driver's bench of the carriage and took hold of the reins.

Ivo gave one last wave before walking to the assembled unit. Finding a spot near the back of the loose order, he did his best to avoid the gazes of the regulars who had neatly lined up at the front. Both the regulars and conscripts were clad in their armour, their weapons hanging at their sides or slung over their shoulders. Ivo was still wearing the same burgundy tunic he had on a week ago.

Feeling satisfied with her inspection, Rook passed on the orders. "Now that you're all here," she said, glaring at Ivo, "we can get underway. Long story short; half of the Rendsheim garrison is being sent to Dalwik, the other half to catch Borig off guard at Stahlsheim. It's official, ladies and gentlemen. There's a war on."

Murmuring spread through the ranks of conscripts, and the regulars exchanged worried glances.

"I know, I'm not happy with the plan either," Rook continued. "We're leaving Rendsheim defenseless. But, according to commander Brutus, the two dukes have been plotting a pincer attack to take us on from two sides. This way, we can draw them into a fair fight."

One of regulars, a tanned man with short hair, commented, "With all due respect, sir, do you trust him?"

Rook shook her head. "Not one bit. But that's not my job, and it's not your job either."

Continuing, Rook began pacing. "Dalwik is at most four days away by foot. We're taking the roads west, then moving down the coastline. No pillaging till we get to the city. We don't expect to encounter any heavy fighting until Dalwik proper. Then, we dig in and get comfortable."

Helena, who was at the far end of the first rank, piped up. "What happens when Dalwik gets reinforcements from Utwic or Petyr's fleets, sir?"

"Utwic is crow pickings, so I doubt we can expect much from him. As for Petyr's fleets, there's not much to be done. Bastard could appear anywhere, at any time."

The regulars grumbled amongst themselves, concerned with the little information they had been given. "Enough of that!" Rook commanded, and just about everyone in the unit straightened up. "You can gripe when you get back. Right now, I need you in marching order. We're over the gap next!"

The 4th Arbalasters marched five across over the stone bridge above Cinder Gap. Behind the 2nd Infantry and in front of Roland's wagon, the group was sandwiched tight. Ivo, stuck in the middle, looked out over the lower burgs of the city, along the wall and up Blacklung road. He could see the billowing pits and kilns that surrounded Rendsheim, and he could just make out the cracked, off-coloured shingles of his modest townhouse. He was finally leaving the living nightmare that was the Charred Hill. Unfortunately, his departure would take him to places he suspected may be far, far worse.

It was a somber march through the narrow streets of Rendsheim. From the other end of the Cinder Gap the army turned north, towards the lower gates by the plaza Ivo was abducted from a week earlier. Bright-eyed and soot-stained children peeked from around corners, and the elderly stood at doorways to watch the mass exodus of soldiers. Ivo was surprised by the lack of fanfare that would usually accompany an occasion like this. No flowers being thrown, no courtesans to bid the soldiers goodbye. Just glazed over eyes bearing down at them.

The stone arch loomed over Ivo as his unit passed through the gates of the city. A small force of sheriffs and watchmen were gathered on either side of the gatehouse, weapons holstered and shoddy helmets held over their chest. They were the soldiers left behind, and soon the only force keeping Rendsheim in order.

Oh, how Ivo envied them.

After a brief plunge into the darkness of the gatehouse, Ivo found himself faced with the vast openness of the outside world. A vista of gently rolling hills dotted with tree stumps was sprawled before him, along with a poorly kept cobblestone road that snaked over the countryside. Ivo could only recall two other times he found himself outside the city, and both of those experiences filled him with dread. Third time was not the charm, however, as the conscript could feel the expansiveness of the outside world consuming him. He would have to get used to it; the road to Dalwik was a long one.

CHAPTER ELEVEN

Ash blew across the choked hills, and from the gate to the horizon, Rudolph could make out his troops in formation. From the ramparts of the Charrec Hill, the duke watched as half of his amassed forces marched towards Dalwik, the last of the second army passing through the gates. His fingers, grasping the cold stone of the crenellations, tapped in a smooth rhythm. In part, this was due to his damaged nerves, but it had more to do with his agitated state. Rudolph was loath to divide up his forces like this because now he would be forced to march into Borig's lands with only half of his army.

Deep down in his drug-addled heart, Rudolph knew Petyr had to be kept away. If the lord of Dalwik managed to move his fleets north, it would be a short march east to the temple. Then, Borig and Petyr would join forces against Rudolph, if only for a time. They would plunder the cache of incanflagarat, leaving Rudolph to a slow, painful death.

Now, Rudolph had to turn his attentions to his own forces, soon to be departing for the lands around Stalsheim. His gaze shifted downwards, to the fields shadowed by the bastion. With the second army cleared out, Rudolph's own forces had began to muster. Row upon row of men-at-arms and heavy infantry, clad in red gambesons and black iron chainmail. Borig was known for the ferocity of his soldiers, but pound for pound nothing could beat Rendsheim forged steel.

A nervous-looking soldier, holding his helmet to his chest, interrupted Rudolph's planning. "My lord..."

Rudolph tilted his head back and sneered. "Do you mind? I'm preoccupied."

The grunt looked at his feet. "Beg your pardon, lord. I was sent to inform you that the second army has just cleared the city gate."

Rudolph rubbed his eyes and spat, "Thank you, I was unaware. Anything else you needed to pass on? Or can I be left in peace?"

"Well, commander Luc of the 8th infantry expressed concern over your choice in troop allocations, lord."

"Again? Can't he let it go?" Rudolph's interest was piqued. "Well, tell him he can make the decisions once he's duke."

"With all due respect, lord...." The grunt was stopped by the emergence of a man clad in a heavy padded jacket, with small iron plates sewn into the fabric. His head was bare, exposing plain features and shaggy hair.

"Ah, Luc. How pleasant," Rudolph said flatly as he turned around.

"Lord Rudolph," Luc bowed, "if you could be so kind as to explain why you have not heeded my advice? Why you've set the siege force up to fail?"

Rudolph raised an eyebrow, and coolly responded. "I can assure you, you are mistaken."

Luc stepped towards Rudolph, and the grunt stepped to the side. "I can assure *you* that you're full of shit! Three divisions of trained soldiers. Three! And over two and a half thousand conscripts. All the while you hoard over twenty of our best divisions to yourself. If I didn't know better, I'd say the second army was an afterthought."

Feigning hurt, Rudolph replied, "My dear Luc, I hold every citizen of my fair city in the highest esteem. I would never place my soldiers in harms way unless faced with the direst of circumstances!"

Luc snorted, and stomped towards Rudolph. Calmly, the duke stood his ground, and soon Luc was inches away from Rudolph's face. "I don't know what you're planning, but I will not stand by it. The 8th Infantry are no longer at your disposal; my men follow me, not you."

Rudolph sighed. "Shame."

Mustering his strength, Rudolph grabbed the collar of Luc's padded jacket. With a swift turn, he heaved the insubordinate over the crenellations, sending him tumbling down the side of the bastion. A cry rang out, but was cut short by a grotesque crack. Leaning over, Rudolph saw the mangled remains of Luc, sprawled across the flagstone below. His neck had snapped on impact, and his ribs stuck through his armour like pallid twigs.

"Oh dear." Rudolph turned to the grunt. "The poor gentleman had a bit of a slip." The grunt's eyes were wide and his jaw agape. "What's your name, boy?" Rudolph inquired.

"E-Einrik," the grunt stammered.

"Commander Einrik," Rudolph said, clasping his hands together. "Congratulations are in order! You've just been promoted!" A look of horror contorted Einrik's face. "Righty ho, off you go then." Rudolph waved him away. "I still have work to do."

Wasting no time, Einrik bolted down the stairs. Over the crenellations came the sound of rising panic. Medics were called, but it was all for show. There was nothing to be done for the fallen commander.

"Shame, really," Rudolph muttered to himself, before heading down the stairs. He would make final preparations for his departure soon. But before that, he needed to see to a matter most personal.

It was in his temporary quarters that Rudolph left his safe. It was a small thing, no larger than a hen, but it was immensely heavy. From a bygone age, this safe was forged with pyroquette steel, and cooled in Wyvern bile. Upon its jet black surface were carved sets of intricate runes, each excruciatingly complex and harsh to look upon, a latticework of scratches. The runes, attuned to the resonances of the world, kept the safe as cold as a mountain stream. A rarity, perhaps the last of its kind; Rudolph knew rune working had been lost millennia ago as selfish masters refused to take apprentices in the hopes of keeping a monopoly. Such an item was priceless, and thus acquiring it required some "unconventional" methods of haggling on Rudolph's part. It had cost the duke far more than just gold.

Stepping towards the stand upon which the safe sat, Rudolph ran his hands over the blackened surface. The metal, though polished to a fine finish, held no reflection. The steel itself was as cold as ice, save for were the runes were carved. Proudly set upon the door was a handle of rose brass, the rich, golden-red colour gleaming under the glow from the candles. It was a more recent addition; the original handle had been broken off at some point. But it suited Rudolph's needs and his taste in brass-work.

Slowly, Rudolph turned the handle, and from within the tenebrous confines of the ancient safe whirred a collection of rune infused gears. The safe recognized its owner and pulled back its hefty bolts. Slowly, smoothly, the door came open, with little effort on Rudolph's part, casting a faint, white light into the room.

Within the confines of the ebony safe was a trove of white powder, glittering in the candlelight. Incanflagarat. All the incanflagarat left in the world, and the last of Rudolph's stash. While the duke kept a minute amount in a snuffbox on his person, he would never leave the rest of his stash protected by conventional means. Theft was a possible issue, yes, but more importantly, such a huge quantity of the drug would become unstable if left in a less exotic safe. And Rudolph could not bear the thought of his precious incanflagarat combusting before his eyes. Kept ice cold, the powder was stable within its rune-bound confines.

Rapping at his chamber door spurred Rudolph to action, slamming his safe shut, and turning the handle. Wheeling, he was greeted by another grunt, wearing a similar uniform to the first. Her brow was drenched with sweat, and she panted heavily. "Lord, commander Luc, he…"

Rudolph cut her off. "Yes, I am aware. Tragic. Now, is there anything else you needed to inform me?" The grunt shook her head. "Good. Now, be a dear and lend me a hand."

Rudolph gestured to his safe, and the grunt made her way across the well-furnished room. Taking the safe in her hands, she attempted to heft it, only to find the safe many times heavier than she had anticipated.

"Now you see why I didn't want to carry it myself," Rudolph jested, slapping the grunt on the back. "Well then, follow me. I'll be taking the safe to my private coach. Well, you'll be taking it, I'll follow."

"Yes, lord," the grunt nodded. Gritting her teeth, she made her way out the room.

Rudolph followed, but took a moment to himself at the doorway. He looked over his quarters one last time before he left. The bed was covered in rich, imported fabric from a kingdom now sunk beneath the waves. Carvings, paintings and other bric-a-brac covered the wattle and daub walls, and on the far side of the room was an ornate fireplace. Shelf upon shelf ran along the walls, covered in books and maps from ages long past, alongside more recent tomes and charts.

Rudolph grew somber for a moment. Too often he was forced to abandon his home over one matter or another. He inhaled then stood to his full height. Plastering on a mask of indifference, he turned to follow the straining grunt and her precious cargo.

The duke continued to descend the bastion, winding through the cavernous guts of the structure as he followed the grunt carrying his precious safe. The floors alternated between manic bustling and dead silence, as more and more units made their way to the courtyard. Camp attendants and quartermasters still fussed over crates and barrels, tallying their sheets before hefting their cargo to carts at the base of the tower. A few were picking over the emptied rooms of the soldiers who had departed with the second army. Bedding was collected, and taken back to storage. Rudolph doubted they would need the same number of beds upon the second army's return.

After a lengthy stroll, Rudolph found himself at the entrance to the bastion, the dull light trickling in from the outside. He inhaled deeply, stretching his arms. "Ahh..." he sighed, "nothing like a walk to get the spirits elevated, eh?" He slapped the grunt on the back, nearly causing her to drop the safe.

Fumbling, she wheezed, "Yes, lord."

Rudolph nodded, before waving for the bastions gate. "Shall we. By the by, it's hardly any of my business, but you really do need to work on your physical condition."

The grunt nodded obediently.

The two stepped through the bastions gate, and Rudolph was greeted with an echoing salute. Before him, in tight packed rows, stood rank upon rank of his soldiers. "My my. Thought they were impressive from a bird's eye view..." he muttered. With a flourish, he bowed before the assembled ranks of infantry, before turning to his right. The grunt, wishing to be rid of burden as quickly as possible, was already working her way to Rudolph's personal cart. Rudolph chuckled, and called out, "Patience is a virtue, dear. No need to rush now." If the grunt heard, she paid no heed, and continued on her way with gusto.

The two finally arrived at Rudolph personal coach. A leviathan thing of brass and painted wood, it dwarfed all but the largest carts gathered around the bastion. Twenty feet long, and nearly half as wide, it possessed all the duke needed for his lengthy journey. Within was a bed of substantial size, a collection of bookshelves with built in railings, and even a small fireplace made from precious metals. Along with an ornately carved table and cushioned chairs, it was a home away from home.

"Ah, there we are," Rudolph waved to the door, situated at the side of the wagon. "Please place it on the nightstand. Thank you dearly."

The grunt huffed, before heading up the stairs and into the well-lit interior. Rudolph took a moment to examine the craftsmanship in the ornately carved exterior, only to be interrupted by a heavy plodding behind him.

"And you said this was a waste of money," Rudolph commented over his shoulder.

Brutus, who had been overseeing the preparations, replied, "No, I said the gold leaf on the interior was a waste of money."

Rudolph snorted. "Pish posh, how am I supposed to think clearly in such Spartan quarters?" He turned around, and waved a finger at Brutus. "You could stand to gain a little flair, my friend."

Stern as always, Brutus asked, "Luc?"

Rudolph stroked his chin for a second. "There were...complications."

"Cold feet?"

"In a sense," Rudolph nodded. "He felt stuffing the second army with our under-qualified conscripts was a poor decision."

Brutus grunted. "They'll be fighting fisherman and net-makers, how qualified do they need to be?"

"My point exactly!" Rudolph replied. "Anyhow, the situation is resolved. Well, once they're done mopping up, but that's hardly my concern, is it?"

Attempting to brighten the mood, Rudolph said, "Care to

join me in my coach? I have a few bottles of 802 vintage red. Made with three types of grapes that are now extinct."

"I don't drink wine," Brutus returned.

"Bloody spoilsport," Rudolph huffed. "I take it you'll be sleeping in some drafty tent then."

Brutus nodded. "On the hard dirt. Wouldn't have it any other way." He nodded towards the coach. "Besides, I'm a married man. Don't much care to share a bed with you."

Rudolph shook his head. "I never said you could sleep in the bed. There's plenty of room on the floor."

"Thanks, but no."

"Suit yourself," Rudolph shrugged. "So, what pressing concern requires my attention?"

"That obvious?" Brutus replied.

"You, my friend, have never been one for conversation. So that leads me to assume there's something else going on."

Brutus nodded. "An individual with a rather…unusual demeanour. Wrapped in stinking rags, barely able to walk, completely blind, has still somehow managed to find a way over Cinder Gap."

"Past the guards?" Rudolph asked, an eyebrow raised. Brutus nodded. Rudolph sneered, "Must of sneaked in as the second army was departing. Have the cripple thrown over the bridge."

"It's more complicated than that, sir." Brutus said.

Rudolph's tone darkened. "Then out with it."

"He asked for you by name. Mentioned your…unusual taste in narcotics."

In a heartbeat, Rudolph was standing inches from Brutus. "What did he say?"

"Calm down sir." Brutus stepped back. "Didn't say it that bluntly. He spoke in riddles. 'The lord of the ember, one whose blood ran with flame. Whose body burned away as he shone ever brighter.' Or something of the ilk."

Rudolph didn't quite know what to think. The man's ramblings were nonsensical, borderline insane. Yet the description seemed to fit all too well. "Were is this man?" Rudolph demanded.

"We had him locked in one of the empty storerooms."

"Show me."

Within the candle-lit confines of the barren storage hall, Rudolph came face to face with the ragged vagabond. Brutus stood behind him and the duke ordered the guard to leave the room, and shut the door behind him. Before Rudolph had a chance to speak, the hooded wretch began to talk. Hoarse and grating, the figure said, "An honour to make your acquaintance, Lord Rudolph Lug. Consumer of knowledge, slave to the burning glass."

Rudolph took a cautious step forward. "You know me?"

The hooded figure cackled. "I know you. As you are, and as you were. A slack jawed, inbred fop."

Brutus raised an arm to silence the figure, but Rudolph stopped him. The vagabond continued, "Yes, you were to go nowhere and accomplish nothing. Until you found the burning glass. And through it, a portion of the old powers."

"Who are you, and how do you know all this?"

"Who am I?" The wretch looked down. "I cannot rightfully say. It seems that I have forgotten. As for what I know..." he turned to Rudolph, and under his heavy cowl the duke saw his gaunt, pallid face. A bloodstained bandage was wrapped around his useless eyes. Baring his rotten teeth, the crippled man continued, "As for what I know, that's a matter between me and my patron."

Rudolph's patience was wearing thin. "Patron? Who do you work for? Borig? Petyr?"

The vagabond chuckled. "No, my patron does not have a name. He has yet to be given one. Tell me, Lord Rudolph, he who burns away, are you a religious man?"

Rudolph spat as he spoke, "No, not I, nor my father, nor any damned cretin and beggar in my damn city! There's been no church or temple in a thousand years! The gods have left us to our own devices."

The ragged man sighed. "You are correct there, Lord of the Ember. The forests have been burned away, the oceans pillaged for fish, and the mountains raped of their bounty. The gods of old are gone." His tone brightened. "But, the power present at creation still lingers. And through it, new gods can be born."

"To the point, madman," Rudolph spat, "before I put your head on a pike."

The vagabond continued, "My patron is one such entity. Though robbed of my sight, I have been granted vision and purpose beyond mortal comprehension. I was tasked to find you, Lord of the Ember, he whose blood burns. Within you is bound the very force that shaped the world. Your mind and soul shine ever brighter, even as your blood boils and your bones burn away." The man turned to meet Rudolph's gaze, sending chills down the duke's spine. "My patron wishes for you to join him. Ascend to godhood, and join the pantheon of those born from man."

Brutus finally stepped between Rudolph and the vagabond. "Sir, I can't listen to this lunatic for another second. I'll have him bound and tossed off the bridge."

Again, the ragged man cackled. "Kill me if you must, my part in this is over. You will still make for the temple, but within, you will find more than your burning glass. With my guidance, you shall find power unending. And salvation from the burning glass."

Brutus once again moved to silence the wretch with a blow to the head, but Rudolph stopped him. "No. Not yet," he said. "Have him put in the prisoner cart, bound and gagged."

"Surely you jest, sir," Brutus said in disbelief. "He's clearly a lunatic."

"Lunatic or not, he knows much about me and my plans. I would be remiss to not press further, find out who he works for and how he acquired the information." Letting go of Brutus' wrist, the duke said, "We shall see if torture helps with his lucidity."

Chapter Twelve

Mucus streamed from Ivo's nose as the biting cold enveloped him. It had been many hours since the army departed Rendsheim. After a short, blood red sunset, the hills around the county were plunged into darkness. Under normal circumstances, the army would have stopped and made camp by now, but the circumstances were far from normal. The five leading commanders, Rook included, came to the decision to push through the night and march until the following evening. In return, double rations were offered, as well as pouches of bitter herbs to keep the soldiers alert.

Ivo spat out his mouthful of herbs, finding the flavour of dead skunk and old boots unappealing. Now, he marched on stress-fuelled paranoia, as his eyes tried to pierce the heavy dark that enveloped the army. One in every five soldiers was given a torch, but such meagre flames strained at the murky reaches of the night. The thick layer of ash and smoke that hung overhead blotted out both the moon and the stars and those below were left clinging to light of their own making.

Ivo had been fortunate; he had managed to acquire his padded jacket as the march progressed. The layers of linen and horsehair were the only things keeping him from freezing solid in the rimy embrace of the night. The regulars faired significantly better, no more troubled by the forced march than a leisurely stroll down Blacklung road would have been.

Over the course of the march, Ivo found himself walking next to Roland's cart. The rotund quartermaster seemed oblivious to the cold, and had the same warm smile he always had. This irritated Ivo immensely. He grumbled under his breath, catching Roland's attention.

"Oh, no frettin' now! Got a few days to go, so it's best to space out your grumblin'."

"I'd love to see you say that after you've walked for six damned hours," Ivo muttered.

"Besides," Roland continued, "you might like Dalwik. Lovely place, really. Well, once you get past the cursed bit of things, but the bathhouses…"

"Cursed!" Ivo jumped.

Roland nodded. "If you're so inclined to superstition, folks say there's a curse on the city. Well, on Petyr's family, but the city was built on their bones. Literally! There's a tour of the catacombs there that'll…"

Ivo cut in again. "Curse?"

"I'm gettin' to it!" Roland's smile broke, if for a moment. "Now, Petyr comes from a long bloodline of occultists. Powerful sort, the kind that could read the resonance of the world around them, tap into it. When there was still primeval energy bound to this world, they bound… something to the city. A god, a dragon, a great sea beast? I have no idea. Suffice to say it was a primeval thing, older than dirt and meaner than a loggin' mule."

Ivo stared at Roland. "Bullshit! The last time anyone has seen a god was while Richart Lug was still making pyroquettes."

Roland shrugged. "Believe what you want to," he said. "All I know is the city has a long record of keeping unwanted guests out. Twelve years ago, I think it was, Utwic made a move on Dalwik. He bought a fleet of cogs.. "

"Cogs? Gears?" Ivo asked.

Roland rubbed his eyes with his free hand. "No, boats," he exhaled, impatient with Ivo's interruptions. "Big, stonkin' boats with wooden fortresses on the prow and aft."

Ivo said nothing, so Roland continued. "Now, Utwic bought a fleet of cogs, outfitted them with ballistae, and paid pirates from Posad to crew them. Fifty ships, five thousand sailors, and twenty thousand soldiers stowed away in the decks below. Petyr's own fleet was heavily damaged in a previous engagement, leaving nothing to stop Utwic from taking the city."

"Then what?"

"Whole damn navy sank. The winds picked up, and blew Utwic's ships against the wave breakers around the city. Fewer than a hundred survived."

"So, it was a freak occurrence?" Ivo asked, uneasy.

"Nothing freak about it, lad." Roland shook his head. "No force has ever taken the city by sea. Or land, for that matter, although no one's made a go by land for an age." Ivo's breathing sped up. "Oh, don't worry, I'm sure we'll be fine." Roland said to reassure Ivo.

"Fine?" Ivo squeaked, his volume and pitch rising. "That mumbo jumbo sank a fleet of boats! What are we supposed to do? Draw pentagrams in the sand and pray to whatever god is listening."

Roland thought for a moment. "Nope. Pentagrams are only good for summoning rituals, I think. We'd probably need to go with some kind of ward or…"

Ivo was shaking, in both fear and frustration. "Burn it all to cinder, answer me seriously for once."

Roland flinched. Several soldiers around the cart turned their heads, checking out the commotion. Ivo apologized. "Sorry Roland, I know you mean well. It's just…I didn't think this mystical bullshit still existed."

Roland nodded. "Well, there's a lot less of it now, I'll give you that. Kinda went with the cinderbark and the wyverns. You can still find traces of it though, locked away in runes and other occult relics. Albeit at a much lesser extent." He went silent for a moment then Roland added, "Sorry for fillin' your head with curse nonsense. By now there's probably no power left in those old glyphs. The city is probably as mystically charged as a pile of Wollok droppings."

"For my sake, I hope your right," Ivo mumbled as a wave of fatigue washed over him. He stumbled, taking a sudden dip to his left. Smacking against the cart, he spun on the spot, regaining his awareness as he regained his footing. As daintily as an overfed boar, he turned himself back around, and jogged back to Roland's side. A few soldiers snickered at his performance but most just kept their eyes locked ahead.

"Bit sleepy there, Mister Ivo?" Roland said, with the same grin he usually wore.

Annoyed, Ivo replied, "Yeah, walking does that to you." *Not like you're familiar*, he added in his head.

"Well, I'm afraid I got no room on the cart for you," Roland said. Then he leaned close and whispered, "But I do have some of my special medicine."

"Appreciate the offer, Roland," Ivo returned, "but I'd rather gargle nails than drink more of that crap." Roland shrugged, and reached for his belt. He pulled free his water skin, and took a quick nip of its contents. Shaking his head, his eyes bulged as though they threatened to evacuate their sockets. Blood rushed to his face, giving him the appearance of a hairy, soot-stained beet.

"Suit yourself, but it's a long night ahead."

Roland's words rang true. Winding through hills in the gloomy veil of night, the second army marched without stopping. Those who dropped were force-fed a hearty handful of the stimulating herbs, sending them into a zombified state, which kept them mindlessly in step with their companions. Food was passed from the mess carts without stopping, and water skins were filled from the great barrels of watered down ale that hung off the sides of wagons.

Many hours later dawn finally broke over the ash-choked land. A vivid, blood red spilled over behind the march, and if one looked hard enough the outline of the sun could be seen. This was a clear indication the second army was swiftly approaching the borders of Rudolph's duchy, and clear skies awaited them ahead.

The scenery around the second army had changed drastically overnight. With the breaking of the dawn, faint signs of life could be picked out. The hills around Rendsheim had given way to a gentle slope as the highlands transitioned into coastline. Saplings, although feeble, dotted the countryside, and every so often a fully-grown tree could be seen. The greed of Rendsheim didn't reach this far—at least not yet. There was a soft chirping; the singing of the few brave birds that dared to call the toxic lands of Rudolph's their home. Even the grass appeared healthier, patches of green mixed in with the vast sea of brown.

Breakfast consisted of half loaves of coarse bread along with several pieces of questionable cheese. Water was boiled over cast iron stoves built into the mess carts, along with chicken bones and a heavy helping of the bitter herbs to delay sleep. The soldiers took turns walking alongside the mess carts as their cups and tankards were filled, and they drank and ate as they walked. Not exactly hearty, but enough to keep a soldier marching until the next meal. Ivo, who had spent most the night walking alongside Roland, found himself pushed to the back of the line as his unit took its turn at the cart.

It was slow going; the cooks were careful with each serving of the soup, not losing a single drop to the loamy soil below. Ivo, exhausted and ravenous, grew impatient. Ahead of him he could count nearly a dozen of his comrades, at least half of whom had shoved him out of the way. Ivo had contemplated finding a way back to his original position, or maybe even the front of the line. Tricking a sleep-deprived soldier would be like tripping a blinded horse; too easy. However, while Ivo questioned the intellect of his brothers in arms, he certainly didn't overlook their physical prowess. Ultimately, he decided a bowl of piss-water and grass was hardly worth his life.

Ivo's turn in line finally came up. The aroma of rank, month-old onions suffused the cart and a steady head of steam rose from the cooking pot. Bits of gristle could be seen floating amongst wilted herbs and starchy cubes of what may or may not have been potato. But it was warm, and it was filling. Holding up his oxidized copper cup, Ivo impatiently awaited his poorly executed breakfast. The cook, a surprisingly lithe thug, grabbed the cup from Ivo's hand, and with a worm chewed ladle, filled it to the brim with the cloudy broth.

The cook was in the process of handing Ivo his meal when a call came up from the front. The entire army ground to a halt, and many carts were forced off the fieldstone road to avoid colliding with stationary infantry. The mess cart lurched to a stop, knocking the cook off balance, and sending Ivo's cup tumbling back into his possession. Hot, oniony broth went flying as he grasped at his breakfast, only serving to further spread the spray of soup. By the time he got a hold of the cup, over half the contents were either soaking into the ground or staining Ivo's person.

He glared up at the fumbling cook, whose eyes were firmly locked forward. Ivo was about to tell him off, when he was interrupted by an all too familiar voice.

"Roland!" Rook called from beyond the mass of troops, "clear some space! We have wounded." The quartermaster, who was scarfing down a bowl of the broth, tossed his meal aside and scrambled over the seat of his cart. Hammers and boxes flew as the portly smith made a bed of crates, stacked with the scrap leather and jacket padding.

Ivo's attention was brought back to the front as soldiers shuffled aside, and two figures came into view. One was a grunt

Ivo hadn't met, and the other was Helena. Between them, a loose bundle of rags wrapped something long and thin.

"Bitch!" Helena called, her grating tone carrying over the murmurings of the crowd, "Get over here and help us out!"

Ivo shook most of the broth off his jacket and made his way over to her as fast as his sleep-deprived body could manage. Once there, Ivo grabbed the middle of the loose bundle and lifted. "For fuck's sake," Helena shouted, rolling her eyes. "Get your hand off her ass! It's a human, not a rug!"

Ivo widened his grip but nearly dropped the injured woman, apologizing to the unconscious pile of rags. He found a sure hold behind her knees and at the small of her back.

"Why is she all bundled up?" Ivo asked as they hauled the woman to Roland's cart. From her head to her toe, she was wrapped in tattered fabric, obscuring her form and leaving her face cloaked in shadow. The hood was deep, and the faint outline of a chin was all that could be seen.

Helena was quick to answer. "She wanted to do her best impression of a caterpillar. How should I know?"

The grunt carrying the woman's upper body asked, "Was she breathing?"

"We think so," Helena replied, "but barely. I bet she nearly froze to death overnight."

Roland was putting the finishing touches to the makeshift cot as the three arrived at the rear of his cart. The quartermaster had rolled a clean piece of cloth over a beat up jacket and used it as a pillow. From there, he assisted in hefting the woman onto the cart.

"Outstanding work, Roland." Rook complimented as she rounded the side of the cart. "Could have been a nurse."

Roland nodded. "Maybe in a past life, sir."

Rook appeared about to say something when another armoured figure interrupted her. A man, clad in a set of steel plates stitched to a blood-red jacket. From the quality of his gear, it was clear he was an officer, matching or exceeding Rook's rank.

"Rook, by all that is scorched, what do you think you're doing?"

Rook spun around, crossing her arms. "I am saving a life."

"You're slowing down the whole convoy! We have lost time to make up!"

"Whether we stop or not is moot. The ships will still be there."

With a huff, the second officer stormed off, barking orders as he went.

Roland leaned towards Ivo from the rear of the cart, and whispered, "Commander Janik, seventh infantry. Bit of a royal prick, if you ask me. Not as bad as his brother Luc, though."

Standing up, Roland made his way to the seat of the cart. "Ivo!" he called, "I need to drive the cart. You need to look after our guest."

Before Ivo could reply, Helena cut in. "Oh please, Roland. For the woman's sake, don't leave her with him. Hasn't she suffered enough already?"

"Come now, Helena," Roland shot back. "Don't be jealous, I'm sure there's plenty of Ivo to go around."

Helena snorted, not dignifying Roland's remark with a response. Tapping the second grunt on the shoulder, the two took off up the convoy.

Ivo pulled himself up into the cart, casting about for a suitable place to sit. He decided on a bit of white cloth, which seemed softer than the surrounding crates. Hunkering down, he looked over the woman. "Uh, Roland. I have no idea what I'm supposed to do here."

"Just give her a once over, check for any open wounds or infection. By the by, if you missed breakfast, I keep a stash of cheese back there. Should be under a white cloth—can't miss it."

Ivo grimaced, and moved to the crate next to the cloth. Finding his new seat suitably less edible, he got to work. The cart, already underway, rattled as he began unwrapping. It was slow going; dozens of layers crisscrossed her body. Ivo would have to cut the cloth to avoid rolling her. Pulling the eating knife from his side, the dull, pitted steel chewed away at the aged linens. "Shouldn't a medic be doing this?" he called to Roland.

"Probably."

After much cutting Ivo had taken away enough fabric to get a good look at the woman's face. She appeared to be perhaps thirty winters. Her dark mane was matted and unkempt. Gaunt cheeks and thin nose made her appear delicate, as though she was made of glass. Her skin was darker than the native daughters of Rendsheim. She was foreign, perhaps from the Black Sands, or the isles of Posad across the sea.

Her eyes remained shut, and even the bouncing of the cart failed to wake her. As gently as he could, Ivo opened the lid of one of her eyes. He was met with an icy stare, pallid blue in stark contrast to her bronze skin. It appeared almost otherworldly, multifaceted as a sheet of ice.

Ivo's examination was cut short as her other eye shot open. He jumped back, nearly toppling over the side of the cart. "Uh...Roland..." Ivo called quietly. "Roland! She's awake!"

Roland turned back to look. "Good work, Ivo. Now check and see if she's okay."

"I...but...you're the medic and..." He turned back the strange woman, who's gaze had not shifted. "Uh.... Hello?" he squeaked.

"Hello." Her voice was soft.

Ivo would have expected a more animated response but the woman's tone was calm, almost cold. She stared at Ivo expectantly. Rubbing his frost-numbed hands together, he said, "Uh...I'm Ivo."

"Hello Ivo," she responded.

Ivo waited for her to continue, and tell him her name. Remaining still, she continued to stare at him.

"Uh…And what's your name?"

The woman's brow furrowed. "My name?"

Ivo nodded meekly. "You assume I have a name then."

Ivo frowned. "Most people have names."

"Is that so?"

"Well, yeah. Didn't your parents give you one?"

"No," she stated.

"Well…I…Roland! A little help!"

"Ask her about her personal life later!" the quartermaster called. "Just find out how she is!"

"Right. So, uh…Are you okay?"

Her brow furrowed. "No, Okay is not my name. As I have said, I do not have a name."

"No, I mean are you hurt? Injured in any way?"

The woman thought for a moment. "I understand your question. I am not injured. I appear to be bundled up, however."

"Yeah…I was going to ask you about that."

"Then ask," she said.

Ivo rubbed his neck. "So, why are you wrapped up."

"I do not know," she replied, her eyes still locked on his.

"I can see we're not getting anywhere here," Ivo mumbled.

"I have to correct you, Ivo. It appears we are currently moving. Where are we going?"

"Do you know where Dalwik is?"

"I am familiar," she nodded.

"We're going there."

The woman nodded. "I understand. Now, please help me out of these wrappings. I wish to move."

Ivo shifted and glanced away then back. "Wouldn't that leave you…naked?"

She shook her head. "No, I have garments under the wrappings." She paused for a moment. "I am confused. You appeared to have little issue with undressing me while I slept. Now that I'm awake, you are averse to the thought."

"Saw right through ya!" Roland roared, laughing heartily.

Ivo sighed. "Not the help I was looking for Roland!" he answered. "Well," he said, turning back to the woman, "I guess we should get started."

Gingerly, Ivo cut the woman's bindings, peeling away layers of linen. She did little to help or hinder him. Rather, she intently watched him work. Her head remained perfectly still, even as the cart bumped and skipped over the uneven roads. Only her eyes moved, slowly and deliberately, unblinking.

Not sure what else to do, Ivo reverted to small talk. "So, where are you from?"

"I do not know."

"You have no idea where you're from or how you ended up on the roadside?"

"Yes," she replied.

"Well, you said you knew about Dalwik. Maybe you're from there."

The woman nodded. "That would make sense."

It was some time before Ivo had undone the last of the bindings. The final layer of linen fell off, leaving the woman free. Under all the fabric, she was lithe. A form fitting pair of red, joined hose and a white, puffed shirt adorned her. Along with a heavy-duty belt, this was all she had with her. She wore no shoes, nor jewelry, and no pouch hung from her side.

Slowly, the woman sat up, stretching her neck and arms out. Turning, she looked Ivo dead in the eye, forcing him to avert his gaze. "Thank you, Ivo."

"Uh, well...you're welcome."

"Don't forget to check for any injuries!" Roland piped up.

"Right, um..."

Without a word, she lifted her arms, giving Ivo a chance to look her over. Shyly, he looked up and down her arms, her neck, and finally her torso. There was no sign of cuts, and her exposed skin was bruise free. Barring internal damage, she seemed perfectly fine.

"Okay, you can put your arms down now."

The woman nodded. "Yes, I can." She remained there, arms outstretched.

"Please put your arms down now." She listened, dropping her arms to her sides. "Do you feel any pain?" Ivo asked, trying to recall medics' procedures. "Like, your ribs or neck? Any knots, or soreness?" She shook her head. "I suppose you want to be let off somewhere near here. Go your own way."

She stared at him.

"I, uh, would spare a few embers, but money's tight, so..."

"Hang on, Ivo," Roland cut in, "this lady doesn't know where she's from or how she got here. We drop her off, and she gets lost. And besides, if she really is from Dalwik, she could...return the favour. Give us a little information about the city."

The woman nodded. "That seems fair. If not for you and your colleagues, I would still be on the roadside. If I can be of assistance, I would be happy to accompany you."

Roland beamed. "Excellent! Now, we'll have to figure out a name for ya. Hmmm..."

"Bitch!" Helena called from further up the column. "Enough of your free ride. Get down here and march like a soldier!" Ivo sighed, and stood up.

"I thought your name is Ivo. Is it bitch?"

Ivo shook his head. "Don't ask." He jumped off the rear of the cart and jogged toward his unit preparing himself for the flak he would catch from Helena.

CHAPTER THIRTEEN

"Remind me to torch the bastard that chose this vintage," Rudolph commanded Brutus. Flames from the oven at the far side of the coach gloomily lit its expansive interior. Night had fallen several hours earlier, but the first army would be marching through until dawn. There would be time to rest tomorrow, once they were at the edge of Borig's duchy. For now, Rudolph had to consolidate his forces at the border—and fast—lest Stahlsheim should empty its forces sooner than expected.

Within the gilded confines of the coach, Rudolph lounged on his feather-stuffed mattress, trying his best to enjoy the wine he brought with him. Brutus sat at the table, pouring over maps and making adjustments with a sliver of charcoal. "I thought you spoke highly of the 802," Brutus grumbled, preoccupied with his task.

Rudolph shook his head. "I was told by my sommelier that it was a superb vintage. Notes of leather, smoke, and citrus."

"And?" Brutus asked.

"Tastes like piss." Rudolph threw the glass to the floor, the contents spilling and soaking into the hardwood boards. "Honestly, anyone who claims to be an expert on wine is either willfully stupid or woefully ignorant." Getting up, he walked towards Brutus. "I spent over a thousand embers on that bottle. 'Last of its kind', he said. I've had bathtub wine that tasted better than that."

"You've drunk bathtub wine?" Brutus raised an eyebrow.

"Long story. Suffice to say, I had acquired some narcotic

fungi, and went for a bit of a bender."

Rudolph sat down across from Brutus, looking over the latter's handiwork. The map, which centred on the border between Rudolph's lands and Borig's, was strewn with arrows, blocks, and lines. In great detail, Brutus had laid out positions for every unit in Rudolph's army, along with fortifications and supply lines.

Rudolph's brow furrowed. "Brutus, this won't take us anywhere near the temple."

The advisor shook his head. "No, this is the diversion. If we set up along the last remaining bridge over the river here," Brutus pointed at the river, "we can force Borig's hand. He'll send his entire force after us and try to reopen his trade routes." Brutus then pointed to a triangle, set north of the bridge. "Meanwhile, you and I, along with a few dozen of your knights, will have already sneaked across and make for the temple."

Rudolph nodded. "And what are the odds of our diversionary force besting Borig's armies?"

Brutus sighed. "Nonexistent. The numbers aren't favourable; we're fighting him one to one on his own turf. The best we can do is fortify up, get them to hold as long as possible, and make a hasty retreat should the need arise. Fight defensively, minimal casualties."

"And leave you and me at Borig's mercy," Rudolph added.

Brutus paused for a moment, then said, "It's doubtful he even knows the temple exists, let alone that it's under his nose. At least not yet. He won't be looking for us, and from there we make our way west, cross the river at its shallowest ford. From there, we haul our loot back to Rendsheim, and prepare for Borig's counter attack."

Rudolph nodded. "Satisfactory."

He was about to continue, when a knock at his door caught his attention. He nodded towards it, and Brutus obediently got up. Undoing the brass latch, he opened the door, revealing a slack jawed soldier, torch in hand. The man was forced to keep pace with the cart as it trundled along the cobblestone road. "My lords, Isaac Miller, military police," he introduced himself. "The prisoner you told me to look after? There's been a few complications."

Rudolph rose from his chair, and walked to the door. "What kind of complications?"

"Well, he...kind of escaped."

Rudolph snorted. "And how, pray tell, does one "kind of" escape?"

"Well, lord..." The jailer thought a moment. "We had him chained up in the cart we usually reserve for deserters. Double locks, solid iron bars, and we chained him down to the bench."

Rudolph nodded, waiting for the point.

"And, well, when we went to bring him some vittles, he was...gone. The chains and cuffs were still locked, as was the door. He just...vanished."

Rudolph frowned. "Well, it seems he made well on his escape then."

The jailor shook his head. "Beg your pardon, lord, but he most certainly did not. We fanned out around the cart to look for him. Imagine the look on our faces when we found him sitting in the mess cart, dining on cheese from your personal supply."

Rudolph was not pleased. "You let a blind man escape? And he was free long enough to raid my pantry?"

"With all due respect, lord, he was there one minute, gone the next."

Rudolph rolled his eyes. "Did you at least apprehend him?"

"Yes, lord. He didn't put up any fight, and we got him back in shackles. But he insisted on having an audience with you."

"To what end?" Rudolph asked.

"He refused to say."

Rudolph mulled the thought over. "Very well, bring him."

He waved the jailer off, and returned to the table. Brutus sat back down, and looked at Rudolph.

"You're taking that vagrant seriously, aren't you?"

Rudolph rubbed his eyes. "No, Brutus, I am not. But for a blind man to break out of a secure cart and into an equally secure pantry raises a few questions, doesn't it?" Shaking his head, he continued, "Either he's exceptionally intelligent, crafty, or truly of a higher power. In any case, I would be remiss to not investigate further."

It wasn't long before another knock came. Brutus, who was already standing, opened the door. Alongside the cart marched a half dozen soldiers from the military police, armed with clubs and bucklers. Each had a chain hooked to a loop on his belt, and in the centre of the grouping was the blind vagabond, his hands bound to his torso. The jailer, Isaac, was at the head of the group. "Here he is, sir," he said, bowing.

"Good. Bring him in, and leave us."

Isaac cocked his head. "My lord?"

Rudolph waved him away. "I can handle a cripple, jailer. Now please, leave us."

Isaac nodded, and motioned for the guards to bring the vagrant to the door. Unhooking their chains, they shoved the blind man to the opening, where Brutus caught him. With one hand, the advisor hauled the vagabond into the cart and closed the door.

Brutus gave the man a hefty shove, nearly toppling him. Twirling, the man caught himself, before turning to Rudolph. "I must admit, oh iridescent lord, that your hospitality is found somewhat wanting." With supreme confidence, the vagrant placed a hand on the back of the chair across from Rudolph, and sat. "But these are dark times, where gods must rule through force."

Rudolph sneered. "You have the nerve to insult me, after you so ungraciously helped yourself to my private pantry?"

The vagabond grinned, the stench of rotted gums and maggot-chewed teeth permeating the air. "I would not dare insult you, lord of men. You verge on apotheosis; your elevation is nigh. To insult you would be most unwise." Leaning back in the chair, he added, "But I will compliment you on your choice in cheeses."

Rudolph raised an eyebrow. "You fail to make any sense, cripple. You speak of godhood in the vain hope to stay your own execution."

The blind man shook his head. "I have no notion of preservation. Should you ask it of me, oh lord, then I would slice my own wrists here and now. My life is ultimately forfeit, I only seek to use what time I have in aiding the foundation of a new pantheon."

"Aid? You seek to aid me?" Rudolph stood up. "Tell me, vagrant, how do riddles and brown-nosing aid me when I have a bloody war to fight, and a bloody temple to secure?"

"Yes, you will wait for Borig, I know. Fortify the bridge and wait. All the while your second army will nip at Petyr's heels." The man nodded slowly.

Brutus moved a hand to his dagger, but Rudolph shook his head.

"That's a military secret. How did you know that?"

The vagabond grinned. "I am a servant, and through my patron, many things have been revealed to me. I know you plan to hold the line at the last standing bridge that divides you and Borig. I know you plan to sacrifice your men in an effort to attain greater goals."

He leaned in, the faint light of the stove revealing his lesioned features. "And I know Borig will not come."

Rudolph cocked his head. "Tell me then, soothsayer, were does my foe lie?"

Hands shaking, the blind man reached over the map on the table, one bony digit landing on the mountain city of

Stahlsheim. "Borig will attempt to resist you, Lord of the Ember. He will hold in his keep, his stores bountiful. Winter will come long before he will need to reach out. And in that time, he will prepare." Moving his hand over the map, he pointed to the mark over the temple. "He knows not what you pursue, simply that you pursue it. Should you make your move, he will strike from Stahlsheim, and slay you himself."

Rudolph stroked his chin. "Brutus," he commanded, "divert a few scouts. I want to know the state Stahlsheim is in."

"Sir," Brutus replied, scowling, "they get caught, the whole operation is blown. Borig will move to the offensive and we'll be on the back foot. Don't be taken in by this freak's jabbering."

Rudolph inhaled. "I am Lord of Rendsheim. I will command my forces as I wish."

Brutus sighed, and replied, "As you say, sir."

Rudolph waved Brutus off, the armour-clad advisor stepping away from the table and planting himself on a stool. Staring intently at the vagrant's bloodied bandages, Rudolph coldly commanded, "Tell me everything you know, and I may spare you yet."

The two spoke well into the morning, Rudolph grilling the blind man with questions and the vagrant responding cryptically. When asked if Borig was conscripting his own force, the vagabond stated the force was gathering itself. When asked of the whereabouts of the late Utwic's treasury, the blind man replied it was lost long before his death. He spoke with absolute surety, no matter how vague or obscure the inquiry. Troop movements, the lay of the land, even the exact whereabouts of Borig himself. He even spoke at length of the second army and their brief delay the previous day. There seemed to be no question beyond the blind man's expansive understanding.

Rudolph's head rested in his hand. "I fail to see your design, cripple," he stated, more to himself than to the blind man. "Every sentence to come slithering past your teeth is utter madness. You attempt to flatter me, confuse me. Hell, I've put greater men down for lesser insults." The duke leaned in. "And yet, here we are. You know what you are, cripple?"

The blind man shrugged. "A servant, and nothing more."

"You're an enigma," Rudolph corrected him, "and I loathe enigmas."

Rudolph stood up from his chair, motioning for Brutus to secure the vagrant. "I will find who you're working for."

"I know," The blind man replied. "I anticipate it."

Rudolph pointed to the door. "Brutus, be so kind as to remove this freak from my sight." Brutus bound the vagrant, who remained passive.

"Can we execute him now, sir?" the advisor asked.

"No." Rudolph turned away. "At the very least he's good for idle chitchat. Something you could stand to learn. Perhaps we'll put a noose round his neck after we uncover his true loyalties." Rudolph waved the two away. "Return him to the prison carts. I hope there won't be another repeat of last night."

The blind man attempted to bow. "As you wish, Lord of the Ember. Your cheeses and meats I shan't consume." Brutus snorted and dragged the blind man out of the cart.

"Now, let's see if we have any decent wine," Rudolph said as he turned to the hardwood shelves. He looked over bottle after bottle, ranging in price from a few embers to those worth their weight in pyroquette steel. One by one, he drew the bottles from the shelf, and ran his hand across their aged labels. "Brennerburg Estates, 902. Wyvern's Roost Vineyard, 985. Hmmm…"

He chose a particularly dusty bottle, whose label had long since been eaten by moths. He rolled it over in his hands, searching for an identifying mark, until finally, he spotted a tiny red blotch on the glass. It appeared to be wax, a deep crimson drop left over from the seal around the cork. Rudolph moved to pick it off, annoyed by the imperfection.

To his surprise, the dot did not peel away. Rather, the crimson drip smeared across his finger, warm to the touch. It was not wax.

Rudolph reached for his face, patting under his nose. Returning his hand he could see his fingers were coated in a thick layer of black blood, shimmering in the dull light. In shock, the duke dropped the bottle of wine and it clattered harshly against the floor. He patted under his left ear and felt a warm, wet patch.

Nausea and haziness overtook Rudolph, his vision darkening and his ears ringing. His heart pounded erratically, threatening to break his ribcage as it desperately tried to circulate blood that was no longer there. His knees gave out next, sending him toppling backwards, sprawling across the wine-soaked floor.

The world closed around Rudolph. His vision narrowed, and all he could hear was the beating of his own diseased heart. Blood pooled in his nose, seeping down his choked airways. His mind raced, urging his overburdened lungs to heave one last call for help. Rudolph attempted to cry out, but only gurgling escaped his clogged throat. Drained of his energy, all went black. The last thing he heard was the sound of a door crashing open.

Chapter Fourteen

By the end of the second day, the second army had departed Rudolph's lands. What they saw was a drastic shift; the trees here grew confidently, having never tasted the blade of an axe. It was Petyr's duchy, uncivilized and unmolested. Ivo was unused to the press of trees. Sprawling forth by the thousands, they choked the landscape. Tall, acutely barbed pines sat alongside squat, rolling oak and maple.

What was worse, however, were the haunting lights set in the sky above. The smog of Rendsheim didn't reach this far, leaving the stars unobstructed. A vast, maddening display of the true scale of creation played out before those brave enough to look skyward. For Ivo, such a sight was rare, and terrifying.

When the call to make camp arose, the soldiers of the second army cautiously fanned outward, ordered to collect firewood and clear areas for bedrolls. Though exhausted, the Rendsheimers were in no rush to leave the relative safety of the road and enter the dark woods around them. Eyes shifted from side to side, and glances were made skyward, lest those brightly shining stars begin to fall upon their heads.

Camp was made off of the road, nestled in amongst a thin patch of trees. Here, the second army could rest in relative obscurity, the only sign of life being the bonfires. Each unit was designated a spit of land, and each soldier a linen blanket and a straw stuffed roll of fabric. A few tents were handed out to officers, but the night was unseasonably warm, and most went without.

The leftover broth from lunch was served cold, along with a cut of salted pork and what may have been yams, served boiled. The poor meal along with the embarrassment of proper sleeping accommodations set Ivo on edge. The mood was foul throughout the camp, the fatigue of a long march having worn down the nerves of even the most timid among the soldiers.

Ivo had been spared the unenviable tasks, such as harvesting timber or digging latrines. His job was to tend the unit's fire, keeping it fed with dead branches and lumps of Rendsheim charcoal. Helena was not pleased. She cried bullshit, stating that Ivo had spent half the day lounging in the cart while the others were marching.

Stretching out before the roaring flame, his back to a sturdy log, Ivo forgot all about Helena's complaints. He deserved a break; after all, he did help save a life. Sure, the strange woman wasn't injured, but that was scarcely the point. And besides, he was on the cart for less than an hour, hardly a lengthy departure from the monotonous marching.

Come to think of it, what ever happened to her? Ivo thought. Last he'd seen of her, she was sitting next to Roland in the cart. That had to be at least three hours ago. His brow furrowed as he ran the day's events through his head.

"Enjoying yourself?" a bark came from behind him. Ivo closed his eyes, hoping beyond hope that his ears were playing tricks on him. "Aw, what's wrong? Too high and mighty to talk to the grunts?" No such luck. He would have to put up with Helena.

Helena, stripped of her armour, sat down next to him and a pungent cocktail of sweat, bitter herbs, and sap assaulted Ivo's nose. Helena had just got back from gathering timber. "I'm curious, bitch," she began. "Who was that woman? Definitely wasn't from around here." Ivo thought for a moment. Impatient, Helena spat, "What? Don't feel like sharing?"

Ivo shook his head, still staring into the flame. "No, I just don't know what to tell you. She was…"

Helena cut in, "Batshit crazy? I got that impression."

Ivo nodded. "She said she doesn't remember much, where she came from or how she got there."

"Couldn't remember her name then?" Helena asked, her tone softening.

"That's the thing," Ivo replied. "She said she didn't have one."

Helena raised an eyebrow. "She's full of shit! Probably a spy or something, wanting to sneak her way in."

Ivo shook his head. "I honestly believe her, Helena. She doesn't seem all there."

Helena snorted. "Takes a moron to know a moron, I suppose." Ivo frowned, and turned back to the flame. Helena continued, "Either way, she's been pulled off to the officer's quarters. Probably going to work her over, see what they can find out."

"Then what?"

Helena shrugged. "Depends on what information they get. In her state, I don't see us setting her loose. So either she's useful and goes with us, or ends up at the executioner's block."

Ivo looked at Helena with disgust. "Wait, so they'll kill her, just because she can't tell us anything."

Helena's brow lowered. "Got a problem with that, bitch? Gonna man up?"

Something snapped within Ivo. A week of pent up fury surged through his veins, clouding his brain and clenching his fists. The days without sleep only fuelled the flame, driving him over the edge. Staring Helena dead in the eye, Ivo replied, "I do. You soldiers think you can make playthings out of other people, that you can shit on whoever you please and get away with it. She's a human being. I'm a human being! If you can't get that through your thick skull then fuck off!"

Immediately Ivo regretted his choice of words. Death was plastered across Helena's face, her stare hotter than a pyroquette forge. She looked ready to kill him, weapon or not. "So the bitch does have a backbone," she growled. "And without your babysitter. I'm almost proud." With a meaty push, she placed her finger on Ivo's chest. "But I can promise you, talk to me like that again, and I'll rip your spine out through your ass." Giving a shove, Helena stood up and departed, leaving Ivo to contemplate the fate of the strange woman and the state of his trousers.

Ivo's solitude was short lived. From behind, the echoes of a slow, rhythmic clap could be heard over the flickering fire. He could tell it was a slowness born less of mockery, and more of fatigue. Looking over his shoulder, Ivo discovered it was Roland. The rotund quartermaster had returned from the gathering of the army's commanders, and by the exhaustion in his eyes, it was a lengthy discussion. Wearily, Roland plodded to the log Ivo lay against.

With a thud, the quartermaster planted himself next to Ivo, and sighed heavily. "Ho boy…" He turned to Ivo. "Never get involved in politics. I swear these officers are worse than the leeches that lurk in Rudolph's court." He shook his head then nodded behind him. "Hell, even Rook turned all proper on me in a second."

"What about the woman?"

Roland's eyes lit up. "Oh, I knew I was forgetting somethin'."

"So you see," Roland started, "we, that is Rook and myself, brought her before the other officers to see if we could decide what to do with her. Half of them wanted to hang her straight up, sayin' she's some kind of spy." He wrapped an imaginary noose around his neck to accentuate his point. "I suggested they do some questioning first, to see what's what. Bad decision. Got chewed out pretty bad for that. I guess talking out of turn is frowned upon in those circles."

Ivo, in the kindest way he could, urged Roland to hurry up with the news.

"Anyway, they decided to keep her for now, considering her knowledge about Dalwik, but they're going through with a more thorough examination. It is a bit concerning."

"Concerning? They're still going to kill her?"

Roland shrugged. "Doubtful. It's just...I noticed a mark, on her left forearm." Roland pointed to his forearm. "Old symbol, hard to describe. Imagine a double headed scythe set in two overlapping triangles."

"Runes?" Ivo asked.

Roland shook his head. "No, older than that. Runes are carved into objects of innate power. That's why you usually find them set in whalebone or pyroquette steel. It's a bit like tuning a violin, adjustin' the resonance just right. Now what she has on her arm is a sigil."

"What's the bloody difference? They both mean the same thing," Ivo snorted.

Roland rubbed his eyes. "To the layman, yes, but in the old arts, no."

"And what, you're not a layman?"

Roland paused. "Sufficed to say I've dabbled in a few...unconventional hobbies. Rune scribing is hardly the worst of it."

Ivo made a mental note to not dig further; the less he knew about the arcane the better. Roland, however, seemed more than willing to share.

"Now, as I was saying," Roland continued brazenly, "that mark's a sigil. Rather than attuning an item of power, they act as a means of transportation...a vent. Allowing power in or out, depending on the mark."

"So, does her sigil let power in or out?"

"No idea. Could stand for reap, could stand for sow, you never know with the older markings," Roland said honestly. "It's not a mark I've come by though. For all I know it could be a mark of a shunned lover, or, hel, she could have carved it herself while she was bored. But it's deep. Real deep. To the bone."

Ivo cocked his head. "Why is that important?"

"Bone doesn't heal like skin and muscle does. The carvings are almost permanent, hold their shape."

Ivo shook his head. "Sorry, Roland, but this sounds made up. If I could just carve a few squiggles into my skull and harness the power of creation itself, why don't we see a cartload of people flying about, flames out their arses?"

Roland chuckled. "Well, for one, most of the symbols have been lost to time. Arse flames included. And second…you don't wield primeval power. You focus it, channel it. The symbol just limits what kind of power flows through you, the rest is beyond your control."

Ivo's face went blank.

Roland looked at him. "What?"

Ivo shrugged, searching for the right words. "Well…to be honest I never really pinned you as…"

Roland's eyes narrowed. "As what? The reading type?"

Ivo smiled nervously, and tapped himself on the nose. He realized he had just talked himself into a bad spot. Roland stared Ivo down. When he had suffered enough, Roland put Ivo's mind at ease with a hearty laugh. "Well, you're no scholar yourself. How many books have you read?"

Ivo wrung his hands together. "Well, I can't really…read."

Roland patted him on the back. "No shame there. Half the bastards in this army can't make heads nor tails of my scribblin'. But despite that, despite not being able to read a lick, you're still a carpenter, right? You could still put a table together, books be damned."

Ivo nodded.

"There you go. When you work a trade, you pick up a few things. I've just had the good fortune to work with interesting people in interesting places."

The two sat there for a moment, silent, then Ivo asked, "So, what else have you picked up?"

Roland's fatigue lifted, and he began to talk. "Well, I spent seven years in Brennerburg studying old stonework—while there was still a Brennerburg. Shame really...but, I met this artist, and sufficed to say she had an unconventional source for her paints..."

The quartermaster continued for some time, after Ivo had fallen into a deep slumber, and long after the rest of the unit had made their return. Soon after, he had finally run out of energy, and his rotund frame slouched sideways as he too fell asleep.

Come morning, Ivo found himself warm, snug, and unable to move. Were he not so tired he would have panicked but, in his exhaustion, he made do with mild annoyance. One eye gummily opened. Through blurred vision, Ivo picked out his surroundings. The strange, blue sky hung over him, and from all around the stink of the trees invaded his nose. Bringing his vision downwards, he searched for the source of his discomfort. He didn't need to search for long; the hefty bulk of Roland lay sprawled across Ivo's legs. The quartermaster had evidently rolled in his sleep, and found more comfort on Ivo's legs than on the cold, grassy earth.

Grudgingly, Ivo forced himself awake. At least as awake as his fatigue would allow. Joint and sinew, stiff after a night on the packed dirt, creaked and groaned into working order as warmth returned to his body. Dormant muscles pulsed into a state of alertness, and Ivo's breathing deepened. Slowly, his mind ignited, and waking thought once again coursed through him. Now he was ready for the task ahead.

Planting his hands firmly onto the unforgiving earth below, Ivo fought to pull himself from beneath Roland. Leaning back and gritting his teeth, he gradually brought his legs out from the lumpy mass of the quartermaster. Heaving, grunting, and exerting muscles he didn't know he had, Ivo pulled himself free. In doing so, Ivo sprang backwards, the back of his head connecting with the log that had served as his pillow. Bone cracked against wood, and Ivo felt himself slipping back into the realm of unconsciousness. This was short lived. The pain, however, was not.

Ivo grasped the back of his head, letting out a muffled cry. His skull throbbed intensely, although the impact had left the skin unbroken. Looking around, Ivo checked to see if he had woken anyone else. The other soldiers of his unit, huddled around the smouldering remains of their bonfire, seemed unfazed by the sudden outburst of noise, and continued to sleep soundly.

"Bastards," Ivo mumbled under his breath. "How the hell am I the only one unable to get a good night's sleep?"

"You're not," came a stern voice behind him. Ivo's head swivelled, and Rook, clad in her mail coat, greeted him. "They don't sleep well either," she said, pointing to the other soldiers. "But they bitch about it less. Good to see you're up, though. I needed to talk to you." She waved for Ivo to join her then she turned and made way for the officer's tents. Rolling his eyes, Ivo hefted himself off the ground and followed the commander.

Once Ivo had caught up with her, Rook began talking. "What I tell you now, Ivo, is to remain between you, me, and the rest of the commanders." She paused for a moment. "Believe me, I don't trust you. And frankly, none of the other commanders do either. But protocol dictates I convey the secrecy of this information anyway."

Ivo nodded dumbly in return.

"Good. Now, regarding the strange individual we picked up yesterday. We had a chance to... talk with her, and she did not disappoint. The exact nature of our conversation is classified, but it has been determined that she is an asset to the cause." Rook paused, waiting for Ivo to give some indication of understanding. Another dumb nod was all she got.

"Now, as an asset, she must be protected..." Rook continued. "It's clear she's not well, mentally speaking. Upon our return to Rendsheim she will be sent to the finest physicians available. Until then she is in need of a guardian. That's where you step in."

Ivo gave Rook a quizzical look. "So...you want me to look after her?"

Rook nodded.

"But, what about all my soldierly duties?"

"You still have those to attend to," Rook replied, trashing Ivo's hopes, "in addition to making sure her physical and mental well being is maintained." Ivo's shoulders sank, the prospect of extra work sullying his already foul mood. "No need to pout," Rook assured him. "Though you still need to fight like the rest of us, your camp duties have been cut back. I hope you use that extra time wisely."

The two had arrived at the officer's tent, the red-dyed fabric blowing lazily in the soft breeze. Over a dozen in total, each tent housed a number of the unit commanders, with a few dedicated to maps and other tools of the trade. Soldiers clad in mail coats patrolled between the two even rows of tents, a bastion of order amidst the chaos of the camp. Ivo couldn't help but feel envious; these fops slept in luxury while he had to spend the night trapped under his unit's quartermaster. He briefly considered voicing his complaint.

Rook stopped at one of the tents near the centre of the column and signalled for Ivo to follow suit. "Wait here," she barked, before disappearing into the darkness of the tent.

Before Ivo could contemplate sneaking off, she returned, the strange woman in tow.

"Your charge, Ivo," Rook said through closed teeth. Contempt was plastered across her face, as well as worry. "Anything happens to her, and command will see you made an example of."

Ivo nodded nervously.

"Now, if you don't mind, I've been awake for three days. I'm off for a nap." With that, Rook returned to the confines of the tent.

Once again left alone with the mysterious stranger, Ivo was forced to make small talk. "Hope they didn't grill you too hard. With questions, that is."

The stranger shook her head. "No, they were quite accommodating. I answered to the best of my abilities."

Ivo nodded. "Good," he said, stalling.

The stranger looked at Ivo, and said, "I was told you would be looking after me. I don't see that as fair. I'm sure you have more important business to attend to."

She really is out of it, Ivo thought.

"Be that as it may," Ivo said, trying his best to appear personable, "I have been tasked with looking out for you until you're well again."

The woman's eyes narrowed. "Well? I was unaware that I was unwell."

Ivo bit his lip, mind racing to cover his ass. "I-I mean once you've regained your faculties, you know, remembering who you are and what happened."

"I remember who I am," she stated. "Although the past is hidden from me. Perhaps you are right. Who knows who left me there at the roadside?"

Ivo smiled ever so slightly, glad to see she was taking this so well.

The woman stared intently at him. He shrank away. "What?"

"Are you protecting me right now?" she asked truthfully. "I apologize. I am unfamiliar with the process."

"Uh…kinda?" Ivo replied.

She nodded. "Good work, Mister Ivo. That is what your companion called you?" Ivo nodded. "Strange name," she stated, "in what land is Mister a name?"

Ivo corrected her. "No, it's just Ivo. I guess 'mister' is kind of a title."

The woman nodded, seeming to understand.

"Well…" Ivo said as he rocked back and forth on his heels. "I really don't know what to call you."

The woman thought a moment. "I suppose it would be difficult to communicate otherwise. Very well, you may call me something."

"I…I don't know. Roland told me you have a sigil on your arm, so what about Sigilina? Sigilana?"

"Sil." She replied.

"Really?" Ivo questioned her. "It seems a bit…"

The woman cut him off. "You asked me what I would like to be called. I am Sil."

CHAPTER FIFTEEN

The room reeked of blood. Rudolph's mind was in a haze; the only thing clear to him was the searing pain in his chest. Stars of agony sparkled before his eyes, and his veins burned as though molten metal flowed through him. His addled brain urged his body to move, to flail. Rudolph wanted nothing more than to claw at his veins, to bleed himself dry of the fire in his blood. But his body failed him, laid flat against the floor of his cart. No amount of willpower could animate his dead limbs, his body shut down in shock.

So this is it... Rudolph thought. *Shame, I didn't have more time.* Rudolph awaited death with anticipation—to burn away and be ripped from this existence. His heart raced, faster and faster, his veins growing hotter and hotter. It wouldn't be long now...

But, death never came. Rudolph was denied the peace of the grave, and he did not understand why. By all rights, his torment should have ended, his body scorched by his blood. But his blood no longer burned as bright, and a soothing coolness flowing through his veins. Starting at his heart, the chill spread through him, cooling his tortured being. Rudolph longingly remembered the summers of his youth, where he and his peers would dip in marbled pools to escape the gloomy heat of Rendsheim.

But the chill ran deeper, nearly frigid. An icy grip surrounded his heart, and soon the pleasant cool was replaced with hellish frost, his limbs going numb. The cold burned his lungs, slowed his thoughts, and froze his eyes. It was too much to bear.

Screaming, Rudolph shot up, frozen drops of blood dripping from his mouth. His breath hung heavy, slowly dissipating into the dark of the cart. Rudolph gasped for breath, his lungs still burning cold. His senses returned to him, the dark clouding his eyes fading away, bringing him back to a familiar world. And a familiar face. Kneeling next to his fallen form was the vagrant, his rotten grin greeting Rudolph.

Rudolph was about to say something, when the vagabond was ripped backwards, out the cart door and into the dull light of the fading sun. Weakly, Rudolph got to his feet, steadying himself on the table. His chest ached horridly, eliciting a moan as he reached for his heart. An intense heat scorched the tips of Rudolph's fingers, and rapidly his hand retreated. Looking down, Rudolph saw his fine robes torn open, leaving his lean torso exposed. Blood trickled down his chest and stained the surrounding fabric.

Scored over his heart was a gaping wound. Blood oozed from the gash, the jagged edges still fresh. Rudolph looked the wound over in confusion. No weapon Rudolph knew of left a mark like this. It appeared to be a crude collection of cuts, short and narrow, but deep. The pattern was unreadable under the flowing blood, but Rudolph cared little for the shaping. Shakily, he made his way to the door.

Outside, the column had been halted, and soldiers began to surround the chaos developing outside Rudolph's cart. Leaning heavily on the doorframe, the duke saw Brutus and a pair of guards from the military police pinning the vagrant to the ground. Brutus looked down in contempt, before smashing his nailed boots into the pinned man's chest. Bone cracked and buckled, but the vagrant didn't make so much as a hiss.

"By all that burns brightly, what's going on here?" Rudolph cried, covering his new wound with his hand. The heat was still too much to touch, but now the duke could hold his hand close without the fear of burning.

"Sir!" Brutus wheeled towards Rudolph. "We thought you were dead! That crippled bastard had you on the floor, knife to your heart."

Rudolph cocked his head.

"If I may, Lord of the Ember..." the vagrant on the ground wheezed.

"Shut your damned mouth! I'm done with you!" Brutus snapped, and, wheeling back, punted the vagrants head. The blind man's neck nearly snapped as his skull was sent twisting to the side.

"Stop!" Rudolph called.

Brutus turned back, his bare forehead wrinkling. "But sir..."

"But nothing!" The duke stumbled from cart door, pushing aside the guards who rushed to help him. One agonizing step after another, he made his way to the fallen vagrant. With bloodstained hands, he grabbed the vagabond by the hem of his robe, and leaned in close. The blind man was still alive, but Brutus had left a massive split in his gaunt cheek.

"You knew."

Weakly, the vagrant smiled. His gums bled where many already rotting teeth had been shattered.

"You came back. You carved this into my chest."

Softly, the blind man nodded.

"What is it?" Rudolph hissed, tightening his grasp. "What did you do to me?"

A soft, strained whistling escaped the vagrant, eventually forming words. "Not...here..." Rudolph dropped the vagabond to the ground.

"You two," he said, pointing to the guards, "pick him up, and follow me."

"Sir?" Brutus stepped in Rudolph's way, before being harshly elbowed aside.

"Not now, Brutus."

A meaty hand on his shoulder stopped Rudolph, forcing him to turn and face his advisor. "Sir, this cripple just tried to kill you. You're not thinking clearly."

Leaning toward him, Rudolph replied, "That cripple just saved my life. You know what flows in my veins. You know my life is already forfeit. I was burning away, and he brought me back." Stepping back, Rudolph regained his composure, and added, "By all means, join us. It's bound to be an interesting conversation." Snapping his fingers, he called to a nearby grunt, and commanded, "Bring me a bite to eat." Wiping the blood from his chest, he added, "I'm feeling a bit peckish."

"A conduit?" Rudolph asked, as he slowly chewed on the crusty loaf set before him.

"Yes," the vagrant wheezed, lain out on the bed at the back of the cart. Brutus stood nearby, his hefty arming sword in his grasp.

"What, pray tell, does this conduit do?"

The blind man wheezed, trying to get the breath to answer.

"Come now," Rudolph said, biting into a piece of dried venison. "Answer my questions and I'll send for the medic."

"It vents…the excess…power…bound within your veins, lord…" The vagrant managed to get out. "Even one…as mighty as…you…cannot metabolize all that is bound…within the flaming glass. The incanflagarat…builds up."

"So, this nasty little scar will keep me alive?" Rudolph asked, dabbing his still-fresh wound with a wet cloth. Steam rolled off his chest as the fabric came into contact with blood, tinged black with soot.

The vagrant feebly shook his head. "No. It was but a temporary solution, lord…"

Rudolph frowned. "So what's a more permanent solution then?"

The vagrant lifted himself to his elbows. "I need to carve more." He tried to get up.

Brutus immediately stopped the blind man with the point of his sword. "Move and you're dead."

"Brutus. We talked about this." Rudolph wagged his finger.

"This crippled prick wants to start carving more nonsense onto your person and I'm the one out of line?"

"Do you have another answer?" Rudolph asked, leaning back in his chair. "I was dead, Brutus. If five more minutes had gone by you would have found a pile of ash in a white robe."

"Sir, our studies on incanflagarat are inconclusive. There's no evidence..."

"No evidence? I wake up with a bloody pillow every morning. I have to take three cool baths a day or the heat begins to make me sick. Fabric, light, hell, even pleasurable company all burn to the touch I don't need any more evidence than that."

"But sir, we can still try weaning you off the powder. We're close with a repla..." Rudolph's laugh cut Brutus off.

"Really, Brutus? Even if I could stop, give up the dirty habit without my heart stopping and my blood freezing, I would sooner die than go back to that slack jawed royal bastard."

"With all due respect, sir, you're putting your life in the hands of a nameless madman who thinks you're a god."

"I'd say he's very astute."

"Be serious sir," Brutus begged.

"Perhaps I was," Rudolph replied. "Besides, I hardly care about his beliefs. Only his skills matter to me."

"But sir..."

Rudolph looked Brutus dead in the eye. "We'll let this cripple do his work, and we'll get to the temple. After I claim what is mine, we can secure the future of my people. And myself, of course."

Brutus shook his head in defeat, getting nowhere with the duke. "Oh, don't be so glum, Brutus," Rudolph berated his advisor. "This is what we've been working towards! This man achieved in moments what we failed to in years. Think of it! This goes beyond pyroquettes and incanflagarat. For the first time since the dawn of creation, the primeval energies of this world can be directed, wielded! By a deity, no less."

Brutus snorted. "You still believe this apotheosis drivel? "

"I didn't believe there were any alive who still practiced runes and sigils. And yet here we have proof." Rudolph pointed out the rapidly scabbing scar on his chest.

"There is plenty of hobbyist sigil makers." Brutus replied.

"And how many of them have saved a duke's life?" Rudolph shot back, picking over an assortment of preserves laid before him.

"The bastard got lucky."

"Lucky?" Rudolph put down the morsel of fruit he was holding. "Brutus, one wrong mark and I could have turned inside out. Remember the testing?" Brutus didn't react. "Come now Brutus, we both remember having to clean up the mess afterwards."

"It was a cadaver. The tests were doomed to fail anyway."

"Be that as it may," Rudolph continued, "this vagrant has proven reliable. I trust him, to an extent. And a man becoming a god is hardly beyond the scope of reality. Remember the stories from Dalwik? Petyr's grandfather?"

Brutus nodded.

"And I'm sure you remember they had a physical link to a god. They had his bones."

Rudolph pointed to the vagrant, who was drifting in and out of the waking world. "We have a rune expert. We don't need a physical link. We'll make one."

Brutus sighed heavily, as he rested his sword at his side. "So, assume all goes according to plan. Assume we pull off the near impossible, and you are reborn a god. Then what? What will you do?"

Rudolph went silent, searching his own thoughts for an answer. "Do you want the ideal answer, or the honest one?"

"That's all the answer I need," Brutus replied.

Rudolph lowered his head, hurt at his friends mistrust. "I don't know what will happen, Brutus," he said softly. "I don't know if I'll go mad with power, or lose my mind, or burn away." Looking up, Rudolph suddenly looked five years older. Nights of study had left his eyes sunken and hollow, and his complexion pallid. "I can promise you one thing, friend. I will do what is right for my people. For Rendsheim."

"By the end, will you remember that promise?" Brutus asked.

Rudolph closed his eyes. "If I don't, I trust you'll take matters into your own hands."

Brutus nodded slowly. Silence hung heavy for some time, neither of them wishing to speak.

Finally, Brutus piped up. "Fuck it," he grumbled, sheathing his sword and crossing his arms. "Too much work to stop now. Besides, if it weren't for this little project of yours, I'd still be training hayseeds how to fight."

Rudolph perked up, his sullen complexion lightening as a sly grin crossed his face. "Knew I could count on you."

CHAPTER SIXTEEN

Ivo spent the remainder of his morning sullenly sitting by the campfire, Sil in tow. Try as he may, sleep eluded the conscript. He was far too alert to just close his eyes and drift off. It didn't help that Sil refused to stop staring at him, her gaze felt like she was boring a hole in the side of his head, as if she expected something to happen, something extraordinary. But Ivo left her wanting, content with lying there on the log until the rest of his unit awoke.

Roland was the first to wake. The rotund quartermaster picked himself up, and with great effort, pulled himself to a leaning position by Ivo. A rank exhalation followed, and if Ivo had eaten, he would surely be queasy by now. Oblivious to his peer's misery, Roland engaged the two in conversation.

"Good to see ya up and about!" He patted Ivo on the back. "And I see your lady friend is out of the officer's tent. Honestly, I was getting worried for a while there." Leaning towards Ivo, Roland whispered, "We figure out her name yet?"

"Sil!" she chimed in. She was beaming, clearly pleased with the name she picked out.

"Oh, that's an interesting one." Roland mulled it over. "I'm not familiar with it. Where's the name from?"

"She thought of it," Ivo cut in.

"Oh. How'd ya think of it?" Roland scratched his head. Sil pointed to her forearm, and the strange mark. Roland nodded. "I've been meanin' ta ask ya were you got that. It's not a symbol I'm familiar with."

Sil's expression shifted to one of confusion, and she twisted her arm to take a better look at the mark.

"I…I'm not sure." Progressively, her demeanour became more panicked, and she studied the mark intensely.

"Calm down, Sil," Roland said. "It's all right. Let me take a look."

Sil obediently handed her arm over to Roland, right over Ivo's sulking form. The quartermaster gingerly took her arm, and looked over the pale marking. "Huh. I think I get what's going on here…"

"I thought you couldn't read it," Ivo barked, staring with irritation at the limb hanging in front of him.

"I can't," Roland assured him, letting Sil's arm go. "But I bet my anvil it's got somethin' to do with her memory loss. A sigil that confusing is bound to mess with memory." The hefty quartermaster leaned back. "The question is whether it was by design, or just a side effect."

"You mentioned you remember Dalwik." Roland said, idly scratching his chin. Sil nodded, absent-mindedly scratching her left forearm. "Doubtful you got that mark there. Hardly the seat of knowledge and understanding." Nudging Ivo with his elbow, Roland said, "If it ain't fish or spirits, it ain't worth talking about in Dalwik." Roland cracked a smile, but Ivo did not share his enthusiasm.

"Unless…" The quartermaster's smile vanished as his brow creased.

Ivo looked at Roland. "Well?"

Roland shook his head. "Probably nothin', but…" Leaning closer to Ivo than the conscript would like, Roland whispered, "Look, this tidbit is for your ears only. Word gets out, and I could be in court-marshalled." Roland paused, then continued in a darker tone. "Then probably tortured, executed, and my remains stuck up on pikes across Rendsheim."

Disgusted, Ivo nodded slowly, a morbid curiosity driving him to listen. Sil nodded too, her expression placid and unreadable.

Satisfied, Roland looked around the bonfire, confirming that the others had yet to wake. Turning back, he began his tale.

"Now, before I say anything, let me just note that all this happened years ago. Before Rudolph took the seat of power in Rendsheim. We, that is, my peers and me..." Flustered, Roland searched for the right words. "Bloody hell, long story short, I used to work in Dalwik under Petyr's brother, Orrik, the Short. Taller than his title would imply, actually. I'd say he came up to my chin, and I hardly think..."

Ivo impatiently snapped his fingers, pulling Roland away from his tangent.

"Oh, sorry. Right, back then I was a smith by trade, and a bloody good one, too. Before Rook had me straightening shoe nails and patching shirts."

Roland's gaze wandered up, his nostalgia getting the best of him. "I had a shop in Dalwik. I was born there, you know, and I had a pretty rough time of it. Work in the city was slow, and war was on, so I could hardly pack up shop and move towns. They'd recognize my accent and have me caged as soon as I got past the gates." Roland sighed. "I was approached by Orrik, may his ashes rest, as the smith on his project. You see, Orrik was a bit...loopy, more so than most nobles. Got it in his head he could reintroduce rune working and sigil carving as trades. Two dead arts, lost for generations, and he wanted us to rediscover them in less than a lifetime. But it paid well, room and meals included."

Took advantage of the meals, I see, Ivo thought.

"I spent ten years of my life working along scholars, alchemists, mystics, even Petyr. Boy wanted to do his lineage proud, and buried himself in work. Admittedly, all that work was for nothing. By the time Orrik died, we had a basic understanding of the art, along with a few crude runes we had etched up on mildly powerful artifacts. Whale bone and the like." Reaching for his neck, Roland grabbed a thin length of string, and pulled a pendant free. It was knucklebone, and by the size, whatever it belonged to was impressive. Upon the bone, Ivo could barely make out a latticework of etches, stained dark with time. The general shape was that of a waning moon, crisscrossed with an intricate network of lines.

"This was supposed to channel the power in the whale's bones, drawn up from the abysmal dark where a portion of the primeval power still lingers. We figured this particular marking had something to do with longevity."

"Did it work?" Sil asked, completely enthralled by Roland's story.

Roland smiled. "Well, I couldn't give ya an exact number, but last I checked, I was fifty somethin'." Gingerly, Roland returned the pendant to under his tunic. Straightening out his clothes, he continued, "Anyway, my point is, Petyr is the only one in Dalwik still alive that knows anything about rune work."

"So?" Ivo cut in, already sick of the drawn-out story.

"So, you think Petyr is the one who carved this on my arm," Sil concluded.

Roland nodded. "So that leaves the question: who are you?"

Sil looked at her arm, flustered. "I wish I knew."

They sat there for a moment, Sil and Roland quietly contemplating. Ivo, who wished for nothing more than a peaceful rest, began to doze off, leaving his charge and the quartermaster to think. For a moment, the world around him melted away, the log upon which he rested his head as soft as a feather pillow. Vistas of familiar places filled him with warmth, his subconscious mind pining for his drafty town home, and the steady pay from his carpentry...the intoxicating aromas of stain and lacquer, the rhythmic tap of the chisel. Through his sleeping mind came imagery of exquisite furniture, which he himself had made.

But, something was awry. Ivo noticed an imperfection upon the leg of a chair, small and unassuming, but holding a significance that drove him to look closer. In his dream, Ivo found himself taking a corporeal form, moving steadily towards the chair. Kneeling, he looked over the finished piece of furniture, attempting to perceive the nature of the flaw. It was too clean to be a nick from the saw, and too out of place to have been chiseled in by mistake.

If Ivo didn't know better, he could have sworn the imperfection resembled a double-headed scythe, set in two overlapping triangles. The dimensions were perfectly measured, a feat even the finest artisans would find hard to achieve on timber. Ivo looked the symbol over. He didn't put it there. He was certain he had never seen the mark before.

Leaning back, Ivo noticed another small nick along the edge of the seat, one that certainly wasn't there prior. To his surprise, it was identical to the first, in both size and shaping. In dismay, Ivo stood, and walked around the chair. It seemed every time he looked over a section again, he would find more flaws, more imperfections. Soon, he found it hard to find a spot on the chair untouched by the symbols.

In frustration, Ivo reached out to grab the chair, with the intention to throw it out the back door. It was rubbish; who would by a marked up chair? But, as he reached for the marked seat, he noticed something. A black, bloody mark upon his hand, the edges cauterized by an intense heat.

No sooner did he notice the wound that he found himself pulling his hand back in agony, a burning shock jumping up his arm and swirling his vision. He grabbed at the mark, the heat of the brand still lingering. His knees went weak, and he dropped to the floor. The urge to wretch from the pain forced him to double over, heaving his lunch onto the dirt floor of his workshop.

His vision clearing, Ivo sought to investigate the wound closely. Shaking, Ivo pulled his right hand away, to reveal the damage done. Struck upon his hand was the bloody, charred mark; a double headed scythe, set on a pair of overlapping triangles.

Ivo's eye's shot open as panic pulled him from his slumber. Frantically, his gaze darted back and forth, revealing that he was still in the camp, propped up against the same log. He sighed, his shoulders sinking slightly, before he shot back up. He pulled his left hand to his face, jerking back the sleeve of his padded jacket. To his relief, the flesh was untouched by iron and flame, every scar and callous where it should be.

"What's up, bitch? Never seen the back of your hand before?" Ivo's shoulders sank, his hand dropping to his side. It was Helena. Bowl in hand, she was returning from the mess carts, and by the smell of things, it was onion and potatoes in a cloudy beef broth. Again.

"While you were sitting here ogling yourself, your lady friend and Roland went on a little tour of the camp." She waved off to the side with her spoon "Doing a damned fine job. Poor girl, I'm surprised she even survived the morning in your care."

"Please, not now, Helena," Ivo groaned, the knot in his back making its presence known.

"Aw, baby had a bad night?"

Ivo looked downwards, fed up with being picked on, but without the strength of will to retaliate. A soft sigh escaped him, causing Helena to roll her eyes in contempt.

"Fine," she said, moving to join the regulars sitting at the other end of the bonfire, "since you asked nicely, I'll bust your balls after breakfast." She nodded in the direction Roland and Sil had gone. "Just man up and do your job."

Elated by this small victory, Ivo stood, his joint creaking in protest, and he made his way off across the camp.

With a rising sense of panic, Ivo paced up and down the rows of carts and tents, drawing sideways glares from regulars and conscripts alike. The day had just started for many who, groggily, made their way to the mess carts and the latrines. Wheels were repaired with whatever spare timber could be scrounged up, and the quartermasters were taking stock of rations, bolts, and so on. Everywhere Ivo went, people were shouldering past in their haste, ignorant of the sunken-eyed conscript. At least it reminded him of home.

Ivo finally caught a glimpse of Roland; his girth was unmistakable. He was standing by his cart, and appeared to be handing a few things to Sil—a wood comb, a bowl and spoon, and a pouch, all standard kit provided by the military. Ivo broke into a jog, ducking and dodging his way through the indifferent crowd of soldiers.

Roland caught a glimpse of Ivo out the corner of his eye, and waved him over. Grinning, he yelled, "Oh, Ivo! Just getting our friend here set up."

Mildly winded, Ivo grunted in response. Sil, who was looking over her new mess kit in confusion, said nothing. Roland opened his mouth, about continue, when a harsh, strained cry echoed from the far side of the camp.

Without a word, Roland sprang into action, taking Sil by the hand and running to the back of his cart. With agility at odds with his heavy frame, he vaulted into the back of the cart, hauling the startled Sil with him. In one motion, he hurried her to a covered spot in the corner, between a two stacks of crates, while hefting a lumber axe over his shoulder. "Ivo!" he called, and tossed something to the startled conscript. Ivo had little time to react, and the tossed item caught him square in the chest. Recoiling, he took a minute to catch his breath, wheezing in pain. Looking down, he discovered Roland had tossed him a blade, still in its scabbard. It was a short, broad blade that tapered dramatically to a fine stabbing point. The simple hilt and straight cross-guard implied a rather unbalanced, if durable, arming sword.

Chaos erupted at the far side of the camp, and steel could be heard rasping against steel. In a panic, Ivo grabbed the sword from the grass, still damp with morning dew. He unsheathed the blade, and tossed the scabbard back in the cart. Sil cried out, having been struck by the wayward projectile, but Ivo didn't have time to apologize. He bolted after Roland, who was already on his way to the commotion. Out of the corners of his vision, Ivo could make out other soldiers preparing for combat, hastily donning arming jackets and buckling on helmets. Crossbows were strung and blades drawn from storage, and all around barked orders could be heard.

As the commotion rose in volume and intensity, Ivo wondered what he was doing. For the first time in his life, he was moving towards a fight, rather than away. Emotions in turmoil, panic drove him away while a combination of duty and sleep deprivation pulled him onward. He cursed under his ragged breath; adrenaline flowed through his veins, sanity an afterthought.

When they arrived at the edge of the camp, the centre of the commotion, whatever had come this way had long since departed, leaving naught but blood and corpses. The grassy clearing that bordered the woods was dotted with the fallen, some crying out, and others silent. At least twenty had fallen, by Ivo's count, most in Rendsheimer uniform. That is, all but two, who were clad in padded jackets, dyed a vibrant purple, with close-fitting skullcaps over yellow hoods. One body was left bifurcated, his legs and abdomen some three feet away from his torso. The other thrashed at the two soldiers attempting to restrain him as they dragged him off to the camp.

Ivo stood dumfounded. The adrenaline surging through his veins had faded, leaving a knot of repugnance in his gut. His sword dropped from his hand, embedding itself in the grassy earth. Before him were blood and limbs and the feeble screams of the dying. One lad, no older than Ivo, desperately tried to keep his innards from spilling forth, cried for his mother. Another, who already bore the scars of a soldier's life, mindlessly picked at the stump of his leg as he stared off into the forest, a glazed look as empty as the void. Another soldier was left impaled, a lance through her sternum pinning her to the ground. Blood gurgled from her mouth as she weakly called for help.

"What happened?" Roland called out, lowering his axe and using it as a crutch.

A regular, with a lengthy gash running down his face, replied, "Cavalry! Purple and yellow, Dalwik! Came riding in, cutting and trampling. We got two of them, the others buggered off!" Holding a rag to his cheek, he woozily stumbled back to camp, searching for a medic.

"Son of a whore!" Roland cursed through clenched teeth. "Petyr never fought his fights fairly." His attention turned to the captured soldier from Dalwik, still trying his best to get the better of his captors. "Oh, the interrogators are going to have fun with that one," Roland said in a bitter tone. "Come on, Ivo. There's still the living to attend to." Roland stepped forward, but when Ivo didn't follow, he turned. "Ivo?"

Ivo didn't respond. The bloodshed before him enthralled him, drew him in. Never had he seen such wounds inflicted in malice, nor had he heard the last gasps of the doomed. It paralyzed him, planted him firmly in place.

"We can't be slackin' about, Ivo!" Roland called, stepping towards him and taking him by the arm. But Ivo resisted his grasp, pulling away and staring daggers at the quartermaster.

"How?" he addressed Roland. "How could anyone put up with this? Live with this?" A panicked desperation filled Roland's face.

"Look, the damage is done. Leave the dead to the dead!"

Ivo shook his head. "I can't," he murmured, looking down at his feet.

Roland bit his lip. From his belt he grabbed a small, copper flask, bound in leather. As gently as possible, he slipped it into Ivo's hand. Ivo examined the flask, running his thumb over the tarnished surface.

"More of your concoction?" he asked.

Roland shook his head, defeated. "No, 'fraid no amount of herbs will help you here. It's moonshine." Ivo looked up from the flask, meeting Roland's concerned gaze. The quartermaster nodded, then turned, and rushed off to assist the wounded.

Ivo's attention returned to the flask. He sank to the ground, his eyes never leaving the leather bound canteen. There, sitting in the damp morning grass, Ivo wished he could cry. But the tears never came. Popping the lid off the flask, Ivo tilted back, and drank deeply.

CHAPTER SEVENTEEN

Rudolph winced, pulling at his bindings. The sharp sting biting at his ribs intensified as the vagrant tapped away, a fine hammer and chisel in hand. They had been at it for some time now, in the confines of Rudolph's wagon. At the vagabond's request, Rudolph had the finest set of jeweller's tools brought to the wagon, along with several clean bandages and a healthy dose of liquor to ease the pain. Then, Rudolph bound himself to the wall of his cart, and let the vagrant begin his bloody work.

"And you said we'd never use these," Rudolph hissed through clenched teeth, jiggling the bindings.

Brutus, who was sitting off to the side, replied, "I said you and I would never use those. And this wasn't exactly their intended purpose." He nodded toward one of the many shelves that lined Rudolph's wagon. "Besides, I'm pretty sure the riding crop and gag haven't seen any use."

"Keep it up," Rudolph said, "and I'll make sure you get to put that gag—BURN IT ALL TO CINDER!" he cried out, thrashing against his restraints. The vagrant quickly drew away, nearly dropping his tools in the process. "For fuck's sake, cripple!" the duke bellowed, his vision blurred in agony.

"My apologies, most magnificent lord. Your nerves are still tender, it will take some time."

"Time is something I'm short on," Rudolph spat. He turned to Brutus, and called out, "More liquor. My head is swimming." Brutus nodded obediently, and rose from his chair. He grabbed a gilded flask from the table, and presented it to Rudolph. The duke tilted his head, and Brutus poured a copious amount of liquor into his mouth. Once the flask was dry, Rudolph exhaled, his breath flammable.

"You know, Brutus..." he said as numbness began to set it, "incanflagarat has not been kind to me. Night terrors, searing pain, heatstroke... But the worst thing is I can't get good and shitfaced anymore."

"Damn shame, sir," Brutus concurred.

Brutus stepped back, looking over the vagrant's handiwork. Half of Rudolph's chest was covered in small, deep wounds, each precisely cut by the vagrant. These wounds ran clean to the ribs, were the vagabond was chiseling into Rudolph's bones. Each sigil was unique, shapes crisscrossed with dozens of lines apiece.

"Still can't believe you let a blind man carve into your chest," Brutus said as he examined the damage. "Do you feel different?"

Rudolph grumbled, as the vagrant hit another nerve. "I feel like someone's digging into my ribcage. How am I supposed to feel?"

Brutus shrugged. "Just let me know if he starts digging too deep." He shot the vagrant a dirty look. "Then we can return the favour." The blind vagrant didn't acknowledge the threat, absorbed in his work.

Morning came slowly for Rudolph. The repetitive tapping of steel on bone rang in his ears, and he felt as if his chest had been torn open. By the dawn, he hung limp from the shackles, consciousness failing him. Brutus, too, had passed out, days without proper sleep finally catching up to him. Lulled to sleep by the rhythmic hammering, he had slumped low in his chair.

Satisfied with his work, the vagrant grinned a rotten grin. With gnarled hands he gently shook Rudolph back into wakefulness. "My lord," he called in a soft, raspy voice, "it is time for you to awaken. My work is done, and you stand a step closer to glorious apotheosis." Rudolph mumbled, his mind slowly returning. With a jolt, he pulled at his bindings, screaming bloody murder. Brutus shot awake, his side-sword drawn before he was even standing. The vagrant stepped back calmly. Brutus was less collected, his hand around the vagabond's throat in seconds. With little effort, he held the cloaked figure aloft, scrawny legs dangling.

"Wait!" Rudolph cried, trying to stop Brutus from doing anything drastic. "Put him down, you idiot! He just startled me!" Brutus stared daggers at the vagrant, before dropping him to the floor. The old man collapsed, wheezing.

Rudolph shook his head. "You've got to stop trying to kill the help. What next, choke out the scullery maid because she dropped some of the silver?"

Brutus turned to the duke, and bowed his head in apology. "Sorry sir. Thought the cripple was trying to do you in."

"Apology accepted," Rudolph spat, pulling at his bindings. "Now shut up and get me out of these." As ordered, Brutus began to undo the clasps around Rudolph's wrists.

Once undone, Rudolph fell forward, his legs stiff and feeble. Gently, Brutus caught him, and pulled him to the bed on the far side of the wagon. With great care, he laid the struggling duke onto the soft mattress. "Remind me," Rudolph said, "to requisition you a new arming jacket." He pointed to Brutus' plus-sized aketon, the bright red fabric stained dark along the front. "I appear to have ruined yours."

Wheezing drew Rudolph's attention and he glanced at the vagrant still sprawled across the floor. "Please help him up, Brutus. And gingerly this time."

Brutus stepped over to the collapsed vagabond, and as softly as he could, hauled him to his feet. The elderly man staggered slightly, collapsing into the chair Brutus had been sleeping in only moments prior.

"Now, apologize," Rudolph commanded as he propped himself up on a number of pillows.

Brutus' scowled. "You can be quite immature when you want to be, sir," he pointed out.

Rudolph wagged his finger. "Tut tut. That doesn't sound like an apology."

Brutus sighed, looked the vagrant in the eye-sockets, and half-heartedly apologized. The vagrant, too weak to respond, simply nodded. Satisfied, Rudolph looked down over the collection of wounds that lined his chest. Taking one of the satin sheets from his bed, he wiped away the blood, revealing row upon row of fresh, red marks, the most recent still oozing blood. Running along each of the ribs and along the edges of the sternum, the newly born sigils were evenly spaced and precisely shaped, to a level of artisanship that Rudolph had rarely seen.

"Seems a bit excessive," Brutus commented, nodding at Rudolph.

The vagrant leaned forward, and softly said, "I did what I had to... Any less, and the power in his blood could have overwhelmed him."

Brutus grunted. "What blood he has left. You could have at least given him time in between, let him recover."

The vagrant shook his head. "Any delay, any interruption, could have put him at risk. You know nothing of what force flows through him."

"Come now, Brutus, it's hardly any worse than that tattoo across your back," Rudolph piped in.

"My tattoo," Brutus replied, turning back to the duke, "wasn't done with a chisel."

"Fair enough. Now stop fretting and bring me some bandages. What time is it?"

Brutus peered out the stained window of the cart's door, where he was greeted with the rays of the rising sun.

"Just after dawn," he replied.

"Ah, then fetch me my robes as well. Have to keep face amongst the troops and all that."

Brutus shook his head. "Sir, you just had an alphabet carved into your ribs. Surely it can wait."

Rudolph snorted. "And miss breakfast? I shall do no such thing."

Freshly bandaged, Rudolph donned a set of modest brown robes and stepped out of the cart. Shadowed by Brutus and the skulking vagabond, he made his rounds of the camp, putting on a smile and greeting every soldier he passed. His army had camped in the field of an old farmstead, along the borders of Rendsheim and Stahlsheim. The farmhouse had burnt down long ago in some forgotten skirmish between Rudolph and Borig, leaving a dead stretch of soil and neglected fencing.

It didn't take long for the three to make to the officer's mess cart. It was a closed in, well stocked canteen, with cuts of fine cured meats hanging from the roof, and artisan cheeses set into shelves along its walls. A step above the slop fed to the regulars, to be sure.

"Ah, you smell that, Brutus?" Rudolph inhaled deeply.

"What? The rank cheese or the overpriced wine?"

"Brutus..." Rudolph rubbed his eyes, "you always have to rain on my parade."

Brutus shrugged. "You know me, not cut out for this fancy stuff. I'll take broth and onions."

"Fine, I'll send someone to get you your peasant fair. Just follow me, we have work to discuss."

Benches and tables were set up to the side of the cart, where officers and high-ranking staff sat and chatted. To the far end of the cluster was a small, round pavilion, stained red and black. This was Rudolph's command tent, were he would look over maps and plan his strategies. It also helped to keep cold wind and unwanted company out during meals.

Impatiently, Rudolph waved to one of the servants from

the mess cart. Without a word, he hastily dropped the plate of food he was carrying, and rushed to the cart to get Rudolph his meal. Satisfied his breakfast was coming, he turned to the vagrant, who stood silently behind him.

"Cripple, make yourself at home. Eat from the officer's canteen, if you so desire. You are to eat on your own. Brutus and I have important business to discuss."

As smoothly as his decrepit body would allow the blind man bowed, and made his way to the nearest empty bench.

Satisfied that they would be left alone, Rudolph and Brutus made for the confines of the tent. Brutus held the flap open, and Rudolph stepped inside. The servant who Rudolph had called for rushed towards the tent, trying to squeeze past Brutus. One meaty fist stopped him dead in his tracks, the food in his hands nearly flying from his grasp. Brutus ripped the platter of food from the servant, and shoved him back.

Brutus wrinkled his nose at the pungent aroma of the cheese arrayed on the platter in his hands. "I'll never understand your tastes," he grumbled as he entered the tent, placing the food on the table. Two chairs sat across from each other, and a number of maps and scrolls lined racks along the walls. "Reminds me of a Brennerburg whorehouse." Rudolph raised an eyebrow. "The aroma," Brutus clarified.

"Ah, charming." Rudolph's appetite subsided slightly.

The chair creaked as Brutus sat down, taking a small wooden bowl from the platter. "Broth and onion. More like it."

Rudolph was occupied with a cut of venison, served raw and sprinkled with imported salt. The two ate for some time, making idle chitchat before getting to business.

"What news from Stahlsheim?" Rudolph asked between bites.

"I read up on the reports when you were out," Brutus replied. "So far, your soothsayer's words ring true. Borig hasn't budged."

"He waits in Stahlsheim. Disappointing."

Brutus nodded. "We'll have to draw him out. Meet him on his own turf. Casualties will be higher than expected. It'll be a bloodbath."

"How do you recommend we proceed?" Rudolph asked.

Brutus rubbed his temples. "I can't rightly recommend anything. We need the distraction to make way to the temple. But we're damning our own soldiers in the process."

"We cannot stop what is in motion," Rudolph commented, leaning back in his chair. "Dalwik will come under siege one way or another. We stall here, Borig will reach out and lift the siege. Rendsheim will be next."

Brutus exhaled through his nose. "How far are we willing to go for this?"

"As far as we need to," Rudolph stated. "You and I both know it's only a matter of time before Borig or Petyr get to that temple. We either sacrifice here, or sacrifice when they move to burn Rendsheim to the ground."

"Can't you bury the hatchet? Make peace?"

"Not as long as Petyr draws breath. Not after the atrocities he's committed."

"We've hardly been saints." Brutus clasped his hands together. "How many people did we test that powder on? How many went mad?"

"A few individuals do not an atrocity make." Rudolph took another bite of venison. "His family has been playing with forces beyond their understanding for centuries. He has no honour, and he will do anything for power."

"Awfully noble of you, to stop a tyrant in the making," Brutus grunted.

"I never said there wasn't anything in it for me. You think Richart dug the pits to further the progress of humanity?" He picked out a finely marbled piece of cheese. "My best interests happen to coincide with the best interests of my people."

Brutus took another sip of his broth, looking blandly at the walls of the tent. He remained silent for quite some time before he finally spoke. "When do we tell the commanders we aren't stopping at the bridge?"

Rudolph grinned. "As soon as possible."

Brutus rose to his feet, turning for the flap of the tent. He was about to make his way out, when Rudolph called after him, "Good to have you on board, friend."

CHAPTER EIGHTEEN

It had been hours since the attack. The dead had been set on a number of pyres and set alight, in keeping with Rendsheim tradition. The fallen horse-rider from Dalwik did not receive such a courtesy, left to rot on the cold grass. His comrade could still be heard, crying foul somewhere in the officer's camp.

Ivo had sequestered himself away behind Roland's cart. The copper flask, long since emptied, lay at his side. But it wasn't enough; he doubted the camp held enough liquor to numb his mind.

Without end, the scene of bloodshed played over in his head. The stink of blood and shit, the piercing wails of the dying and the jagged, cruel wounds. That people could wreak such terrible mayhem was deeply horrifying.

Soldiers and support staff filed past Ivo, some assisting with the cleanup, others packing up camp for the march. All ignored the slumped form of Ivo. Save for one familiar face.

"I can't believe it."

Ivo looked up, seeing Helena looming over him. "Sons and daughters of Rendsheim lay fallen, and you're snivelling under a cart."

Ivo paid her no mind, deeply rooted in his own torments.

"No good response. Figures." Helena crossed her arms. "You're pathetic. Each of those soldiers who died out there were worth ten of you, but here you are, still alive while they burn." She sniffed. "Do I smell booze?"

Ivo weakly nodded to the discarded flask by his side. Helena bent down, and picked it up. "Roland's? You stole this from Roland?"

Ivo shook his head. "He gave it to me," he mumbled. "To ease my nerves. It didn't help."

Helena looked back at the flask. "Bloody hell, you really that shook up about this?"

Ivo nodded. "It was the first time I've seen a body, Helena. The gore..." His head dropped again.

Helena shook her head. "Look, kid, we all get the first time jitters, but you got to get over it. Get up and start helping!"

"The screams, Helena..." Ivo slurred his words slightly, heavily inebriated.

"Burn it all to cinder," Helena muttered under her breath. "Stop feeling sorry for yourself and get moving!"

Ivo didn't respond.

Helena sighed, and leaned down to Ivo's level. "Look, Ivo. You're worthless. You're pathetic. But have some dignity. Get up, dust yourself off, and work through it."

He didn't respond. Helena rolled her eyes, and continued, "I get it. You're feeling sick. You think I was cheery the first time I took a life? You think I forgot the sound he made as his lungs collapsed, my sword through his chest? I remember, Ivo. Every single son of a bitch, I remember." She pointed at the flask. "I spent three years going from tavern to tavern. But you know what? I got over it. Life isn't all fine and dandy."

Ivo remained silent.

"Fine." Helena stood up. "You want to mope like the bitch you are, go for it. I got work to do." With that, she turned and left.

Not that Ivo minded, really. All he wished for was solitude, and strong drink. Anything to numb the horror raking at his mind, to silence the screams. What he got, however, was another uninvited visitor. Silently, Sil crept towards him, and softly sat to his side. A tilt of the head was the only acknowledgement he gave, and all the acknowledgement she needed.

"You seem troubled, Ivo. I asked Roland, but he would not say why."

"There's no point telling you," Ivo mumbled. "You wouldn't understand."

"And why is that?" Sil followed up.

Ivo shook his head. "I don't want to talk about it." He eyed the empty flask. "I just want to forget it all."

Sil frowned. "You're wrong, Ivo. I believe you would mind forgetting very much."

"Doubtful. The worst part is remembering how life was. Sure, it was a shit job in a rundown shack, but it was *my* shack, *my* shit job. I had a calling. I knew where I fit in this running joke we call life. Now..." His head sank.

"You're not the only one," Sil said. "Imagine, waking up in the company of strangers, unaware of who you are or how you got there. I have no past, Ivo, no clue how I fit into things. But I can either move forward with life, or mope behind a cart for the rest of my days." Ivo lifted his head, and saw Sil holding a hand out to him. "You can get through it, Ivo. I'm here to help."

Hesitantly, Ivo reached out, and took Sil's hand. She stood, pulling the groggy conscript to his feet. "One step at a time," she said. "Now let's help pack camp."

The rest of the morning was spent packing and preparing for the long march ahead. The horses were harnessed to the carts, and the tents were neatly tucked away. By noon, the army was ready to march. The delay caused by the attack had set the schedule back drastically, and word around the camp was another night of forced marching. However, the usual grumbling accompanying such an order was absent. Most of the regulars were ready to get to grips with Petyr's soldiers, ready to enact a grisly revenge for their fallen comrades.

As Ivo packed away the last of Rook's tent, he wondered what happened to Roland. His usual place at his wagon was empty, and Ivo hadn't seen him around the camp. It wasn't until he looked around that he finally caught a glimpse of him. The corpulent quartermaster was hurriedly following Rook, the two in a heated discussion. The quartermaster's leather apron was flecked with dark droplets of arterial blood, no doubt a grisly reminder of the impromptu first aid he was forced to deliver.

Ivo ran off after Roland, Sil in tow. As they approached, they caught a few snippets of conversation.

"... not right, Rook. We promised we'd let him go!" Roland's breathing was ragged, and he was having a hard time keeping up with Rook's pace.

"I never mentioned when," Rook called over her shoulder. "He knows more than he lets on, Roland. We have to push him harder. I will not discuss this further."

Roland stopped in his tracks, taking a moment to catch his breath. Ivo could see the quartermaster muttering to himself, mouthing a number of vile curses. The scowl on Roland's face lifted when he saw Ivo. "Oh, Ivo! Good to see you! Sorry I ran off like that." He pointed to his bloody apron. "I had to..."

"You had medic duty?" Ivo asked.

Roland grimaced. "Not quite. You know that bastard we took alive? Well, Rook was trying to persuade him to give us a bit of information."

Ivo raised an eyebrow. "So..."

"I was there to hold him down while the interrogators...well, let's not talk about it." He cheered up a little bit. "Good to see you in decent spirits though. I was worried you'd still be a bit traumatized. It's never an easy thing to see, that."

"I'll survive." Ivo said.

"Good. Then you can give me a hand with the forge!"

"That's not what I..." Roland grabbed Ivo by the shoulder, and pulled him along as he made his way to his forge.

"So, did you learn anything from him?" Ivo asked.

"Well, we did learn he was a conscript. The whole cavalry force is, apparently. Looks like Petyr is takin' a hint from Rudolph. Petyr knows we're here, but it's doubtful he'll be takin' us head on."

"Anything esle?"

"Well, he did hint at a number of units sprinkled about the forest here. Local hunters and the like, probably goin' to be plinking away at us, but we're not too worried."

"Is that it?" Ivo asked.

"'Fraid so. They didn't give much information to the grunts, kinda kept 'em in the dark. Bet you can relate."

You have no idea, Ivo thought.

"Oh, by the by," Roland continued, "you forgot somethin'." Arriving at the cart, Roland hopped into the back, and began to rummage through the crates stacked there. After a moment, he produced a broad, tapering blade, stowed away in its scabbard. "Seemed a shame to leave it stuck in the ground," Roland said, and tossed it to Ivo. "Hopefully you won't need to be usin' it. But better safe than sorry."

Ivo looked at the worn leather scabbard, the faint aroma of age coming off the shabby surface. Ivo was about to thank Roland, but the quartermaster was already busy preparing the horses for the march ahead.

"He really treasures that sword, you know," Sil said from behind Ivo. "It's his brother's. Roland made it for him for his coming of age."

"Would explain the heft," Ivo thought aloud. "Anyone the size of Roland could swing this thing, no problem."

"Make sure you take care of it," Sil chided him.

Ivo nodded, once again looking over the blade. He ran his hand over the pommel, feeling the rough oxidized finish of the metal. He undid the binding of the blade, and looped it around his belt. The sword hung heavy at his side, encumbering and reassuring in equal measure. A semblance of confidence flowed through Ivo, a feeling unfamiliar to him.

"Might want to leave that in the cart!" Roland called, pulling Ivo from his short-lived measure of personal worth. "It's a bit heavy to be luggin' around all day!"

Camp was packed in short order, the commanders barking the order to make haste. It was a short jaunt back to the road, and from there the march continued. Between the looming boughs of the towering trees, the road to Dalwik stretched far into the distance. The heavy scent of pine sap and earth rot hung low in the sunken road, a far departure from the aroma of smoke and ash Ivo was used to.

The tension among the soldiers was palpable, many eyes darting in many directions. The clustered trees cast long shadows, giving ample opportunity for an ambush. Heavy branches blocked the noon light, creating a stark contrast between the illuminated path and the shadowy clutches of the trees. From the arching branches, foreign birds cried their haunting songs, the shrill echoes putting the Ivo in an ill mood.

Occasionally, a rustling could be heard from the edges of the road, faint glimpses of long legged, horned beasts and beady yellow eyes. Bushy-tailed rodents chittered as they observed the passing procession, lobbing pinecones and twigs at the interlopers below.

Civilization was absent from this place. The road was caked with dirt and pine needles, the few patches of fieldstone overgrown with creeping vines and choking grass. Small, white flowers grew in patches at the roadside, breaking up the expanse of green. Such growth would be pleasant within the finery of a royal garden, but here, they spread thick and wild, adding a pungent floral punch to the cloying odor of sap.

Even now, Ivo could feel eyes upon him from the inky recesses of the woods. Whether or not it was idle paranoia, he could not say. From nook to shadowy nook, he watched. For anything, really—anything that would betray the presence of something sinister. To Ivo, it was all sinister. Even the smallest of these woodland creatures was alien to him, a strange and potentially threatening form of life unknown to the oil-slicked surfaces of Rendsheim.

Sil, on the other hand, seemed delighted by the change of scenery. Her eyes were wide open, trying to take in as much as possible every second. Her head pivoted with every new sound, it seemed in the hopes of glimpsing one of the myriad beasts within the woods. She began asking questions, about the names and natures of the life at the borders of the road. Ivo had no answers, responding to each new inquiry with a dismissive, "No idea."

On more than one occasion, she made her way to Roland's cart, walking alongside and asking questions of the quartermaster.

Of the natural world, Roland knew little. Ivo knew his forte was with steel and fire, not the living things of the woods. But that did little to stop him. He spun lengthy yarns about the fur-tailed rats, who would pounce upon the horned dogs from the branches above and sink in their wicked fangs. Ivo figured it was nonsense, but Sil continued to listen, nodding every few seconds.

Sil's light-hearted mood was contagious. The terror of the forest seemed to lessen as soldiers began to chat with one another about the unusual sights and sounds of Petyr's lands. A few cracked tales of far away lands and even stranger beasts from abroad. There was chatter and argument in equal measure, as is the norm for any gathering of soldiers. Even the stern, proper regulars began to rub shoulders with the conscripts.

With spirits raised, the lengthy march ahead seemed less strenuous, if only slightly. Lunch was served on the go; reheated broth and course bread. Age did not improve the flavour, but it was filling, and it facilitated further conversation. Even Ivo, who had remained silent for most of the march, found himself in the mood for chit-chat after eating. As he walked alongside Roland's cart, the two spoke.

"Really, you don't need to use many nails in furniture," he explained to Roland. "I join most of my furniture with peg and socket. Holds together just fine."

Roland nodded, taking in the information between sips of his soup. "Sounds like a lot of work," he mused. "Does it pay well?"

Ivo shrugged.

"Oh, come now, it's not like you make fifteen embers a week."

"Twelve, actually," Ivo replied, face stern as stone. Roland bit his lip.

"Well, I guess it's not about the money, it's about doing what you love," Roland said, trying to cover his ass.

"Yeah, I guess," Ivo mumbled.

"Believe me, at your age, I was happy to…" A shrill whistle cut Roland off.

A storm of white fletching and barbed steel glinted in the noon sun. The jagged arrows found their mark in the flesh of soldiers, who in their conversations never heard the rustling in the woods. Half a dozen dropped, injured. Others grabbed at the arrows embedded in their armour, trying to dislodge the projectiles. For every arrow that found its mark, a dozen stuck firm in the packed dirt, or clattered off of the aged cobblestones. The quantity of arrows alone betrayed a sizeable, if untrained, force of archers hidden within the trees.

Wayward arrows dug deep into the wood of Roland's cart as he rolled over the side for cover. The regulars, who had opted to march with their crossbows over their shoulders, took cover behind the wagons, and opened fire into the darkness of the woods. A flurry of bolts answered the hail of arrows, the thunk of spring steel audible over the shouting.

Ivo dove behind the cart, joining Roland and Sil. Roland still held the reins of the horses, which threatened to pull away in panic, taking the cart with them.

"What the hell do we do?" Ivo called to Roland in panic.

"We have to get to the shields! We won't be able to get anywhere without them!" Roland pointed a meaty finger down the column towards one of the weapon carts.

It was a good fifty feet away, over open ground. The regulars, who were closer to the cart, had already grabbed a number of pavises, planting the hefty shields on wooden stands.

"It looks like they got this handled!" Ivo said, nodding towards the soldiers.

Then a stray arrow caught the flank of one of sturdy draft horses hitched to Roland's cart. To an animal that size, an arrow would be an annoyance, but the sting was enough to push the already frightened mare to panic. The horse snorted, eyes wide, and pulled with all the force she could muster. Her partner followed suit, and the cart began to creak forward. Roland and Sil got to their feet in an effort to remain behind the safety of the wagon.

Ivo was not so alert. He didn't notice the cart behind him moving until one of the wheels collided with his side, nearly running him over. Ivo jumped into a low, ape like stance, half running half crawling after Roland and Sil. Roland pulled at the reins of his horses, called out warning, and hoped the soldiers could hear him or the wagon rumbling towards them.

The horses began to gain momentum, not stopping for anything in their blind flight. Regulars and conscripts leapt out of the way, still fighting the unseen enemy. A few were forced to abandon their pavises, unable to pull them free in time. The horses simply trampled over them, breaking reinforced timber as easy as kindling. Splinters flew, the crack of wood joining the commotion of the battle.

"Ivo! Grab the bloody shield!" Roland called back, preoccupied with reigning in the horses. Ivo saw what he meant. A pavise stood loosely locked in a patch of dirt. Several light arrows stuck firm in the shield's cover, but it was still in good condition.

Ivo grabbed the shield as he ran past, nearly pulled backward when the pavise refused to budge. It took another hefty yank to dislodge it, the stand falling free. Ivo was now lugging a large, heavy piece of protection. Not as practical as he had hoped, but still. Clumsily, he fumbled with the leather straps, tightening until they held firm on his right arm. He threw the loop of leather over his shoulder, distributing the weight of the pavise. At least that was one problem solved.

"Now what?" he called to Roland.

"You're the shield bearer! Go bear the damn shield!"

Ivo just kept running.

Frustrated, Roland spat, "Find Helena!"

Reluctantly, Ivo slowed down, bringing the pavise up to cover him as the cart rolled past. His timing was impeccable. No sooner had he raised the shield than an arrow struck home, embedding itself at chest height into the canvassed timber. The impact was substantial, albeit deadened by the heft of the pavise. But it was still enough to stop Ivo's heart for a moment, as he stood dumfounded. Another arrow whistled past him, and another. He realized that the unseen attackers were, indeed, shooting at him.

He dove into a kneeling position, keeping the shield between himself and the flurry of arrows from the edge of the woods. At the very least, he could make himself as unappealing a target as possible. Sitting as he was, he left no flesh for the arrows to pierce, and the concealed archers began to choose other, less ready targets.

One problem down, Ivo now debated seeking out Helena. True, he was her shield-bearer, but she seemed more than capable of caring for herself. Really, it would be in both their best interests if Ivo just stayed where he was. *On the other hand...*

Ivo didn't have time to mull it over. A heavy thud on his shield signified an impact, but not from the front. Looking up, Ivo could make out a steel-spanned crossbow resting on the rim of his pavise, cocked and loaded. Craning his neck backwards, he saw it was Helena, clad in her mail coat and staring down the bolt she had nocked. Oblivious of Ivo, she peered into the blackness of the woods, unblinking. With slow, shallow breaths, she lined up a target. Her finger wrapped around the trigger.

In a flurry, the crossbow sprung into life. The arms cracked forward, faster than the eye could perceive, sending the bolt hurtling into the woods. Immediately, Helena ducked down behind Ivo, the catch still rattling as it rolled in the stock. Already, her foot was in the spanner, and with the hook laced to her belt, she spanned the crossbow, locking the string in place. From a pouch on her side, she retrieved a second bolt, a length of ash with a black ring painted around the centre.

The bolt was placed in the notch of the stock and she was ready to fire again. The crossbow was again laid upon the pavise, and Helena took another shot. This went on for several minutes, Helena loading and firing while Ivo squatted behind the shield. She was mechanical in her motions, each action perfectly executed to maximize speed without causing fatigue.

Ivo, on the other hand, found his arms and legs locking up, in particular the arm holding up the massive shield. He was tempted to readjust himself, but was certain as soon as he did, an opportunistic archer would put an arrow into whatever he placed outside the confines of his shield.

Blood began to pool in his locked limbs, and away from his brain. He was on the verge of passing out when Helena stopped firing. The arrows had ceased a minute earlier, but the regulars kept slinging bolts into the black reaches of the trees. Now, it seemed their attackers had either fled, or lay slain. It was safe to leave cover.

A soft kick to his thigh made Ivo look up, Helena standing over him. "You can get up now," she said, followed by another, harder kick. Ivo winced. "Next time we come under attack," she spat, "actually make an effort to find me. Or my next bolt is going through your balls." With that, she slung her crossbow over her shoulder, and made towards the regulars farther down the column.

Finally able to move, Ivo heaved himself to his feet. His limbs burned in protest, limiting him to a glacial pace. Using his shield as a crutch and holding onto it with both hands, he pulled himself up. It was then he saw the full extent of the fighting.

The ground around him was littered with arrows, stuck in dirt or shattered against stone. Relatively few managed to find their mark. Compared to the events of the morning, casualties were light. Those being tended to suffered minor injuries, most had been struck in the limbs, and those hit in the torso had enough armour to at least slow the arrow. One soldier had been nicked in the neck, the jagged edge opening veins and causing profuse bleeding. The field medics were already at work stanching the flow.

Roland's cart, however, was in worse shape. Far down the road, Ivo could see him and the confused Sil attempting to right the tumbled wagon. The horses were gone, free from their harness, and the right wheel was shattered. Whatever they hit, it left its mark.

"What do you see, Helena?" Ivo heard. It was Rook, coming down the road. Helena, who had joined a group surveying the edge of the woods, jogged towards the commander.

"You're not going to like it, sir," she nodded toward the tree line. "Most of them are too old to be soldiers. No uniforms or armour. Hell, even their bows look old."

Rook nodded. "Conscripts. Explains why they only ambushed us from the one side. Petyr's throwing his people's lives away. He hopes he can scare us off." Rook called to the column, "Tend to any wounds, and restock any ammunition. Leave the dead to the Dalwikers. We've lost enough time already."

CHAPTER NINETEEN

"Scarring up quite nicely sir," Brutus commented. Within the confines of his wagon, the duke allowed his wounds to breathe. In a pair of black and white hose, he looked over the collection of markings. Much of their shape had been lost, fallible flesh unable to hold such intricate design. But the wounds were clean, devoid of rot or puss. To his credit, the vagrant had taken steps to avoid infection, and recommended Rudolph rub the wounds with strong, clear spirits to keep gangrene away.

It had been three days since the duke subjected himself to the lengthy, agonizing treatment. But the effects of the sigils were apparent by the first. Rudolph's nerves, aflame for decades, had cooled to a point the duke would almost consider normal. He could bear rough fabrics and tight fitting clothing, if only just. Even his failing senses seemed to return, smell and taste now regaining some semblance of acuteness.

But his newfound scars did little to decrease the severity of his withdrawals. Even now he felt scratching at the corners of his mind, a creeping desire to consume more incanflagarat. He craved the manic burning, coursing through his veins as his mind elevated to higher planes of thought.

But there would be a time for that. For now, he had a war to wage. "So, how did the officers take the new orders?" he asked, dabbing at his wounds with an alcohol soaked cloth.

"Mixed," Brutus grunted back. "They seem reluctant to fight Borig in his own back yard. But most are just happy they won't be hunkering down by a shit-choked river for the next week."

Rudolph nodded.

"And any more insight from our soothsayer?" Brutus turned his head to the far corner of Rudolph's cart. The vagrant, secreted into the dark corner of the wagon, stepped into the dim light of the fireplace. His hands clasped together, he blankly stared into the ironbound flame.

"I see much, scorched lord, but little has changed in Stahlsheim. Borig still awaits your challenge, and he has not sat idle. He has found something...old."

Brutus cocked his head. "What kind of something?"

"Probably just that pyroquette suit of armour he used to brag about," Rudolph remarked, "Bloody thing cost him a fortune."

"No, it is no creation wrought of steel. I fear my lord's enemies have themselves tapped into the powers that be."

Rudolph cocked his head. "Elaborate."

"I feel...a void. Much like your markings." The blind man gestured with his hands. "It's an empty space, through which the old powers are funnelled."

"Runes? Didn't think Petyr would share that kind of knowledge," Brutus cut in. "If I recall, his project was a failure."

Rudolph nodded in agreement. "The most valuable thing to come out of that workshop was self heating cookware. We have nothing to worry about."

"I am afraid I must correct you, burning magister. We have much to worry about." The vagrant peered into the dying embers of the fireplace as the logs crackled and twisted. "I may see much, but my vision is crude. Rough. I can only see that which is obvious."

"Obvious? You could bloody well clarify a bit better." Rudolph crossed his arms.

The vagrant nodded slowly. "This is no middling trinket, lord. Borig is in possession of something far greater than I can construct. I fear he has acquired an advisor of his own—one who understands the working of the ancient powers."

Rudolph frowned. "There are more of you? How many arcanists are there?"

"I am flattered that you present me such titles, lord, but I am but a humble servant."

"Arcanist, servant, bloody pontificate, it doesn't matter! You're saying Borig has a crippled savant as his own?" The vagrant nodded. Rudolph inhaled, holding a hand to his temple. "And you can't be any more clear?"

"All I can say, lord, is this power was made for a war long over. For a foe long dead. And now, your enemies would use it against you."

"Bloody fantastic. Borig's got mystical powers and a suit of pyroquette armour and I have a cripple with an obsession with flesh carvings."

Brutus piped up. "We're sneaking away from Borig. He won't get a chance to use his pet."

"If he's got one of those," Rudolph pointed to the vagrant, "he already knows where we are. He'll be after us."

"There are ways to deceive the eldritch eye. Ways to make you appear where you are not." The vagrant held his hands together.

Rudolph inclined his head. "And how would you go about that? How does one appear somewhere else to a being with divine vision? Swap souls? Transfer essence of being?"

The vagrant remained silent. Rudolph's eyes opened further. "Wait, it really was one of those?"

The vagrant nodded. "In a sense. We need not transfer your whole soul."

"Wait," Brutus cut in, "you can't be serious. Why do you put up with this drivel, sir?"

"For once, I agree with you, Brutus." Rudolph stared at the vagrant. "I've put up with much. I've been patient, and you've delivered on your promises. But now...do you realize what you're suggesting?"

The vagrant held up his hands. "I assure you, lord, it would be no more intense than the sigils, you..."

"You're tampering with my soul! That sounds wee bit more invasive than digging a few squiggles in my chest!"

"I have no intention of tampering, lord. It is not my place. What I suggest is to create a puppet of sorts."

"A puppet? Really?" Rudolph remained unconvinced. "How do you plan on making this puppet then? Shall I inquire the quartermasters for some timber and string?"

"This would be a puppet of blood and bone. A puppet of its own will, unaware of its strings. But to our unknown adversary, it would be you."

"Blood and bone? You intend to use another person as a dummy?"

The vagrant nodded. "A vessel for a shard of your soul. To create the link, I would need to place sigils upon a medium of bone," he held a hand over his chest, "and place it within your heart."

Disgust and contempt where chiseled on Rudolph's regal features, glaring as he held his breath. Exhaling, he grumbled, "You would do well, cripple, to make no more mention of your... abominable practices. Even I have my limits. Runes and sigils I can understand, I can harness. I will not mess with that which is beyond my control."

"As a god, you shall need to understand the soul. But I shall not press the issue, if it so displeases my lord." He bowed as elegantly as his aged body would allow. "Do you wish for me to take my leave, lord?"

"Deposit yourself in some other corner of the convoy. I shall call if I have need of you."

His head lowered, the vagrant slunk out the door, and into the dark of the night. Rudolph closed the door behind him, flipping one of the brass latches and locking the door. He turned back to Brutus, shaking his head. Brutus mumbled,

"Bloody lot of information to take in at once."

"You don't say," Rudolph remarked, striding towards the far wall of his wagon. Sequestered in the many racks were a number of wine bottles, along with the occasional spirit. Reaching to the bottom shelf, Rudolph produced an old, worn out ceramic vessel, the paint long since peeled.

He swirled the bottle, a wet slapping assuring him the container was indeed full. "Ah, just what I need."

"878 Cinder Gap, sir?" Brutus asked.

"1024 Moonshine, my personal still."

Brutus nodded, grabbing the copper cup from his belt and placing it on the table with a hefty thud. Rudolph grabbed his own brass mug from the shelf, and sat down at the table. He pulled a small dagger from his boot, and used the blade to cut the wax seal off the vessel. The smell of alcohol burned his nose, a sensation he relished. Inhaling deeply, Rudolph suppressed the need to cough up the toxic fumes. Shaking his head, he poured the clear liquid into his cup, then Brutus'.

The two clinked their respective cups together, nodded, then shot the liquid back. The pleasant, numbing burn filled Rudolph. This wouldn't be enough to get him drunk; years of incanflagarat abuse had left him immune to most intoxicants. But at the very least, it left him feeling warm. Brutus, despite years of building a tolerance to booze, already looked a bit flushed.

"Burn it all to cinder, that's a bit much, isn't it?"

Rudolph shrugged. "I kept having the batch tested till the tasters stopped going blind. It should be fine. Why, the big bad Brutus can't handle his liquor?"

With a harumph, Brutus leaned in. "If this is you trying to get me drunk, it isn't going to work."

Rudolph smiled. "The night is young, friend." He poured himself another draft.

The morning came too soon. Rudolph, sprawled across his

bed, felt the sting of light upon his eyes, the rays of the morning filtering through the stained glass of his wagon. The duke moaned in protest, covering his head in an attempt to keep back the day. He was not hung over. His altered constitution wouldn't allow for it, but he was unwilling to leave the comfort of his bed. Although the smell of burning timber did pique his interest, no doubt the cooking fires being stoked for breakfast.

He rolled over, turning away from the intruding light, and finding comfort in the dark of his carriage. Once again, he was at peace, the burdens of life slipping away into the embrace of slumber. A serene calm fell over him, and he returned to the void of sleep. His return, however, was short lived. An annoying, insignificant noise pulled him back into the waking world. It was almost like...rapping.

Perhaps it was the heavy plodding of draft horses, or an overzealous soldier training on a nearby dummy. In either case, it had little to do with the duke, and he decided it not worth his time to investigate. Besides, he was sleeping.

Despite his dismissal, the noise droned on, repeating over and over. It didn't take long for the duke to become annoyed. Slowly, his eyes opened, and he was greeted with the warm glow of a fire. Quaint, really, almost like home...

Something was off. He was certain the fire had gone out late in the morning, just as he was dozing off. It seemed unlikely Brutus would have relit it; the advisor was too sloshed to stand let alone rekindle a flame. This begged the question: who lit the fire? Rudolph looked groggily over to his stove. The iron grated thing sat dead, devoid of spark or ember. Odd, then where was the glow coming from?

Rubbing the sleep from his eyes, Rudolph looked around his cart lazily. It all seemed in place, nothing unusual. That was, until he saw the far wall of the cart across from his bed. There, from the window trim spread a meagre flame devouring its way through the timber of the cart.

In an instant, Rudolph was awake, shooting up from his bed. He got to his feet, pushing aside the curtains of his bed, and made for the door, passing a blacked-out Brutus. The advisor was out cold, his face firmly planted on the table. Even with the commotion and the heat of the spreading flame, he remained motionless. Rudolph was almost at the door when he looked back, and cursed under his breath.

Not thinking, the duke wheeled about, and reached back for his advisor. Preparing himself mentally and physically he grabbed Brutus under the armpits, the course fabric of his arming jacket scratching Rudolph's skin. Rudolph paid no heed to the discomfort, gritting his teeth and hauling Brutus to a sitting position.

"Burn it all to cinder, how much do you weigh?" Rudolph grumbled to the unconscious Brutus as he tried his best to move him from the table. With a heavy crash, the advisor fell to the wagon floor, nearly pulling Rudolph down with him. Recovering, the duke inhaled deeply, and heaved. Nothing. Again, he heaved. Finally, the bulk of Brutus shifted, if only a bit.

The short trip to the door seemed to take forever, the effort of moving his advisor and the encroaching flame skewing Rudolph's perception of time. He wheezed with exertion, never stopping. By the time he got to the door, the smoke pouring into the wagon began to overtake the duke, and he felt his vision fading. Putting Brutus down for a moment, Rudolph struggled with the latch that had locked his door shut.

The latch flew open, as did the door, and Rudolph flopped forward. He was fortunate. A startled soldier stood before the door and instinctively caught the tumbling duke. The soldier stepped back, and, realizing who he had caught, escorted the duke to safety. Rudolph, however, pushed away, and standing on his own two feet, weakly barked, "Leave me, you moron! Go get Brutus!"

Waving to the doorway, were the hung over advisor lay sprawled, Rudolph got his point across. The soldier, along with another who had been nearby, both sprinted to the door, and shunted the weighty Brutus out the door. By no means a gentle exit, Brutus rolled down the stairs, and impacted hard with the dirt road. The two soldiers dragged him face first a safe distance away from the wagon as it was consumed by flame.

Rudolph heaved, doubled over after the great exertion of moving his friend. He had little time for himself, though. No sooner was Brutus safe, than the soldier at his door sprinted over to him.

"My lord! Are you injured, lord? Shall I call for a medic?" Rudolph held up a hand, still catching his breath.

"Just...some water..." The soldier obediently grabbed his water skin, unclasping it from his belt and handing it to the duke. In a swift motion, Rudolph took the skin from the soldier, and began downing its contents. Once the vessel was emptied, Rudolph handed it back, and wiped the excess from his chin.

Reinvigorated, the duke decided an explanation was in order. "What bloody happened? Who lit the fire? I'll have the moron flayed alive!" He paused, and his eyes went wide. "The cripple! That two-faced freak tried to do me in. Guards!"

"I'm must correct you, oh lord of lords." That raspy, broken voice. It was the vagrant. Rudolph turned about, eyes aflame. In his tattered robes, he approached the duke.

"He's telling the truth, lord," the soldier butted in. "I was with him all morning. He told me to come get you. Lucky he did, I saw the flame and did my best to wake you, lord."

Rudolph stared daggers at the soldier. "If it wasn't him, who was it?"

"A saboteur, lord," the vagrant answered. "Your enemies seek to undo you off the field of battle, to end your ascent before it has even begun."

"Borig...."

The vagrant agreed.

"And you didn't see fit to warn me then? You seem to have a fair grasp on the situation."

"I did warn you, lord. Borig knows precisely where you are. I sensed the rogue agent as he was executing his foul deeds. And he won't be the last." The soldier raised his eyebrows, confused. Rudolph waved him away.

"Attend to Brutus. Leave us."

The soldier bowed, and did as his duke had ordered.

"Where is this saboteur?" Rudolph demanded. "Or is that beyond your vision as well."

The vagrant rubbed his hands together, uncomfortable. "I know the man's name, his face, and where he was from. But I cannot see where he has gone. It is certain, however, that he has returned to his master."

Rudolph rolled his eyes. "Sounds like the soothsayer Borig recruited is a damn sight better at this than you."

"Which is why I implore you, oh Lord of the Ember, to allow me to assist you in the best way I can. My vision may be weak, but my hands are steady, and my mind etched with sigils. I can conceal you from my wayward kindred, keep you safe from their prying eyes."

Rudolph exhaled, rubbing his eyes. "I'm a bit more inclined to believe you," he mumbled, "but it still sounds like bullshit." Looking back up, Rudolph said, "How dangerous is this procedure of yours?"

The vagrant smiled a rotten-toothed smile. "Not at all, my lord."

The duke shook his head. "Tell the quartermasters what you need. I'll procure a suitable specimen for a puppet."

The vagrant nodded, and shuffled off. Thoroughly disgusted with the blind man, Rudolph turned his attention to Brutus.

The veteran lay flopped onto his back, his head lazily lolling to the side. The other soldiers had departed, tending to the fire, leaving one haggard field doctor by his side. The doctor, white apron stained from years of bloody work, was prying Brutus' eyes open in an attempt to illicit some kind of response.

"How is he?" Rudolph asked, kneeling next to his advisor.

"Out!" the doctor mumbled, his arthritic fingers shuffling through the pouch at his side.

Rudolph gently rolled Brutus' bald head around, checking for injuries. Save for a bruise over his left eye, he seemed relatively intact.

"Hell of a headache when he comes to?"

The medic nodded, producing a corked vile of yellow crystals. "Sal ammoniac." He popped the cork.

Rudolph clapped a hand over his own nose. "Smells like a piss bucket at a Brennerburg brothel!" he exclaimed, reeling from the stink.

"That's the point," the medic stated, and brought the foul vial to Brutus' nose.

With great ferocity, Brutus awoke. In one swift motion, he reached for his belt, grabbed for his dagger, and began jabbing upwards. Fortunately for the medic, the dagger was absent, but he received a fist to the gut for his efforts. The doctor keeled over, the wind knocked out of him. Brutus shot up, staring at the doctor. His gaze then moved to Rudolph, who knelt by his side.

"What just happened?"

"You, my friend, just punched our medic in the chest."

Brutus raised one eyebrow and spied the fallen medic. He halfheartedly apologized, then placed his head squarely in his hands.

"My head feels like an overripe melon…" he moaned.

"And yet half as full," Rudolph remarked, standing.

Brutus looked around. "Where'd the bloody cart go?"

Rudolph pointed over his shoulder. The cart was now fully consumed in flame, the structure giving out and collapsing inwards.

"Burn it all to cinder, please say it wasn't me..." Brutus moaned.

"No need to worry, friend. You were out cold before I went to bed. Didn't move an inch. But we have a few ideas on who did it."

"The cripple! Bastard had it out for us from the start!"

Rudolph shook his head. "Our associate had nothing to do with it. He has a good alibi. There were mentions of an unsavoury individual under Borig's employ."

"Saboteur?"

"Yes. Our soothsayer said as much. It seems our enemy has eyes in more places than we thought."

"What do you do about it? It's not like...wait!" Brutus suddenly recalled the previous night's conversation. "You better not be bloody going through with it."

Rudolph shrugged, looking into the burning wreck of his cart. "Don't suppose you have any other ideas. If Borig can pinpoint me at a whim, I'm as good as dead anyway. And I'd hate to lead that madman straight to the temple."

Brutus slowly rubbed circles on his temples. "What about your safe?" he asked, his one good eye bugging out of his head.

"Fireproof. Remind me to get you to dig it out once you're done moping."

Brutus grunted. It was clear he had nothing more to say on the matter that would make a difference. "Did you manage to save any of the booze?" he queried. "I need some hair of the dog."

"'Fraid you'll have to make do with whatever they have in the mess carts."

Brutus heaved a great sigh. "How many embers worth of wine were in that cart?"

"More than a boat of charcoal."

"Well, shit!" was all the advisor could say.

CHAPTER TWENTY

The second army was in disarray. The ambush staged by the Dalwik militia, while failing to inflict casualties, successfully forced the entire march to come to a halt. Wounds were few but Roland's cart more than made up for that in collateral damage. In their panic, the horses veered the wagon into a sizeable stone once used as a marker. The right wheel, rimmed with iron, was cracked clean down the middle, the spokes knocked free and sent flying from the force of the impact.

By the time Ivo had made it there, Roland was chewing his beard in frustration. He had already gathered various stray pieces, and managed to chase down the wayward horses. But the entire wheel was scrap, and they would have to mount a replacement. No small feat, considering Rook wanted the column moving in ten minutes.

Ivo placed a hand on Roland's shoulder attempting to calm him. It had no impact; he continued to fret and fuss. The replacement wheel was brought in from the engineer's cart. However, the engineer was absent. Roland turned to the soldier hauling the replacement, and asked about his whereabouts.

"Caught an arrow to the knee. Won't be walking anytime soon."

"How am I supposed to mount this bloody thing? We need gear to fix the cart!"

The soldier shrugged. "Get creative, I guess."

"Get creative! I hope a badger "get's creative" all over his face." The quartermaster rolled the wheel over to the axel. The axel itself was dug deep into the dirt, sunken in a soft spot in the run down road. Thousands of pounds of forge gear pushed down on the timber, meaning it would be tricky to dislodge without completely emptying the cart.

"Well, were do we start?" Roland muttered aloud. "I suppose we should find the missing bits o' wheel. Ivo, see what you can scrounge up while I...I don't know."

Ivo nodded, and set off, scrounging through the tangled growth of bushes alongside the cart looking for spokes of the wheel. One by one, he dug out the timber rods from the foliage, hissing as the thorny brushed grabbed at his hands, nicking his fingers, and pulling the sleeves of his jacket. With much sniveling, he finally recovered all the spokes he could see, half a dozen in total.

When Ivo returned to the cart Roland had disappeared, supposedly having run off to retrieve materials to affix the new wheel. Sil was the only one there, a length of rope tied in her hand. The rope, heavy duty, was slung over a nearby branch, a loop dangling idly just above Sil's head. Ivo looked at it, confused.

He called out as he walked "What are you working on?"

Sil looked up from the knot she was tying at the other end of the rope. "I had an idea how we can get the cart unstuck. Why do you ask?"

"How's this supposed to work?" he asked, placing the spokes gingerly on the ground beside the broken axel.

Sil tugged lightly on the rope. "We can use our weight to our advantage, and lift the cart from the mud."

"Weight is Roland' biggest advantage," he claimed with a grin. "Where is Roland anyway?" Sil pointed, and Ivo turned to find Roland, face red and beard frazzled, making his way back to the cart with a small hammer and a handful of shoe nails. His lips moved under his moustache, no doubt mumbling curses and obscenities in frustration. Ivo made a quick note that, despite his jovial demeanour, it was unwise to upset Roland.

Exhaling heavily, Roland looked over the setup Sil had prepared while she silently awaited his approval. She didn't need to wait long as a broad grin brightened up Roland's flushed face.

"That'll do perfect! Take the lifting gear out of the picture entirely! Good thinkin'." Sil beamed. Ivo, not to be outdone, retrieved the spokes, and presented them to Roland.

"Oh, and the spokes." The quartermaster frowned. "There were eight…ah well, we'll make do on six." Stepping past Ivo, Roland placed his tools on the road and tested the heft of the rope. Satisfied the branch wasn't about to snap, he waved at Sil. "Be a dear and get a crate or a stump to prop the axel once it's in the air. Ivo, I need a little extra weight here."

Didn't think it possible, Ivo thought to, trudging towards another thankless task.

Sil returned with a crate as Roland and Ivo took hold of the rope. Roland nodded, and proceeded to pull down on the rope with as much force as he could muster. Ivo joined in, lifting himself off the ground as he tried to add his own scrawny weight to the balance. It seemed to be just enough, as the cart slowly rose from the confines of the soil. The branch above crackled and groaned in protest, but held firm. As soon as there was enough clearance, Sil jammed the crate beneath the axel. About a foot of air was all that spaced the gap between the two. Satisfied, she gave Roland the go ahead to stop.

The hefty quartermaster released the rope, allowing the axel to settle onto the crate. Unfortunately, Ivo found himself still hanging, unable to hear Sil's words through his own exertion. As the cart fell, Ivo rose at an equally uncomfortable speed. While his flight was short, it was enough to pull the rope from his hands, leaving a raw sting in his fingers, followed by a dull crack to his back. Stars wheeled overhead, and Ivo could feel his brain jostle in his skull. The world went black.

Ivo came to, hauled up by big, meaty hands. His head swivelled freely on his limp neck, coming to rest on Roland's stained shoulder. The quartermaster patted him on the back, trying to revitalize the stunned conscript.

Ivo shook his head. Now he heard the raucous laughter of those close enough to witness his tumble. He looked around, confused. "Don't worry, Ivo," Roland assured him, checking the back of his head for any lumps. "Just a little fall. You're fine."

A small hand was gently placed on his arm and he found Sil looking at him with concern. "Are you well?" she asked softly.

Words failed him but a jeering spectator broke the silence. Insults and jokes flew his way, before sergeants and officers called off the cackling crowd.

"I do not understand," Sil said. "Why do they laugh? Why do they not come and see if you are all right."

Roland shook his head. "Trust me, Sil. They're a crude bunch, and will laugh at anything to lighten the mood." He set Ivo down, and went back to the cart. "Certainly don't have to be so rude about it, though," he mumbled as he went. With Roland gone, Ivo found himself alone with Sil.

She continued to look at him, awaiting a response. Ivo's brain had completely crapped out on him; the situation was alien in the extreme. The only people who had cared about him before were his landlord and the tax collector, and neither exactly fawned over him with concern.

Ivo gently pulled away from Sil. "I'm okay. Thanks for asking." He stepped beside Roland, Sil following behind, curiously eyeing the raised axel.

"That was some good thinkin'," Roland complimented her. "How'd you figure it would work?"

Sil bit her lip. "I'm not sure. It just kind of…came to me."

"If that's the case, you'd make a better engineer than half the coal-shovellers in this army."

Sil smiled, thanking Roland.

"Tell you what," Roland said. "How about I let you hammer on the new wheel?" She nodded excitedly, picking up the hammer and nails Roland had set down.

Ivo went to gather the spokes he had left on the ground, but Roland called, "Just throw those in the cart. The old wheel's too buggered to be fixed. We'll use 'em as spares as need be."

Ivo's shoulders slumped. All the effort of digging the damn things from the brush had been for naught. At least he didn't have to do any hammering.

Sil made quick work of the new wheel, the hammer flying as she pounded in nail after nail. It was a hasty, manic rhythm, but a rhythm none-the-less. Before Ivo could get back, she had exhausted her supply of nails, and the wheel was firmly in place.

Roland tested her work, pulling with all his might to dislodge the hub from the axel. Satisfied it was going nowhere, he moved to the back of the cart.

"How are we supposed to get it off the crate?" Ivo asked.

Roland tapped Ivo on the shoulder, nudging him to the side as he stepped forward with a massive sledgehammer. While easily twenty pounds of steel, Roland carried it like a carpenters hammer.

He tapped the top of the crate with the butt of the haft. Satisfied it was empty, he stepped back, choked up, and swung at the crate. With a hearty crack, steel met timber, and the box disintegrated. The cart fell heavily to the ground, rattling the contents of wagon as splinters flew every which way. Roland triumphantly set his hammer down and leaned on it.

"There we go!" he said, grinning. He called out to an unseen soldier further up the convoy to bring him two sturdy, fearless, draft horses.

Two beasts were pulled from reserve equines and harnessed to Roland's cart. His previous horses were of little use to the army as animals of such poor nerve ill suited to the campaigning life. They were allowed to go free, slowly plodding back down the path towards Rendsheim.

The quartermaster was back in business, and by the time he had taken his seat, the rest of the convoy was prepared to move. The wounded had been dealt with or placed on carts, and the crossbowmen returned from the forests, having retrieved their bolts. A few brought back trophies as well: new boots or daggers, and scraps of gear with which to supplement their own. One particularly enthusiastic individual had two armfuls of hunting bows, no doubt hoping to supplement his pay with a visit to the requisitions officer.

"I be damned, we came out of an ambush better off than before," Roland mused as he watched the returning soldiers.

Helena, too, had emerged from the woods, carrying a handful of ash bolts encircled with a ring of black paint. Outside of a few extra pouches, she had no loot with her. Rather, she appeared somewhat ragged, her brow drenched with sweat and her jacket littered with pine needles. Rook was there to greet her.

"Lost them," Helena called, waving towards the woods. "Tracks run back to Dalwik. Guess they didn't have to stomach to stay and fight."

"It matters little," Rook replied, looking up and down the tree line. "Petyr will make an example of them. We don't have to be too worried. The city is still a ways off, we should make haste." Rook then called to Roland: "Hope you got your act together, we're moving out!"

The second army was once again underway, the commanders eager to make up for the delays. Lunch was served on the march, as it had been the day before. The soldier's enthusiasm to get to grips with their foes had been rekindled, putting a fire in their step.

By evening of the third day, Dalwik was in sight.

Ivo first caught a glimpse of the city as he crested a small hump in the road, expecting to see yet more forest. What he saw, however, planted him firmly in place. To either side, the trees ceased in a neat, even line, twenty feet between the woods and a short drop. At the bottom of the drop strange, ebony dirt shone like broken glass in the setting light. Black sand. Ivo's eyes followed the sand outwards, the ebony expanse finally giving way to the great, green sea. Beyond that, a crimson horizon, obscuring lands unknown to the humble carpenter from Rendsheim.

Ivo stood, awestruck. In Rendsheim, there were no great bodies of water, only oil choked culverts and drains. Ivo wished he had paid attention to the poets and singers that frequented his favourite dives. Maybe one of them could find the words for something so vast as the ocean he now saw.

An impatient shoulder sent Ivo stumbling forward. The sea's spell broken, Ivo shook himself of indignantly and took one last, longing look at the sea, before moving ahead with the others.

The road veered sharply to the left, breaking from the forest and sitting between the tree line and the drop. The quality in construction appeared substantially better here as sharp stones sat flush with one another in an unbroken mass. One only need to look down the road to see why. Far down the raven-black shores was the largest port city in the kingdom.

When the kingdom was still a kingdom.

It seemed to be an impossible site, so perfect was its layout. A craggy cliff face jutted outwards in defiance of the sea, squat and circular as the water daintily kissed its edge. How such a landmass had yet to sink into the waves Ivo couldn't begin to guess. The only thing more stunning than the outcropping itself was what was placed upon it: a great, white crown.

Above the waves mighty alabaster walls and towers rose, breaking an otherwise unbroken horizon. Such massive edifices conjured wonder and intimidation in equal measure, for few would believe such grand monuments still existed. The city itself was built from marble, the stone polished by the sea and dyed a faint red in the setting light. Even here, miles away, one could see why Petyr was the undisputed lord of the waves.

Beyond the city, the vast sails of cogs and caravels, merchant ships, and military vessels dotted the green ocean and surrounded the port like bees to a hive. Flags of purple and yellow hung proudly from masts and bows, declaring loyalty to Dalwik and Dalwik alone. The stature of the largest cogs rivalled that of the cities towers, larger than a city block and crewed by hundreds. Ballistas and catapults lined the decks of these floating fortresses, prepared to fend off any foolish enough to prod the hive.

How the second army was to break such an imposing bastion was beyond Ivo. Knowing nothing of tactics, even he was aware that attempting to starve out the city was futile. The sea provided everything, bringing food and weapons and soldiers in unimaginable quantities stowed in the holds of colossal cogs. Even if the ships were to sink, and the sea fail to bear bounties of fish, such a fortress would no doubt have stocks of dried meats and grain to last months, if not years. And with walls as thick as most roads were wide, there would be little chance of getting through by force.

"The most beautiful city in the world," he muttered, "and I'll be stuck outside getting shot at."

His moping was not without justification, as one by one, small pillars of flame rose from the great towers, their own feeble light joining with the setting sun. This didn't bode well.

"Shit, they've seen us," Ivo heard a soldier behind him say.

"Of course they saw us. There's nothing between us and them," another barked. "Besides, if they need to send up a warning, it means they weren't expecting us. Probably thought their little ambushes would slow us down."

The soldier's words rang true. No sooner did the fires go up than the great merchant ships pulled away, heading towards safer waters. The warships, however, began jockeying for position, nudging towards shore in an attempt to intimidate the attacking force. Such a show of force was more bark than bite, however, as great, jagged rocks jutted along the shoreline surrounded the city. Whatever force churned up the flat outcropping no doubt also heaved up the surrounding stone.

Still, the sheer scale of the warships put Ivo off, even if there was little chance of a ballista bolt finding a home in his torso. Nervously, he kept his eye on the fleet while avoiding running in the soldiers in front of him. He decided it was time he talked to Roland to ease his panicked mind. He picked up the pace, squeezing through the unwashed, onion-scented soldiers. He neared Roland's cart. Sil sat next to the quartermaster. Rook hung off the side of the cart, sharing an animated conversation with Roland. As Ivo approached, Rook stepped down, and marched off in haste. Ivo took her place along the side of the cart, carefully hauling himself up.

Sil greeted him with a smile. "Hello, Ivo. It appears you have the effect of making woman want to leave."

Ivo cocked an eyebrow at the unusual wording of her comment.

"Sorry, Ivo," Roland said with a chuckle. "I've been teaching her about jokes. She wanted to try it out. Not bad for a first try."

Sil was suitably pleased, happy to know her first attempt at joke telling a success. "I'll make sure she doesn't make a habit of it," Roland added.

Ivo snorted. Nodding towards Rook, he asked, "What was that about."

"Rook and I had a...disagreement," Roland replied cautiously. "The scouts claim the city is prepped for siege, but even with the crews of those warships, they're short on numbers." Roland nodded towards the city. "Rook thinks we need to make a push tonight, get the engineers to fill in the ditch they dug so we can get our ladders up."

"Meaning?" Ivo asked.

Roland sighed. "Well…you may have to play babysitter to the engineers while they do their shovel work." Ivo felt the blood drain from his face as a familiar terror gripping his chest.

"Don't worry, Ivo…" Roland said.

"You always tell me not to worry. When should I worry?" Ivo's temper flared; the day had been far too long.

"You'd be surprised how few people die in combat these days," Roland told him. "Mind you, you'll probably be worse for wear. Might be missing an eye or digit. I knew one soldier, really more scar than man, and he…"

"That's supposed to be reassuring?" Ivo yelped, cutting Roland off.

"My point, Ivo, is you're hardly running into the meat grinder here. The only thing you'll need to watch out for is caltrops and hurled rocks."

Ivo stared at Roland.

"Oh, right, I keep forgetting you're new here. Caltrops are these nasty, metal spikes, stick in your foot and don't come out easy. Think fishhook for your feet."

Sil, until now silently listening, spoke up. "People would use something so…horrific? I know we are fighting, but certainly we can be civil about it, attempt to avoid any undue harm."

Roland shook his head. "Sorry, but that's not the way of the world. War's about dukes and kings and to the nobility, the end justifies the means." He trailed off for a moment. "The things Rudolph made me build for Rendsheim…well, I pray they never see use…" A moment of uncharacteristic melancholy fell over the hefty quartermaster, his head hanging low. It didn't take long for the moment to pass.

"Whelp, could be worse. You hear stories of the old days, when wyverns and the like were still around. I know of one chieftain, back before the kingdom was a kingdom, who decided…"

Roland's story ran on, going into colourful detail during the more violent moments. Sil was captivated, and Ivo did his best to keep his imagination from running away with him. By the time the city drew near, he wrapped up the tale.

"...suffice to say, when the chains did break, the wyvern weren't too happy. Surprisingly vindictive for a lizard, made straight for Duke Horris and crushed his head with its talons. Gave rise to the old Dalwik saying, "taming the lizard". Course, it means something else now, but that's a different story. It all started..."

Ivo cut Roland off with a raised hand. He had ceased listening minutes ago, more concerned with the hulking white walls rising before him. It was as if the bleached stone had sneaked up on them, the mountainous bulk hiding the fading sun as the second army passed. Even beyond the range of any siege weapons, the walls were able to smother the sun. A chill ran down Ivo's back, whether from the shadow or the fear brewing in his soul, he could not say.

Roland, too, had ceased his prattling, his eyes drawn skyward. "I remember these walls..." he said softly, his eyes glassy. "Been a long time coming..." He shook his head, a smile crossing his face. "No need to rush, Ivo. Take it in at your own pace, we'll be here a while."

A ways from the walls, the column came to a stop, and began to wrap around itself as more and more soldiers and carts marched down the narrow road. Coiling like a serpent, the army came to rest, a half mile from the city. Here, they would be safe from anything mounted on the castle, and the great stone teeth flanking the narrow causeway to Dalwik would bar any warships from closing in with their ballistae.

The engineers were already at work by the time Roland's cart trundled into the newly formed encampment. Ragged, aged masters held aloft instruments of copper and glass, directing hopeful apprentices and burly labourers. Wood stakes, pulled from the carts, were being hauled to the edges of the army. Sil leaned towards Roland, pointing towards the activity. "What are they doing with those posts? Do we need that many signs?"

Roland stifled a laugh, biting his thumb hard until the urge had eased. "No," he said, "they're building a wall out of stakes, to keep out any unwanted guests."

Sil raised an eyebrow. "Why would guests be unwelcome? It would be nice to have...Oh, that was one of your jokes."

Ivo jumped as Sil let out a raucous laugh, her voice cutting through the noise of the busy camp. A few soldiers turned their heads, expressions ranging from confusion to contempt.

"Er...not quite. We'll work on that." He turned to Ivo, who was also easing the ringing in his ears. "Ivo, help me tether the horses. Looks like we're making camp."

Ivo stepped down from the cart. He did not get far, however; as failed to see Helena standing behind him until his face was square in her bosom. She was taller than Ivo thought. A quick shove resolved the situation.

"Nice try, bitch," she glowered at him. "Lucky for you, I need your scrawny ass alive. Rook's given the order, we're moving. Grab your pavise and let's go." Before Ivo had a chance to reply, Helena had an armoured hand on Ivo's back, leading him towards the arming cart.

"Wait!" Roland called, the wagon creaking as his weight shifted. Plodding his way to the back of the cart, Roland grabbed the sword he had left Ivo. "Don't forget this!"

Ivo and Helena both stopped, watching Roland approach them as fast as his frame would allow. Heaving, he handed Ivo the sword, still in its scabbard.

"Really?" Helena sneered. "You're giving the scrub your sword?"

"Nothing personal, Helena, but I think he'll make the most of it."

Helena snorted. "Say what you will, when the bitch drops dead I'm taking the sword."

Roland shrugged and turned his attention to Ivo. "Just remember to keep your head down, your helmet on, and your shield up." He set a heavy hand on Ivo's shoulder as the conscript looked over the weapon. "I'll see you when you get back to the camp."

Begrudgingly, Ivo followed Helena to the armoury, having been unpacked and laid out near the centre of the camp. From the many racks, Ivo retrieved his helmet, and Helena donned her coat of mail. Finally, Ivo was given a new pavise, his original shield lost during the attacks earlier that day. The new shield was much like the old, save for a few nicks in the canvas cover. Still as heavy, though. Ivo tightened the strap around his shoulder, putting the weight on his torso.

Clad in his ill-fitting armour and lugging his hefty shield, Ivo joined the collected mass of soldiers near the edge of the camp. Assembled was a force of two hundred; a hundred pulled from the various ranged units in the army and a hundred sappers from the engineer corps. They were easy enough to spot; thick, high collared arming jackets were crisscrossed with straps and belts holding tools and pouches. Thick leather aprons protected their torsos from stray bolt and wayward nail alike. They wore heavy kettle helmets, much like Ivo. Unlike Ivo's helmet, these were marked out along the brim, numbers and ticks running along the edge much like a protractor. A weighty spade was either slung across their backs or at their sides like a poor man's sword, and beefy mattocks were used as crutches and canes.

A vulture-like fellow, clad in the engineers garb without the helmet, stood discussing something with Rook. What they were discussing, Ivo couldn't say. All he knew was it involved a map and some serious excavation. Soon, the two were satisfied, and Rook moved to address the soldiers.

"Listen up!" she called. The regulars snapped to attention, and the conscripts did their best to straighten their backs. "As you can see," she said, pointing to the walls of Dalwik, "our opposition has been busy. In the time it's taken us to get here, they have dug ditches, placed stakes, and spread caltrops over the ground. Hard going. Our friends in engineering are going to help us fix that."

The sappers cheered in acknowledgment, earning a stern look from the senior engineer.

Rook continued, "This is our best chance to undo our enemies hard work. The garrison is weak, they'll be hard pressed to keep us from working. It will be some time before we can begin a full-scale assault, and by then their force will likely increase. We fill the pits and remove the stakes now and it will make the final assault that much smoother. Your job is to make sure the sappers get there in one piece. Draw fire, cover them with bolt fire, the usual song and dance. Don't expect more than token resistance, but don't get cocky, and don't die."

There was a grunt of acknowledgement from the regulars, and nervous murmurs from the conscripts. Rook, satisfied with her briefing, gave a quick salute, and allowed the engineer chief to step up.

"Right," he said in a curt, dull voice, "get to it."

The regulars lined up, "encouraging" their shield-bearing counterparts to stand in front of them. Ivo was no exception. Helena roughly guided him to the front, near the far right of the line. The sappers, in a much less organized fashion, moved behind the soldiers.

Their gathering had not gone unnoticed. High upon the crenellations of the city guards congregated, their dark outlines easy to spot against the dying light of the sun. One by one, a sizeable force gathered upon the pinnacle of the walls, cautiously waiting for the Rendsheimers to approach. And the Rendsheimers would not keep them waiting. Shields raised and crossbows strung, the soldiers began their advance towards the alabaster towers of Dalwik.

It was easy going the first few hundred feet or so. While uneven, the footing was stable and the path clear of obstacles. It seemed the defenders of the city were caught off guard, having failed to lay their traps so far from the city. If it weren't for the blinding rays of the setting sun, it would have been a simple task.

That is until the first of the arrows were loosed. The first Ivo heard of the incoming volley was the impact upon his pavise, barbed hunting arrows bouncing off the reinforced timber of his shield. He lifted his arm a fraction, covering his face before another arrow struck harmlessly against the canvas. At this distance, the feeble hunting bows of the militia would do little more than aggravate the incoming attackers, as long as their shields remained raised.

A call came up from the walls, commanding the militia to cease their futile efforts. The modest stream of arrows abated, the last of their number finding purchase in the soil ahead of the force. "Don't let the calm trick you!" the head engineer called from the rear rank. "They'll be waiting for you to screw up. Make sure they wait a while!"

True to his words, the militia on the wall held their fire, and ducked behind the sea-smoothed ramparts. Save for a few prying shots, they remained hidden. It proved a boon for the Rendsheimers. As the walls loomed ever closer, the faint gleam of steel was visible in the short grass covering the land bridge. These were the caltrops Roland had mentioned earlier, scattered over the field like seeds, leaving one wicked spike pointing upwards at all times. Progress slowed, as the conscript shield bearers attempted to navigate the field of metal and keep their shields up.

The force, having navigated the clumsily laid trap, neared the wall. At this distance, one was able to pick out minute details of the militia high upon the walls, the large nose of one and crooked eyebrow of another.

"Pick your spot!" the chief engineer called out, motioning to the crossbows in the middle rank. A number of soldiers scattered throughout the column tapped their pavisiers on the shoulder, giving their partners the order to place their shields down. The conscripts complied, brushing away any wayward caltrops and kneeling behind their shields, allowing the arbalester behind him both a source of cover and a stable place from which to aim.

Helena gave Ivo a push, instructing him to move farther up in the hopes of finding a superior position from which to fire. Ivo stumbled, narrowly missing the steel barbs in his path, and glanced at Helena. She angrily pointed forwards, her crossbow held over her shoulder and a bolt between her teeth. Ivo glanced over his shield and found a suitable place to plant himself. He placed his shield down a few feet ahead, and knelt down.

"What part of go forward don't you get, bitch?" Helena shouted, placing her bolt onto the stock of the crossbow.

"What difference does it make?" he called back. "You can get a shot from here!"

Nervously, a number of engineers moved past the arguing pair, marching into the teeth of an enemy stronghold. Shovels bit into dirt as they hastily proceeded to fill the ditch at the base of the wall.

Helena spat to the side, and stamped past Ivo. "I don't need this. If you decide to grow a pair, you'll know where to find me." Ahead of Ivo, Helena levelled her crossbow, keeping an eye on the ramparts for any wayward militia.

Ivo was relieved he'd got away with as little backlash as he had. His position was quite comfortable, truth be told. Peeking over the pavise, Ivo watched as any Dalwikers brave enough to stick his head up received a bolt for their troubles. Most bolts clattered harmlessly off the stone parapet, while a small number embedded themselves in the torsos and limbs of the city's defenders. It was a gruesome game of hide and seek, with anyone caught in the open punished for their failings. All the while, the engineers piled dirt into the gap between them and the wall.

Ivo spotted one militiaman, braver than his peers, who lifted his bow over the lip of the rampart, a barbed arrow knocked. Ivo waited to see when the arbalesters below would pick off the poor bastard. The bolt did not come however, and Ivo looked down to see why.

Helena, unaware of the soldier above her taking aim, was aggressively attempting to fix her crossbow. It appeared to Ivo the trigger had failed to fully depress, leaving the wheel stuck in place and the bolt unfired.

Ivo looked at her for a moment, then back up, then back to Helena. Horror pierced his heart. She was about to be shot.

Without thinking, Ivo sprang to his feet, pulling his shield from the dirt and barreling towards Helena. In moments, he closed the distance. His shield held above him, he tackled Helena to the ground, keeping the pavise upwards. She sprawled across the grass, Ivo's elbow wedged in her shoulder blade. A loud crack, and Ivo registered he was at the base of the wall, lying on Helena.

It took Helena a moment to realize what happened, and another moment to realize that Ivo was on her like soot on a streetwalker. "Are you bloody mental?" she hollered, rolling over to berate Ivo as he shuffled to let her move.

The glimmer of steel stopped her.

Ivo's shield, held over both of them, had caught the barbed head of an arrow lodged in the overlapping layers of timber and canvas. Only the point was visible, inches away from Helena's head.

Ivo yelped in pain.

"Did you get hit?" Helena said trying to get a better look at the kneeling Ivo.

He shook his head, teeth clenched. Keeping the shield up, he nodded towards his left foot. Helena craned her neck, and saw the problem. A length of iron, sharpened to a horrific point, was protruding through the top of his standard issue shoes.

"Fuuuck!" Ivo spat, trying to keep as much weight off the foot as possible. "I stepped on it trying to get to you. Burn it all to cinder, this hurts!"

"Medic!" Helena called, drawing attention to the strange scene playing out. "Get us some cover and get him out of here!" Several soldiers called back in acknowledgement, and bolts began to fly as two engineers dropped their tools and made for the pileup. One ripped the shield from Ivo's arm, holding it in front of them as the second pulled Ivo off of Helena. Helena pushed herself up, still holding her crossbow. "Get him back to camp. He's got a caltrop through his foot. Make sure Roland takes a look at it, keep him away from the butcher surgeons."

She clapped Ivo heavily on the shoulder, causing him to wince further. "Thanks," she said, turning back to her crossbow. With a hefty whack, the lock freed, and once again she was aiming towards the walls.

Ivo limped off the field, assisted by the engineer. Despite the lack of a shield, there was little chance an arrow would be flying their way. Judging by the cry of agony, Helena had "thanked" the militia who had shot at her with an exchange of projectiles.

Not that Ivo paid much attention. Woozy from shock, he pulled away from the engineer, who was forced to bring him back into line. Again and again Ivo nearly stumbled and the engineer kept him up until they reached the trappings of the camp.

In his absence, the palisade had been completed, with ten-foot stakes rising around a city of tents and carts.

Roland was inspecting the hinges on the gates when Ivo caught sight of him out of the corner of his eye. The quartermaster's hammer hit the grass as he bolted towards his injured peer, nails and tools dropping from his belt. Sil stuck her head around the reinforced door, checking on the commotion. She let out a small gasp, and sprinted to catch up with Roland.

"I got 'im!" Roland grunted, picking Ivo up like a puppy and nearly bowling the engineer over. The engineer, done with his duties, shrugged and left him to Roland. Sil caught up, out of breath, as Roland turned and trundled back to camp. She opened her mouth to speak, but Roland had moved past her, forcing her to run back to the camp.

"Where's it hurtin'? How bad is it?" Roland asked as he made way for the medic's tent.

"I stepped on a caltrop at full sprint. Hurts like a bitch," Ivo groaned, blood dripping from his foot. Roland let out a sigh of relief.

"Well, at least it won't kill ya." Roland glanced at Ivo's foot, seeing the length of steel stuck through his shoe. "You may wish it had though."

It was a short walk to the medic's tent, but it might as well have been a mile for Ivo. Every jostle moved the iron spike lodged in his foot, a quarter pound of metal tearing the flesh and shooting pain up his leg. As Roland set him on the table his vision darkened.

"Sil, grab the heaviest shears you can find, over there!" Roland pointed to the far side of the plain tent, were was sat a rack of tools that could pass as instruments of torture. Among them was a set of steel cutters, with long handles and short, heavy blades. Sil struggled to lift the instrument and drag it over to the table as Roland looked Ivo over.

"You're goin' to want to close your eyes," Roland told Ivo as he moved the blades of the shears over to top part of the spike, as close to his foot as he dared. Ivo, woozy and blacking out, had his mind elsewhere. Roland inhaled, and with all the force he could muster slammed the shears shut on the protruding metal, sending the barbed length flying, where it embedded itself in the ground. Ivo cried out in pain, forcing Roland to drop the shears and grab a hold of his leg. He turned to Sil as he subdued Ivo.

"Sil, I'm gonna need ya to pull the bottom bit out for me. Just grab and pull!" Sil nodded, shakily grabbing hold of the bottom spikes of the caltrop. Avoiding the wicked barbs at the ends, she pulled with all her might, dislodging the cut length of steel and reeling backwards.

Ivo was silent as Sil tumbled to the floor. The pain had been too much, and he had passed out. His head rolled limply to the side. Blood oozed from his foot, giving Roland a slippery surface to work with as he did his best to peel the shoe away. Finally free, Roland threw the bloody piece of footwear, narrowly missing Sil as she scrambled to her feet. She hoisted herself up to the table, watching Roland apply the bandages.

Her voice quivering, Sil asked, "Is he all right? He's not moving. Why isn't he moving, he should be moving…"

Roland held up a bloody hand. "Calm down, Sil. He'll be all right. Can't say I've seen anyone pass out from a caltrop before, but I can't imagine it feeling too good." Roland wiped his hands off, and gave Ivo one last look over. "He'll be fine, I'm sure of that. Just give him some time to rest."

Chapter Twenty-One

Rudolph tugged lightly at his bindings. He chided himself for insisting on the metal clasps, as the cold steel began to chafe. Hardly the worst of his concerns, however. The duke lay sprawled on the stump of a Cinderbark tree, the timber still warm against his bare flesh.

It wasn't the only stump, either. All around, the corpses of the ancient trees marred the gentle roll of a once dense wood. A legacy left by Rudolph's ancestors.

It was midnight; a thick, murky haze obscured the sky above, leaving only the light of the torches and the faint glow of the fallen trees. Gathered around the duke were a small group of his personal guard and Brutus, the vagrant, and the recently promoted Einrik, who was unconscious. A spiked bowl of soup had renendered the new commander perfectly compliant.

"Why did we have to march all this way?" Brutus grunted, his side-sword drawn and at the ready.

"Our radiant lord has a unique aspect," the vagrant replied, working on a small knucklebone with an awl. "The power that flows through him is one in the same as these trees."

"All I see are stumps," Brutus snorted.

"And yet they still reside here. Centuries later, and not a spot of rot." The vagrant wiped the excess shavings from the knucklebone. "These trees still hold their power, if but a fraction. It provides a…purgatory of sorts."

"Explain."

"The crossing of power here acts as a net, one capable of holding the soul of our lord."

"You mean to kill him?" Brutus raised his sword slightly.

The vagrant lowered his work, and attempted to pacify the Cyclops. "He will not die, but if the power in his blood overwhelms him in his weakened state, it will be ripped from his body. Along with his soul. This net will keep his divine power in check, holding him together until I can finish my work."

Brutus lowered the sword, before addressing Rudolph. "You sure you want to go through with this? You can bloody well count yourself lucky for surviving all the other "treatments" this cripple has given you."

Rudolph nodded, gazing into the deep reaches of the night sky. "If Borig can follow me to the temple, this whole project will be for naught. Years of planning, hundreds of lives...I'm not about to let my own selfishness get in the way." The duke smiled, glancing sideways to Brutus. "Don't worry, friend. I'm not about to leave you here. It takes a lot to kill a Lug."

The Duke bit his lip, his confidence masking a deep, languishing terror.

"I am ready, oh lord," the vagrant declared, holding a needle sharp piece of bone between his skeletal fingers. The knuckle had been shaved down, the entirety of its surface covered in a latticework of lines and figures, many too small to see unaided. "Upon this shard I have placed all the wards we will need to blind Borig. All I need to do is place it." His free hand reached into the enveloping folds of his robe, from which he produced a long-bladed dagger. "Allow me to begin my work."

Rudolph closed his eyes tightly and nodded.

The duke remained as relaxed as the situation allowed, knowing any tensing could end his life in seconds. The vagrant brought the dagger up to his own head. Sliding the blade under bandages around his eyes, he flicked his wrist. The blade sliced through the tattered wrappings, the fabric blowing away in a soft breeze. He opened his milky eyes, devoid of iris or pupil. In their place sat a set of overlapping triangles, upon which were set the image of a flower sheathed in barbs.

Slowly, the vagrant lowered his knife towards Rudolph's bare chest, until the razor-sharp tip sank into yielding flesh. Gently, carefully, he cut between the myriad of scars embedded in the dukes ribs, blood trailing the knife's gruesome path. Rudolph grimaced as he felt the knife slide leisurely over his ribs, scraping against bone as it severed the meat of his chest. The blood boiled as it met air, steam venting forth as the vagrant ended the cut just above the duke's abdomen, exposing alabaster bone. Flesh peeled away far easier than it had any right to, the tissue lifting with no effort. Detailed runes lined Rudolph's ribcage, running down the bleached protrusions before terminating at his sternum.

His bones exposed to the world, the duke's indomitable will finally gave out. Rudolph succumbed to the gathering dark. There he found himself suspended in a void with no light, nor sound, nor the tangibility of his own person. Nothing, save for his drifting consciousness. He reached to clear his eyes, only to find both his hand and head missing.

Strange, how little his formlessness concerned him. It was refreshing.

A bolt broke dark, the world filling with light, sound, smell, and touch. Rudolph felt himself tumbling, rolling in an unbound sea of chaos. The formless world around him swirled, tossed and rolled as it battered against its unseen confines. The madness was short lived as pockets of stillness began to form, congealing into greater and greater masses of substance. Shapes and colours broke white haze, shades of browns and reds, and eventually greens.

Set around the duke was an unending stretch of grass, beyond the bounds of vision or reason. It was all there was save for piles of jet-black stone and bleached saplings. The sun and stars wheeled overhead, day and night passing into one another as the world below shifted and evolved. Small hills formed beyond the grove of burgeoning trees, sporting their own groves. These groves sprouted far faster than the pallid saplings that accompanied Rudolph, broad, simple boughs and jagged needles grabbing at the life-giving sun.

The hills shifted in the distance, rising above the patches of lesser trees and shedding their coatings of dirt. Jagged stone was pushed forth, ripping from the womb of the world, piercing the sky in their pompous grandeur. These newborn mountains were soon dusted in a powdery coating of snow, settling in place until the ending of the world.

A quick glance of his surroundings revealed to Rudolph his sapling peers had sprung upwards in a dramatic fashion, crackled white bark and black leaves set high above the forest floor. Below, the duke sensed the first trappings of life, a faint singing of birds and the rustle of little clawed feet through the trees. A breeze blew through the grove, and Rudolph swayed gently from side to side. It was peaceful.

Time passed. How long, Rudolph could not say. It mattered little, the past and the present flowing seamlessly into the future. Rudolph found himself deeply content, a feeling with which he was unfamiliar.

His newfound peace would not last. Violently, he was dragged from his trance by a deep, sharp agony at the base of his being. Rhythmically, the pounding wore away at his sturdy form, drawing his fiery blood and loosening his iron grip on the world. He was sent tumbling, moving for the first time in millennia, and left sprawled out on the muddied earth below. Iron. All he saw was iron, severing his being, ripping his soul apart. And the heat. *The heat!*

Rudolph's cry echoed through the barren patch of stumps, his restraints ripping from the packed earth below and sailing through the air. The stink of blood and torched flesh permeated the stagnant air, the reek of copper and fire. Bug-eyed, the duke inspected his surroundings, every minute detail as he remembered. Save for the state of his torso.

Looking down, the duke witnessed his own mangled chest. His once proud physique left a collection of scars, dominated by a thick, brutal cut clean down his sternum and branching under his pectorals. The jagged wounds were seared black, sealed with fire and iron. The pain had subsided to manageable levels, leaving Rudolph with the shock of the aftermath. ˎ

His breath was heavy, his arms shaking. He wheezed, his tortured lungs struggling to fill. "I'm alive," he managed to get out before falling back.

A pair of hefty hands caught him, laying him gently back onto the stump. Brutus held his friend for a moment, before calling, "Get the shackles off, and bring me some water!" The giant kneeled down, and caught the duke smiling. "Still awake, sir?" Brutus asked softly.

Rudolph nodded slightly. "I think," he whispered. "Thanks for catching me."

Brutus smiled. "Glad to be of service, sir."

A shadow slid into view, hovering over Rudolph as he wavered in and out of the waking world. A bloody knife was set in the thick leather belt of the vagrant, heart-blood congealing on the blade. His eyes covered once again by his ratty bandage, he leaned close to the duke. "My lord, all has been set into place."

Rudolph opened his eyes, spotting the hooded figure looming over him.

"My work here is done, lord. My services are no longer required. This is where our paths diverge."

Rudolph raised an eyebrow. "You're leaving? After all the work you've done, you're leaving? Bit dramatic, don't you think?"

The vagrant stood to his full height. "I will miss basking in the glow of your presence, Lord of the Ember. And I wish to bear witness to your ascension. But I feel a calling elsewhere, a familiar voice with an unfamiliar command. I shall take my leave. Farewell, lord."

The vagrant looked towards the ebony expanse of the night, and without hesitation, set off. Rudolph watched him disappear into the dark. He then cast his gaze to Brutus, who was following the hooded man with his one good eye. "Not going to follow him?" the duke inquired.

"Are you ordering me to?" Brutus replied. When Rudolph said nothing, Brutus added, "Good."

The vagrant had long since vanished into the night, and still Rudolph sat, staring into the darkness. "Hard to believe that just happened," he mused, picking at his scarred chest.

"Strange times we live in, sir."

"Too true."

"Still think you're going to be a god?"

"More so than I already am?"

Brutus snorted. "In all seriousness, sir."

Rudolph chuckled. "I thought you didn't believe him."

"Believe me, sir. I saw what that bastard did, and by now I'm willing to believe anything."

"That bad?" Rudolph asked.

"He shoved a glowing shard of bone into your heart, and yet here we are."

Wishing to linger no longer, Rudolph clapped his hands, signalling for his knights to attend him. "Gentlemen, if you would be so kind as to fetch me my cloak, the crimson one. I'd rather not let anyone see me bleed."

As the nearest knight stepped aside, Rudolph pointed to the unconscious Einrik. "I doubt he'll be walking anywhere. Mind grabbing him?"

Brutus nodded, plodding towards the downed commander. "And be gentle!" Rudolph called after him.

A steel clad knight strode forth carrying a crimson mass of fabric. Rudolph garbed himself in his robe, the red velvet helping hide the blood still oozing from his chest. The cauterizing had done its job, but such an injury would take time to close. Rudolph absent-mindedly scratched at his chest before producing a flask from the depths of his robe. He made sure to keep at least one bottle of spirits on him at all times, for just such an occasion. He drank deeply from the ornate flask, emptying the contents in a matter of seconds.

"Blackbush Cognac, 954." Rudolph mumbled to himself, looking over the gem encrusted flask.

"Seven hundred embers a bottle," Brutus called as he approached, Einrik slung over his shoulder.

Rudolph tipped the flask to Brutus. "Well worth it." The duke then nodded to the unconscious commander. "He okay?"

"Should be. His head'll be sore tomorrow."

"What did the cripple do to him?"

"Tapped a shard of something into his temple. The hole scabbed up quick, he should be back up soon."

Rudolph instinctively grabbed the side of his head. "Bloody hell, that's a bit much isn't it? What do we tell him?"

"He had a little tumble, banged his head. Give him double alcohol rations and I doubt he'll inquire much further."

"Always in tune with the common man. I like that."

Compared to the events of the night, the trip back to camp was uneventful. There was a bit of a panic once the guard spotted the incapacitated Einrik, but it was short lived. Brutus left the poor sod in the hands of the duke's personal physician, who was told in private not to pry.

No one asked the whereabouts of the hooded vagrant.

With Einrik deposited, Brutus joined Rudolph in the tent that served as his temporary quarters. With the cart a pile of cinder and gold accents, it was the best the duke could do. By comparison, the furnishings were Spartan, the room dominated by a large table upon which sat a number of maps and letters. Rudolph was already pouring over the maps as Brutus closed the flap behind him.

"A pigeon arrived while I was out," the Duke stated, holding up a small note.

"We use pigeons?" Brutus asked.

"We have to import ravens, and I'm not made of money." The Duke threw the note down. "The second army has made camp around Dalwik. Acceptable casualties, minimal resistance."

Brutus hummed, then asked, "And Stahlsheim?". Rudolph bobbed his head and Brutus plodded to the space on the far side the table to examine the map.

The area was bordered by a crescent of rock, a vast mountain range encompassing an expanse of flat land. The city of Stahlsheim had been dug into the side of the mountain, dead in the middle of the arc.

"Borig knows he has the advantage. He won't leave his city unless we enter the killing fields."

"Could we rush the city? Keep him locked behind his walls while we make our way for the temple?"

Rudolph shook his head. "Old goat's got more siege weapons than Petyr and me combined. He can get to us well before we get to him."

Brutus rubbed his eyes. "Shitty situation all around then."

"I've looked over it every way possible," Rudolph claimed. "If Borig has already set out for the temple, our forces stand a chance. But if he gets there first..."

"We're fucked royally, sir?"

"Royally."

Brutus hefted himself off the table, timber creaking as he pushed away. "Better make your mind up. We'll be there by tomorrow."

"Right now, I just need to rest," he said, hand clutching his chest.

The duke stood, stretching. "You're relieved for the night, Brutus."

"You sure you're fine, sir? You had a rough night."

"While touching, your concern is not needed. I will be fine. Unless you'd rather spend the night. Bed is big enough for two."

Brutus snorted.

"All right, duly noted. Off to your cot then."

Rudolph waved his advisor away before taking another look at the map. His hand settled on the field set before Stahlsheim. "I'm coming for you, you bastard."

The first rays of morning broke the hold of the night, lighting the camp and rousing the inhabitants. Rudolph was still hunched over his desk, a pose he had adopted halfway through the night. He was used to long spans of time without sleep, the drugs in his veins keeping him awake.

And yet the duke felt horrible. Hour after hour he poured over the charts, playing out battles in his head and on the table. He drew from experience upon the field of battle, both personal and from the teachings of others.

In every situation played out before him, his armies were massacred. No matter where he placed his reserves, or how defensive a stance he took, Borig would crush the force assembled against him. While a loss was to be expected, what was left of Rudolph's humanity drove him to preserve as much life as possible. And exact a grisly revenge upon Borig.

In frustration, Rudolph swiped the pieces from the map, the small, wooden figures landing on the rug below. Reeling back, the duke smashed his fists into the table. "BURN IT ALL TO CINDER!" he bellowed, veins bulging as his heart and mind raced. Blood began to drip on the map, the massive wound carved into his chest reopening in clefts.

Rudolph stepped back from the table, mentally calming himself before his injury worsened. He propped himself against the footboard of his bed, leaning back and breathing deeply. His eyes closed as he tried to focus on a happy place, searching for that serene calm that came with years of meditation and contemplation. When that failed, he patted down his robe, searching for another flask of spirits.

The duke found his query sewn within the hem of his crimson coat, just beneath his left hip. In a hurry, Rudolph didn't bother undoing the seam. He desperately tore into the fabric and produced the flask.

"Out of style anyway..." he muttered as he undid the stopper. Swiftly, Rudolph emptied the gold-plated flask, tossing the empty container to the ground.

A familiar calm began to fill the duke, the spirits deadening his frustration and calming his mind. He exhaled, alcohol heavy on his breath.

An old, familiar feeling washed over him. Tingling numbness in his digits. His head, usually clear as crystal, becoming ever so fuzzy, dulling his senses. He was becoming...drunk.

"By all the whores of Brennerburg..." he murmured, looking over his fingers. "I haven't felt buzzed since...I can't bloody remember."

"Say something?"

Rudolph looked to the flap of his tent, were Brutus was making an entrance. "Long night sir?"

"That's beside the point. Brutus, I feel..."

Concern crossed Brutus' face. "Are you unwell? Is it the wound?"

Rudolph held up a hand. "Brutus, I'm buzzed. On booze."

Brutus stopped in his tracks. "Sir, I thought you drank...heavily. Maybe this was a stronger spirit than..."

"I can't get drunk Brutus!" Rudolph exclaimed. "It put me at ease, but never got to my head like this! The incanflagarat...it numbed me, made me immune..." He looked back at his fingers. "I don't like this, Brutus."

"Do I need to fetch a medic, sir?"

The duke shook his head. "A medic would do little. This goes beyond medicine. I've been feeling more and more like my old self, Brutus. Ever since that vagabond started working on me."

"Sounds like a good thing, sir. You look healthier, you're not sick as often, and how long has it been since you've needed to imbibe another dose of incanflagarat?"

Rudolph chuckled. "The old me was an idiot—slack-jawed dullard with as much ambition as a decorative squash. And I'll be damned if I'm to sit idly by as all my aspirations sink into a morass of mediocrity and decadence."

"You still seem to have your wits about you," Brutus observed.

Rudolph waved at the map. "That so?" he spat. "Rudolph of Rendsheim, the siegemaster, who studied under the greatest warmongers of his time." He sat down heavily. "And the old dog still has me bested. I'm losing my edge, Brutus."

"Well, it seems like we'll have to move quickly then, sir."

Rudolph stared at the maps.

"You shouldn't concern yourself with battle plans anyway. You and I both know war is won and lost by the soldiers fighting it. And you have legions of the best and brightest out there, they believe in your cause."

"How could they? I'm beginning to question the ethics of this venture, Brutus. I am willing to do many things to maintain the order of this world. Perhaps sending two armies to die is too much." Rudolph exhaled heavily. "Maybe I was wrong. Maybe I've been lying to myself. I'd seek to further my own ends and dress it up to appear far nobler. I brainwashed my people, I raised a force of craftsmen and labourers, and I'm condemning thousands to death. If there's any justice in this world, I'd be remembered as a tyrant."

Brutus remained expressionless, his mind turning behind his cyclopean gaze. "Perhaps you don't believe the cause you set out to achieve, but I do. They do."

Rudolph looked up.

"We've done the investigating, the research. We know what may reside in that temple. We've just witnessed it firsthand." Brutus motioned to Rudolph's scars. "Yes, people will die. Yes, you are the one with the most to gain. But if it keeps power of that magnitude out of the hands of madmen like Borig and Petyr, so be it. I would much rather see it in the hands of madmen like yourself."

A smile broke through Rudolph's glum visage. "Perhaps you're right, perhaps some good may come of this yet."

Rudolph shot up, producing a sheet of parchment from a stack on the table. He grabbed a stained quill from its perch, and began to scribble. "Have this sent to Rendsheim as soon as possible. To the guild-masters' hall."

Brutus cocked an eyebrow. "Bit of an odd time to be ordering a new set of jewelry."

"You know I detest the stuff." Rudolph replied, still scribbling. "You're right, Brutus. And about politics, for once. I'm proud. If we are to be ruled by the mad..." Rudolph flicked his hand rapidly as he signed the document, "Then we can at least be discerning about their madness. This note states that, should I not return, rule of the city is to be handed over to the guild-masters. I'm terminating the line of succession."

"You're ending a line going back to Richart on a whim? How will the nobility respond?"

Rudolph snorted, sealing the letter with wax. "Who gives a damn about the nobles? Think about it: if I didn't sacrifice years of my life to that damnable drug who would have gotten the throne? The eldest, Rupert? Rupert can't even read! We've had enough of these knock kneed, inbred dunces who spend more time fornicating in the lavatories than studying economics. And we've certainly had enough egomaniacal apes participating in a continent wide dick-swinging contest!"

"Yourself included?"

"Myself in particular, old friend." Rudolph handed the rolled up note to Brutus. "Now let's get this sent off. Then we have a battle to win." The duke rushed past Brutus, his chest as puffed out as his wounds would allow

Outside, soldiers and staff were busy preparing for the battle ahead. The harsh, metallic screech of grindstones permeated the air, and tailors were busy mending padded jackets. Hurried quartermasters rushed about with crates and barrels, the occasional mail ring or arrowhead scattering behind them. Despite the chaos, everyone who passed Rudolph stopped to give a stiff salute, the duke following suit with a salute of his own.

The duke passed a groggy Einrik, who stumbled from his own tent. He did his best to salute, but ended up holding his throbbing head in his hands. Rudolph patted the worn-out commander on the back as he passed, forcing Einrik to retch onto the packed earth. Apologizing profusely, he crawled back into the dark, quiet confines of his tent.

Brutus caught up to Rudolph as he marched towards the courier's tent, flicking his thumb back at the sorry commander. "He okay?"

Rudolph shrugged. "I'm sure he'll be fine. By the smell of things he took advantage of his bonus spirit rations. Give him a few minutes."

Reaching the edge of the camp, Rudolph arrived at the courier's station. A small, aging man was grooming a compact horse when he spotted the duke. He saluted, setting down the brush and drawing a disappointed whinny from the horse. "My lord."

"Tut tut, none of that now, Mr…"

"Miller, lord."

"Miller! Good man. Now listen, Miller, I have a rather urgent letter I need delivered to Rencsheim. Specifically, to the guild-masters. Don't bother with the local mail service, just hand it over yourself."

The smaller man's head bobbed up and down. "Your will be done, lord."

"Superb!" Rudolph beamed as he produced a small satchel, handing it over along with the letter. "Here's a little something extra. Consider it a retirement fund. Buy yourself a nice little cottage and put that old horse out to stud."

The old man's eyes nearly popped out of his head as he felt the weight of the pouch in his hand. "I…I…"

Rudolph held up a hand. "No need for thanks. Best of luck on your trip."

The courier wasted little time saddling his horse, and in a matter of minutes, he was racing down the road. Brutus and Rudolph watched as he disappeared over the rolling landscape, at which time Brutus leaned over and whispered, "You do realize that was a mare?"

Rudolph snorted. "You bloody well know I hate horses. Buck toothed, bug-eyed monsters. And what, no compliments on the charity?"

"That would defeat the purpose, sir."

Rudolph shook his head. "Enough of your nonsense, I'm off to the armoury. It's about time I got my coat of plates adjusted."

It was a lengthy trip, the panicked armourer frantically cutting and reshaping plates from Rudolph's brigandine. The duke took his breakfast by the forge, conducting the last preparations for the upcoming battle as he dined on an assortment of candied fruits. After a brief meeting with the commanders, including the heaving Einrik, the final deployments were decided, and a plan devised.

They would force Borig into a charge, and on the commander's mark, the front line of spearmen would step back, catching the Stahlsheimers on the wrong foot and neutering Borig's ferocious assault. All the while, arbalests would rain forge hardened bolts, hopefully punching through the formidable armour of Stahlsheim's finest.

By the time the commanders were dismissed, Rudolph's armour had been finished. A new, black layer of velvet covered the plates, along with gold-plated rivets and a thick, mailed collar. The duke looked over the smith's handiwork, before stepping behind a changing curtain to try it on. Donning a crimson arming jacket with splinted sleeves, Rudolph slipped into the iron confines of the brigandine. He was surprised at its light weight, and once he had wrapped a belt around his waist, the comfort of the fit. In part, thanks to the fine work of the smith, and to the absent burning sensation the course fabric of the jacket usually had on his drug-abraded nerves.

Rudolph stretched to his left, then his right, testing the flexibility of his new brigandine. The interlocking plates slid past one another smoothly, leaving Rudolph with the same level of flexibility as he possessed uninhibited. Satisfied, the duke stepped out from behind the changing curtain where Brutus was watching the smith wring his hands anxiously. Sweat accumulating on his brow, he watched for Rudolph's approval. And approval he got as Rudolph grinned at Brutus.

"Miracles never cease. You were right, Brutus. This is a damn sight more comfortable."

The smith let out a sigh of relief, and Brutus replied, "Looks good. Less foppish than before."

Rudolph looked the piece over again. "It does lack a bit of flair, doesn't it?"

Brutus pushed himself away from the table, and tilted his head toward the bustling commotion taking place near the mustering ground. "We can address that later," he said impatiently. "For now we have places to be."

"To Stahlsheim then," Rudolph replied.

"To Stahlsheim."

The assembled masses of troops filed into neat units, each ten wide by ten deep. Black iron sat upon red jackets, and the sharpened edges of axes and billhooks glinted in the rising sun. Dew rolled off high leather boots as soldiers marched with drilled unison. Unit by unit, Rudolph's private army departed camp, leaving behind the supporting craftsmen and accompanying tradespersons. Either the soldiers would return by nightfall, or not at all.

Rudolph marched proudly at the head of the column, flanked by Brutus and a number of his loyal knights. Blowing in the breeze overhead was the Scorched Banner, the flag of war of the Lugs since Richart. The black fabric was still as dark as it was the day it was dyed, pyroquette dust permeating the heavy fabric. Upon the field of jet was emblazoned the ember of Rendsheim, an intricately flowing flame that appeared to flicker in the breeze.

Ahead stretched Borig's land, an expanse of craggy peaks and deep gorges. The choked, brown grass so familiar to Rudolph was thin here, a few hearty patches finding purchase in the jagged slate and crumbling granite of the dramatic landscape. Upon a horizon of clearing skies loomed a proud, snowcapped mountain range, the last and largest of its kind.

Rudolph recalled reading of this place, before the mines and quarries pocked the rocky landscape like the diggings of worms. The foothills that sprang from the mountains were once much greater, both in domain and stature. While as devoid of life as it was now, a wealth of minerals and metals permeated the stone. Great veins of iron and copper, spat up from the bowels of the earth, gave hulking stones a marbled appearance, greens and browns breaking the grey visage of the hillside.

Gems of varying qualities and sizes could be found in jagged growths. There was an old saying that one would need to throw his pick in the air, and start digging were it landed. And the saying held true, for a time.

With the coming of man, tribes of hill folk began to spring up, finding shelter in the nooks and crannies of the dynamic terrain. These people were the first to mine metal, selling crude ingots of bronze and the first iron tools in exchange for food and timber. As their tool working was refined to an art, they brought back greater hauls of gleaming metals, until the surface was all but devoid. It was at that time, when the first pyroquettes made their way into the mountains, that the hill folk began to delve below the earth.

Like moles these people tunnelled under the stony hills, leaving snaking passages. Greater and greater quantities of metals and gems were pulled up from the depths in iron braced carts, set upon a clever system of tracks and drawn by sturdy Wolloks. Once a tunnel failed to bear fruit, another would be dug, and the cycle would begin again.

It was a prosperous time for the hill folk, their systematic rape of the land yielding gross quantities of precious commodities, which in turn were traded for copious foodstuffs. Even as the earth they stood upon and under began to crack, they toiled away by candlelight in the deep.

Until the earth itself, stripped bare and dug through so thoroughly, finally gave out. Hundreds of miles of hill and dale collapsed in unison, bringing an unimaginable amount of stone upon those in the mines. Fully half the population died that day, leaving the remaining tribes to eke out a living further up the mountains. Hauling their stocks of goods, they left the crumbling land, and settled on what was now Stahlsheim.

Years of toil had hardened the Stahlsheimers as a people, broad shouldered with heavy features. Their sun-bleached lands, unlike the shrouded fields of Rendsheim, left their skin a much darker hue, and leathery in texture. Rudolph had traversed these lands a time or two, when the animosity between lords was but a simmer. He watched as Borig put on a military display, the expansive parade grounds at the highest peak of the city covered in mailed warriors. Rudolph did his best to keep an image of collective calmness, hiding his growing concern with a noble indifference.

Rudolph knew his opposition would be tenacious, having advantage in both numbers as well as being on home turf. As the craggy countryside rolled by, he mulled his strategies over and over.

Brutus took note of his growing concern as he plodded alongside the duke. "Troubled?" he asked over the din of marching feet and clanking steel.

"More so than usual," Rudolph responded, keeping his eye on the mountains on the horizon. "Too late now, we're almost there."

By noon, Rudolph's forces crested a ridge overlooking a shallow incline, emptying into a colossal basin encircled by dramatic mountains. At the far side rose the tallest peak, the Stahl, upon which Borig's city sat. Stepping off to the side and allowing the rest of his forces to march, Rudolph took in the lands before him. Brutus, close behind, pointed towards the bulk of the mountain a few miles off, upon which sat the carved city of Stahlsheim.

Solid stone terraces, hard-edged and lofty, were spotted with houses and hearty trees. Streets and gardens intermingled with sprawling homes and open air forges, so massive were these stone flats. The houses themselves were made of stone coated in plaster, grey slate shingles set upon cracked alabaster walls. As the terraces rose higher, these homes grew larger, integrating rare metals and a growing quantity of wood in their construction.

Navigating the terraces were great cranes, crafted with steel-studded timber, hauling platforms up and down the sheer faces, and powered by streams of mountain runoff. These provided transport for goods and people.

In particular, the lowest and broadest terrace was a bustling hub of chaos. Dozens of cranes wheeled about, hauling great platforms lined with row upon row of figures. At the base of the cliff, these figures would disgorge and array themselves in orderly rows.

"Like clockwork," Brutus grumbled. "Bastard's gotten predictable in his old age."

"I doubt he'll move far from the city. He's going to want his people to bear witness to his victory. Arrogant prick."

Brutus grunted in agreement. "When do you plan on leaving?"

"Shortly. It will take him time to muster once he realizes I'm not among the dead. We'll have a day on him." Rudolph rubbed his eyes. "I sincerely hope we aren't just chasing ghosts here. I'm not getting away from this without repercussions. No doubt I'll be labeled a traitor, or worse, an idiot." He shrugged. "Better the people know nothing about our true goals."

Brutus thought a moment. "Couldn't we just block the road? Force Borig to stay put."

Rudolph shook his head. "Doubtful. He'll know something's up, and there is more than one way out of this basin. He'll send riders out to survey the surrounding area and they'll have our tracks in hours. This way, Borig is forced to commit his entire force."

The two were silent as rank after rank of red clad soldiers filed past, until Brutus piped up, "What if things go our way? If we route the Stahlsheimers back to the city, are they to set up a siege?"

"I doubt that's a decision we'll need to make. I have left written instruction, should I be absent, that states we encircle the city until they surrender. I won't chance a frontal assault;

Borig uses his people as shields, and the lower levels would be torched as soon as we set foot upon the first terrace."

"You sound a wee bit disappointed."

"Well, I've always wanted a manor on the high terrace. But a massacre would devalue the place."

"Damn shame, sir. Now, if we're done here."

"Yes, yes. Let's get to it then."

CHAPTER TWENTY-TWO

Ivo gasped at the rasping at his diseased foot, pus infused flesh sloughing off in green, putrescent hunks. "Burn it all to cinder!" he spat, nails digging into his palms as his grip tightened.

He was laid out on a hard, bloodstained table in the medic's tent, receiving the best treatment the second army could afford. Which wasn't saying much; at the other end of the knife, Roland was doing his best to clean the rot from Ivo's wound. "Steady now, not my fault you didn't bother to clean it," the quartermaster commented as he rinsed the blade in a bowl of spirits next to Ivo's foot.

"Just be glad it's not spreadin'," Roland told him, dipping a length of linen bandage in the blood tinged spirits of the bowl. Wringing the excess liquid, the quartermaster gingerly wrapped the alcohol infused bandage around Ivo's pierced foot. "You're going through more booze than three regulars!"

"How about a flask of it to drink?" Ivo replied, hoping for the numbing relief of whatever alcohol he could get his hands on.

"If you don't mind foot drippin's mixed in. You've already gone through both your weeks rations and mine."

Ivo grumbled at Roland's dismissal. Raw flesh stung intensely as the chemical burn of the spirit seeped deeper and deeper into the wound. Thanks to Roland's constant digging, the green stayed confined to the sole of Ivo's calloused foot. But all the fussing and scraping left Ivo unable to perform most of his duties. The elation at a free ride was swiftly overtaken by the agony that left him hobbling about the camp.

Roland tied off the ends of the bandage, giving Ivo's foot a hearty pat. Ivo winced, eliciting an apology. "Oops, force o' habit," he said, grabbing a nearby length of timber. Roland had repurposed four feet of ash from an old spear shaft as a walking stick for Ivo. A bit roughshod to be sure, but it was sturdy and reliable.

Table and bone creaking in unison, Ivo rose from his timber bed with the assistance of his friend. On his feet, Ivo gave Roland grumbled thanks, stiffly bending his aching neck, and rigidly hobbled to the door. An hour planted on a dense pine table did that to a body, in particular one working its damnedest to stave off disease.

Pushing aside the troublesome flap of the tent, Ivo emerged into the midday sun. The dull rays forcing him to squint and he looked up and down the sloppy row of carts and tents that ran to either side, the line curving as it went. Camp had been roughly assembled in a circle, concentric rings housing progressively more important personnel and equipment as they neared the centre. Ten-foot palisade walls surrounded the vaguely round mass with sharpened posts of splintery timber that kept the outside, outside. At the core, like in an exotic fruit, were the personal quarters and armouries of the unit's commanders and accompanying bodyguards.

It was at this fortified core that Ivo would find Sil. Despite being taken off combat duty he was still in charge of keeping an eye on the strange woman. Not that he hadn't tired to eliminate the remaining labor; the day after the incident, he had limped to Rook and pleaded he be left to recover from his injuries. In addition to a few harsh comments, Rook stated bluntly that Sil wouldn't allow it.

Despite regaining most of her faculties and integrating splendidly with the campaigner's life, Sil insisted on keeping Ivo around. While she spent the days working with the camp staff or talking with the commanders, she met with Ivo and Roland come sunset, almost habitually. Roland was thrilled with this arrangement, the camaraderie doing wonders for his mood. He and Sil would talk into the wee hours of the night, with Sil asking Roland question after question and the quartermaster answering to the best of his abilities. All the while, Ivo lounged on his cot, or glowered into his meal. Quiet seemed to elude him, save for the confines of slumber.

It wasn't all bad, however. Roland, for all his rambling stories, provided significantly better company than the soldiers. Even after his daring exploits, Ivo was still the butt of more than a few jokes. And Sil...well, Ivo didn't know what to think. She was odd, truly a blank slate. Everything was new to her, even the most mundane of the day-to-day life. Every joke was fresh, and often requiring a lengthy follow-up explanation. Every story had her teetering on the edge of her seat, waiting to hear its conclusion. It was...Ivo wouldn't go as far as to say refreshing, but it was certainly the right train of thought.

Ivo was pulled from his idle contemplation as he approached the core of the camp by a rattling, metallic din from the collected tents ahead. A series of curses went up, and Ivo increased his feeble pace in an effort to glimpse the chaos. A number of staff filed past and by the time he got to the action, a sizeable crowd had accumulated.

From what Ivo could glimpse as he approached, one of the many armour racks set around tents was toppled over, coats of blackened mail and pieces of pyroquette-forged armour lay strewn across the grassy earth. A crestfallen lad, no older than fifteen, was receiving the berating of a lifetime. Rook personally took the time to chew the poor bastard out.

From the wrathful tirade, Ivo had deduced that the lad was tasked with fetching one of the commanders a helmet, to get a new lining sewn in. It seemed the lad, to quote Rook, "completely fucked up", and toppled several sets of pricey armour. While it was doubtful such solid pieces of protection would be damaged in any way, a recent rain meant the forge-blackened steel would have been given a fresh coat of mud.

Satisfied the boy had had enough, Rook gave him the unenviable job of collecting, cleaning, and setting up of the stand in as pristine an order as it once was. Happy to be let off lightly, and keeping his head down, the lad dove to the ground and began collecting the mail coats and wayward pieces of plate. Rook, in the meantime, told the crowd to "shove off" in a manner quite at odds with her usual demeanour. Taking it as a sign, Ivo turned to go with the crowd. Rook, however, had other plans. "Not you, hobbles."

At least hobbles is better than witch.

Ivo wheeled, using his crutch as a pivot. He jumped slightly once he saw Rook standing a few feet in front of him. She must have moved up to talk to him while he'd tried to sneak off.

Up close, Ivo could see how ragged she was. Purple bags hung under her sunken grey eyes, from many nights spent in the company of maps and charts. The rim of her padded jacket revealed a number of reddish welts, and Ivo wondered if she had even removed her armour since the campaign began. Once he caught a whiff of the stink coming from the padding, he was certain she had not.

"I apologize for the disorder," she said, indicating her condolences. "We've had setback after setback. Minor issues, mostly. Equipment breakages, missing gear, misread orders. I've never seen a campaign run into this many problems…" The commander trailed off, her gaze drifting into nothingness.

She shook her head. "Be that as it may," she continued, assuming a more stilted, military pose, "it certainly does *not* imply you are free to skip your assigned duties."

"She's doing pretty well by herself," Ivo commented. It was a bit of a gutsy move to talk back to the commander, but Ivo was certain she wouldn't reprimand someone in Ivo's condition.

He was wrong.

A heavy hand landed on his shoulder, the platted fingertips digging into his burgundy tunic. He was nearly taken off his foot as Rook pulled him close. "I am in no mood to deal with wayward conscripts, hobbles. Do not test me."

Ivo's eyes bugged out. "Okay, okay! Where is she?" he squeaked. Rook released Ivo, who immediately began rubbing his shoulder.

Glancing over her shoulder, she barked to the lad picking up armour. "Boy? Where did Sil go?"

The lad looked up, dropping a gauntlet as he pointed towards a cart across from the clearing in the centre of the cart. "She was helping me get some boxes of whetstones, sir."

"Better get to it then," Rook snapped at Ivo then, hands behind her back, strode to the largest tent in the cluster.

Ivo sighed, looking down at the lad, who shrugged and continued his work.

The lad had told the truth; Sil was still working away at the cart. She was oblivious to the chaos in the camp; more concerned with the tasks she was given than the goings on around her. Ivo found her digging through one of a dozen crates, counting the brick-sized stones for sharpening blades. A neatly stacked pile was to her side, and once stock was taken, these would be handed out to the quartermasters for further distribution.

Sil was marking down another tick on a crude sheet of paper when she caught the hobbling Ivo out the corner of her eye. She shot up immediately, waving enthusiastically as he took a few more laboured steps forward. "Oh, hi Ivo!" She smiled. "I hope it went well."

"Oh, just lovely…"

"Really? I thought it'd be painful."

Ivo sighed, in no mood to correct her.

"Well, I'm just about finished here, so I suppose I could leave early." Sil called behind the cart. "Miss Brewer?" A thin, twitchy woman in her forties appeared from behind the cart, several logs rolling away from her. Sil put a hand to her mouth. "Oh, I'm so sorry!"

In a thin, worn out voice, the quartermaster raised a hand and said, "Just…go do what you're going to do."

"Roland wanted to meet with me once I was done here," Sil said. "Let's go!" She grabbed Ivo by the forearm, nearly toppling him, and forced the grumbling conscript to hop after her. Several camp staff chuckled as they passed, enjoying Ivo's discomfort as the two made their way to the mess area. Most of the soldiers were either on patrol or guarding the engineers as they plied their trade at the base of Dalwik's marble walls. Ivo couldn't' recall seeing Helena since the first day of the siege.

As a result, the mess area was empty. The narrow benches and clear tables were preferable to the lowbrow humour and frequent brawls that often followed large groups of soldiers.

Roland was already at one of the many stained benches surrounded by linen tarps and hanging meats. Roughly twenty feet in radius, this was one of the smaller eating areas, making it all the more attractive to Ivo.

Around the eating area, camp staff rushed to and from various stations, strewn with stale bread and maggot riddled hunks of meat. Their tables, covered in tarps and backing onto tents, were blanketed in a cloud of flies and stink. Ivo mused on stories he'd heard, how nobles would pay extra for particularly riddled cheese and consume it alongside raw meat and wrinkled fruit. Strange tastes to a carpenter, who often ate spoiled food out of necessity rather than desire.

Roland, however, didn't seem to have the same reservations on the food. The quartermaster was oblivious to Sil and Ivo's approach, occupied with a hunk of bread and a gob of so-called cheese. It wasn't until the two had sat down across from him that the quartermaster noticed them, and even then only after he drained his copper canteen.

"Well, just in time for lunch," he said, wiping froth from his oily beard. "Here, have a nibble o' this." He pushed his plate forward, presenting Ivo with the questionable dairy product.

"No, I lost my appetite."

Roland moved the plate over to Sil who curiously poked at the off yellow mass.

"Can't say I blame you," Roland agreed. "I lost my appetite a while back."

Ivo raised an eyebrow.

"I've been worried sick about my family's anvil. Things gone missin', and no one seems to know bugger all! How does an anvil just up and disappear?"

Ivo shrugged.

Between mouthfuls of bread, Roland absentmindedly murmured, "Didn't think Petyr actually followed through with it..."

"With what?" Sil asked, pushing away the pungent plate of cheese.

Roland suddenly began coughing violently. Clearing his throat, Roland leaned in close, his eye's watering. "Let's just forget I said anything."

This was the first time Ivo had seen Roland refuse to follow up on a question.

"Petyr is the man within those walls, yes? Please Roland, I must know!" Sil pleaded.

Roland sighed. "Not a word of this to anyone, right?"

Sil nodded enthusiastically. "Look, this curse business, it's a bit more founded in reality than you might think. When I was working with Petyr, he had a bit of a side project. The curse had been a legend up to that point, nothin' but a story really. Petyr wanted to change that." Sil sat enthralled, and even Ivo had begun to listen closer. "He came to me in the dead of night, and asked me to make him a few tools—a chisel and hammer of a very unusual design. Even let me work with an ingot of pyroquette steel, fancy stuff to be sure."

"Maybe he wanted to take up carving," Ivo mused.

"Oh no, no good would come from these. He instructed me to inscribe these tools with some old, very…wrong runes. Ones we had reservations 'bout workin' with."

"Why did you do it?" Sil asked.

"What choice did I have? Work was work, and I was young. I never thought his ramblings would come to fruition."

Sil frowned. "You still helped him."

Roland's broad shoulders sank and he looked down to the table. "I'm afraid I did, yes. And now, I'm regretting it."

"So the curse is real?" Ivo inquired, growing agitated at all this mystical talk.

"I believe so," Roland claimed. "I'd like to count our misfortune to a streak o' bad luck, but I fear it's all part of that madman's machinations."

"Shouldn't we tell the commanders?" Sil asked. "Warn them?"

Roland shook his head. "All that would do is send me to the gallows as a traitor. Rook'll never believe me, doesn't matter how well she knows me."

"We're fucked then," Ivo blurted, setting his hands down on the table. "My foot's going to turn green and fall off because thirty years ago you made magic tools for a madman. Great."

"It was more like seventy," Roland blurted, before wincing at his own mistake. Both Ivo and Sil stared at him.

"Just how old are you, Roland?" Ivo asked cautiously.

Roland inhaled deeply. "Closer to a hundred. I lost count a decade or so ago."

"You're a hundred!" Sil blurted, drawing unwanted gazes from various staff at the mess stations.

"Yes, I am, now keep your voice down!" Roland hissed, motioning for them to do the same. "Like I said, a couple of our experiments came to fruition. I was thirty somethin' when we first started, and I managed to sneak off with one of the only successful projects we had."

"So you're older than Petyr? The bastard is ancient!" Ivo exclaimed.

"The years haven't been as kind to him as they have been to me, I must say."

A small twitch had developed in Ivo's left eye, his brain not fully accepting Roland's claim. "There's no way. People don't even live to be seventy! You're lying."

"Almost wish I was," Roland replied softly. "I used to think livin' this long would give me a chance to do all I wanted to."

"And have you not?" Sil asked.

"Oh, I have. I've studied under the greatest masters of three generations. I've seen the lands beyond that emerald sea. I've done it all. Doesn't leave a whole lot to look forward to."

"Can't you remove the amulet? Won't that let you die?" Sil looked at Roland sympathetically as Ivo sat shaking his head.

"To tell ya' the truth, the amulet doesn't work so well anymore. Anythin' bound to it passed to me years ago. It's just a fancy bit o' whalebone at this point. Which means I either go ahead and wait it out, or..."

"This is like a fucking fairytale," Ivo mumbled. "Either you're nuts or the world's nuts. You sure you just didn't crack your head at some point? Forget a chunk of your life?"

Roland chuckled. "Well, I took a bump or two, but I can remember the past fifty or so years clear as..."

"Why would Roland lie to us?" Sil inquired, staring at Ivo.

"I'm not saying he's lying," Ivo explained, "I'm saying he's banged himself on the head!"

"Believe what you want. Don't matter much to me," Roland said. "All I'm sayin' is Petyr's bound to have done somethin' crazy over the past few years. And I'm gonna figure out how to undo the damage he's done."

"How?" Sil asked.

"No idea. Can't be sure the exact nature of the curse, beyond what runes he used. I can still see 'em, burned into my brain." He shuddered violently. "Just gotta figure out what he carved 'em into, see if I can get the resonance right."

"Could we be of any help?" Sil volunteered herself and Ivo, who looked at her with disdain.

"Just keep an eye out for any strange stones around the camp. He'd either need to make smaller items of power to act as boosters, or this curse it much more powerful than I had anticipated."

"So that's it then? We have to find some rocks?" Ivo snorted.

Roland looked at him with a tilt of his head.

Ivo rubbed his eyes, and then stood up. "Okay. Yeah, okay. A hundred-year-old blacksmith is telling me to look for magic rocks to lift a sea-curse. Righty then."

"Actually, a sea-curse would manifest as more of a fog…" Roland's voice trailed off as Ivo hobbled away, deciding he'd had enough crazy for one day. Not that he didn't believe Roland, at least in part. It didn't make it any less crazy though. He looked back and saw Sil listening intently to Roland, for which Ivo was grateful. Time to put all that mystic mumbo-jumbo behind and have brisk, four-hour nap in the midday sun.

Ivo rounded the bend leading to his quarters, near the far north edge of the camp. Here, a linen tarp had been raised using a number of gnarled branches, and served as shelter for the entire unit. A hundred or so bedrolls had been laid out beneath the stained expanse of the tarp, which Ivo figured had served as a sail earlier in life. Cheap blankets and straw gave the whole area the comfort of a pigpen, which made it almost homey for Ivo.

Unsurprisingly, Ivo found the filthy bedding unoccupied; the 4th Arbalasters were serving on the front, keeping the militia on the walls pinned. The engineers were busy putting the finishing touches on a number of wooden pathways leading to the wall. This left Ivo with a choice of bedrolls, and he picked out the least grotty as he limped down the rough aisles. No easy feat, mind you; no sooner did the army lay down their camp that a horde of parasites rose from the ground, from mites smaller than a grain of sand to leeches the size of small snakes. The latter being the more rare, but still far too common for Ivo's taste.

The most inviting bedroll lay near the centre. Usually such spots would be hotly contested, men and women twice Ivo's size staring one another down for the right to sleep on a clean bed. But now, the midday sun filtering through the rough canvas above, Ivo had no competition. Gently laying himself down, Ivo sprawled across the cheap blanket, and softly floated in and out of wakefulness.

Despite the heat, stink, and scratchy fabric, Ivo had nearly drifted off to sleep, when a boot toe in his side roused him. He grunted and gummily opened his eyes.

"Enjoying your nap, Ivan?" Helena asked.

"Please, not now Helena. It's been a long day."

"Oh really? So how many fishermen tried to put an arrow through your torso?"

"You know what I mean." Ivo whined, his foot beginning to act up again.

Helena wiped her nose with the sleeve of her padded jacket. "How's the foot holding up?" She spoke with a sincerity Ivo wasn't used to. He got up to his elbows, looking at her curiously.

"You want the truth or is this some kind of joke?"

"Oh, don't worry. I'll still take every chance to bust your balls," Helena assured him, "but I never really thanked you for saving my ass a few days ago. Didn't think you had it in you."

Ivo raised an eyebrow. "So…"

"So you've been promoted from bitch."

"So no more nicknames?"

"No such luck, hobbles."

Ivo sulked. "Why are you back? Shouldn't you be at the front?" He hoped she'd leave.

"'Fraid not, your replacement ran into a few problems. Bastard wasn't as lucky as you. They're still trying to pry the arrow from his skull."

"Replacement?"

"Mm-hmm. That's why we have more shield bearers than crossbows. You expect a few to drop every once in a while."

Helena looked from side to side, before squatting next to Ivo. From here, the smell of sweat and blood coming off her nearly made Ivo gag. "Look, between you and me, last thing he did before leaving camp was getting that Sil character to help him with his pavise."

"Your point being?"

"Look, the girls bad news. Me and the regulars been talking, and ever since we picked her sorry ass up, we've had nothing but problems."

"Oh, so now you feel chummy enough to "warn" me. After all the shit you put me through. The one decent person in the camp, and you make her out as a monster."

Helena raised a gloved hand. "Watch it, hobbles. Don't let that new backbone of yours get you in trouble." Lowering her hand, Helena stood to her full height. "Just a friendly warning. Enjoy your nap, Igor. I'm getting lunch."

CHAPTER TWENTY-THREE

"There he is." Brutus lowered the brass telescope. One of Rudolph's favourite toys, it incorporated a number of lenses crafted from the great crystal pillars that once dotted the far fields of his land.

"Let me have a gander," Rudolph said, taking the telescope from Brutus' gauntleted hands.

Brutus waved towards the mass of Stahlsheim infantry, three and a half thousand easy. "There, dead centre. Bastard even had his palanquin brought out."

Rudolph lifted the eyeglass, scanning the assembled ranks for Borig. It was a short search. Borig stood on platform of wood and brass, carried aloft by four of the largest guards Rudolph had ever seen. And they needed to be, as Borig himself was clad head to toe in black steel, sharp, arching lines drawn over the fluted plate. Gold trim ran the edges of the pauldrons, cuirass, and tassets, and a great, sweeping helmet fit over a perforated neck guard. As much as Rudolph hated to admit, it was a good look for him. He silently made a note to get a hold of that suit someday.

The platform upon which the ironclad brute stood was wide enough to allow for an animated speech. Rudolph couldn't hear Borig, but from his theatrical gesturing Rudolph could guess.

"Bet you fifty embers he's tarnishing my good name," Rudolph chuckled, lowering the scope.

Brutus shrugged. "We did just blockade his city. With an army. Without a formal declaration of war."

"To be fair, he started it."

Brutus raised an eyebrow. "Real mature, sir."

Rudolph turned his attention to his own troops, hundreds of arbalasts spanning their weapons with steel tools and equal numbers of infantry checking the straps of their shields as they lined up at the front. The lines were thin. Rudolph had been concerned with covering the gap in the mountains. This would leave his formation weak, but hopefully fewer would be crushed by the press of bodies come the inevitable retreat. Behind them, a hundred hobilars—lightly armed cavalry bearing lances—sat bunched in groups of twenty. Ideally, they would exploit breaks in the enemy lines. Now, Rudolph hoped they could harry Borig's thugs, making the prospect of chasing the routed Rendsheimer's less appealing to the bloodthirsty mob.

"He's bound to charge soon." Brutus remarked. "Bastard's anxious."

"Of course he's anxious," Rudolph replied. "He's been wanting a go at me for decades."

"You think he would figure something's up. Hold off his charge."

"Hubris. Hell of a thing," Rudolph mused. "Might as well use it to our advantage."

Brutus didn't reply. Instead, he motioned for Rudolph to pass him the telescope.

"What is it?"

"I think we found our crippled friend's counterpart."

Brutus handed the brass tube to the duke, who followed his advisor's pointing finger. His gaze took him back to the duke, who was awkwardly squatting on his timber platform. Below him, a brown robe hung heavily around a frail frame. Perched on a bent spine was an elongated, pallid head of an ancient hag, eyes sunk too deeply to spot from this distance. Her snowy, wispy hair clung to her spotted scalp, and upon her forehead a dark mark was set. It was difficult to tell, but Rudolph was certain he could make out a set of overlapping triangles.

"Well, I suppose that explains things," Rudolph murmured, looking down the length of the brass tube. "Guess that blind fellow was right. You owe him an apology."

"I'll make sure to give him one next time I see him," Brutus grumbled. "See where she's pointing?"

Rudolph followed the crone's skeletal finger, extending from the sleeve of her baggy robe. Even from across the field, it was clear she was marking the 8th heavy infantry to Borig, the unit under the recently promoted commander Einrik.

"Son of a whore, right to him." Rudolph straightened, collapsing the brass telescope.

"Brutus, I do believe we've overstayed our welcome."

"Couldn't agree more sir. Your guard is waiting just over the hill." He turned to go ahead of his lord. "No speech?"

Rudolph shook his head as he moved next to the advisor. "The commanders are giving their own speeches. All very personal and such. Besides, I'd rather not give Borig an easy time of spotting me."

Rudolph stepped down from the small rise then looked back at his army.

Gently, the duke bowed his head, eyes closed. "Best of luck to you, sons and daughters of Rendsheim. Give him hell."

Rudolph quickened his pace to catch up with the hulking Brutus, who already had crested the rise behind the army. Their departure was sure to go unnoticed, and for that Rudolph was grateful. On the other side of the hill, down the rough gravel road, Brutus waited with a dozen of the duke's knights.

"Something wrong, sir? You took a moment," the advisor inquired.

"Just..."

"Gotcha," Brutus interjected, gesturing towards the foothills of the mountain. "No roads to the temple; got some pretty tough terrain ahead."

"What, the Cyclops of Charred Hill afraid of a little cardio?" Rudolph jested.

"Let's see if you're making that joke after twenty miles of hills and ravines."

"No worries there, friend. I have a strenuous regime of stretching and endurance training. I'll manage."

The advisor shrugged. "What you do in the privacy of your bedroom is your own business, sir."

Brutus' words rang true; seven hours into the trek and Rudolph was wishing for death. The brigandine wasn't helping much, either. Though flexible and light, the extra weight began to wear him down immensely.

The scree-covered slopes around Stahlsheim gave way to an equally uninviting tree line, where old growth still flourished. Rudolph had seen forests before; on more than one occasion he surveyed Petyr's lands for new logging operations, of which Petyr was neither present nor privy. And for all their fantastical charm, they could not match the mystery of the woods bordering the mountain. Pines and firs were few and far between; oak and walnut dominated these lands, covering the narrow paths with dark green leaves and gnarled, twisting boughs. Deep ravines and sharp drops to slate-strewn death were frequent here, where the sudden void of trees was startling. Were it not for a set if maps and a gold-plated compass, Rudolph's away party could have travelled the woods for an eternity. Now approaching dusk, the duke insisted they put a stop to their forced march.

The knights, each carrying a travel pack, got to work setting up a simple camp in the confines of a craggy ravine, long devoid of water. Rudolph set down his own pack, given to him by Brutus as they set off from the battlefield, and drew a leather water skin. Breathlessly, he popped the cork, and imbibed.

Lowering the flask, he turned to Brutus. "What is this?"

"Water," the advisor replied as he produced a small, pitted tinderbox.

Rudolph hummed then took another swig. "Could use a little kick, but it'll do."

Brutus sat next to Rudolph under the lip of the embankment, assembling a pile of dead twigs. The knights continued their work in silence, each setting up their own little fires and putting down rolls of bedding. Mail coats and padded jackets rested on stands fashioned from branches, drying by the meagre flames.

Brutus didn't have quite the same luck, however; try as he might, the pile of dry moss and kindling wouldn't take a flame. It wasn't until he handed the flint and steel to Rudolph that a fire was finally started.

"Lucky," he grumbled as Rudolph smugly warmed his hands over the fire.

"My family's been starting fire since the dawn of civilization," the duke stated, smirking as he gloated. "You could say fire's in my blood. Well, more literally than I meant, but you get the gist."

Brutus grunted. The two looked at the dancing tongues of flame for a time, the stars slowly wheeling above, before Rudolph spoke. "You've never told me much about your family. I mean, I've known you what, twenty years?"

"Twenty two and a half," Brutus confirmed.

"You kept track?" Rudolph inquired, raising an eyebrow.

"For the pay records."

"Ah, naturally." Rudolph nodded. "Still doesn't answer my question, though."

"Still, not much to know. Don't even have a last name."

Rudolph raised a finger, opened his mouth to reply, but found himself drawing a blank. "Well, your family had to have some kind of work."

"Beggars both," Brutus grunted. "First memory is my father coughing to death. Worked odd jobs after that, supported my mother's addictions, right up to the day she died. From there, I joined the army under your father. You know the rest."

"Well, from humble beginnings. And look where it got you."

"In some backwards ass woods with a drug addled madman," Brutus replied sardonically.

"You don't do yourself enough credit, my good man," Rudolph said, smiling. "There's a reason I promoted you."

"I'm guessing appearances had nothing to do with it?"

"Well, you were a lot thinner back then. And you had the most luscious head of hair I'd ever seen."

"Easy now," Brutus said, holding his left hand up and wiggling his ring finger, upon which rested a brass band.

"Right, right. How is Delilah anyway?"

"Expecting our firstborn."

Rudolph clapped Brutus on the back. "Well, bloody congratulations! Didn't think you had it in you!"

"You've been trying to find cut for years," Brutus mumbled.

"Oh come now, I'm serious. Manor house is a wee bit empty, it'll be nice to have a little one running around."

Brutus nodded, the reflection of the flame dancing in his one good eye. Rudolph tilted his head. "Why so glum?"

Brutus inhaled. "You do realize this is my formal declaration of resignation."

Rudolph's brow furrowed. "I don't follow."

"I'm going to be a father, Rudolph," Brutus said. "I can't keep putting myself in the line of fire. I have more to live for than just myself."

Rudolph exhaled, biting his lip in thought. A heavy hand fell on his shoulder, and as he looked up, he saw a small smile under

Brutus' massive moustache. "We bought a little farmstead just outside the city. I hope you won't be a stranger, sir."

"I wouldn't dream of it."

A short respite was all the party was afforded. After a day of treacherous trekking through tumbled trees and trenches, Rudolph was loath to pick himself up from his lumpy bedroll. Even after he removed his plated brigandine and padded jacket, the weight still dug at his shoulders, making sleep tenuous at best. Combined with the meagre pickings of food his escorts had packed, Rudolph found his energy sapped.

He snorted as he hoisted himself off the lined leather bedroll, finding little relief in the change of posture. He ran a hand through his unkempt hair, attempting to fully awaken but failing spectacularly. It seemed he would have to make do with sluggishness. Unwillingly, the duke opened his pale eyes, and surveyed the little ravine hideaway.

A faint light trickled in through the twisting boughs of the great trees, illuminating the forms of his guard. Each had already done away with his bed, having been conditioned to function on little sleep. No doubt they had already spent a good few hours getting ready for the day's march before Rudolph awoke.

"How was your night, sir?" Brutus called softly.

Rudolph rolled his eyes lazily. "Miserable. Splinter of slate lodged firm in my side when I went to roll over. I think it broke the skin." He rubbed his eyes. "And you, Brutus?"

The advisor gave no reply.

Rudolph adjusted his tunic, and stood up. "That bad?" the duke inquired, turning to see Brutus inspecting the haft of his hammer.

"Didn't sleep," he grumbled, his fatigue evident by the bags under his eyes.

"Your bed?"

Brutus shook his head. "Never lay on it. Been sitting up all night."

"About the battle?"

"Yep."

The duke sighed. "That's been on my mind as well. If I could still dream, I don't think I would have dozed off either." He paused. "And the ravens?"

"Blotted out the sky come dawn," Brutus grunted. "Wind must have brought the stink of death this way. Need to be a lot of gore to draw them from this far."

Rudolph cursed under his breath.

"Better get moving," Brutus said, shouldering his hammer as he stood. "Make sure they didn't die for nothing."

The path of Rudolph's entourage once again wound itself through the choking roots of ancient trees, aged timber, and wilted leaves blending into one great, homogenous mass of brown and green. Save for the occasional brief breaks amongst the gathered boughs, the trails were clad in an artificial twilight, half seen things haunting the edges of Rudolph's vision. What was real and what was sleepless illusion, the duke could not say. Corporeal or not, he dismissed the skittering shapes and bounding leaps, too occupied with his own thoughts. Regret, guilt, anger, directed towards Borig, and toward himself in equal measure.

If not for the loathing, both self and otherwise, it would have been an uneventful trek for the duke. Save for a growing number of jagged, rocky outcroppings, the space was stagnant. The outcroppings themselves were rough and coated in a thick layer of moss, leading one to believe them to be purely natural. Rudolph, however, picked up subtle lines and a vague sense of symmetry that betrayed a more manmade appearance. Curiosity finally pulled the duke from his melancholy. Beyond the temple itself, he couldn't recall any information on architecture of this type. The more intact examples, while crude in both shape and design, had an almost mathematical quality to them. The stones were measured out with painstaking precision, perfect in their imperfect shapes.

The importance of the stones became apparent as the trees thinned, opening into a circular space strewn with a broken, primeval rock and prying saplings. The strange, geometric stones sat at intervals surrounding the empty space, creating invisible lines crossing the root choked stone of a place long forgotten. Tumbling, pallid rock created a primitive wall dead in the middle of the clearing, polygonal stone interlacing in a maddening fashion. The structure was squat and octagonal in design, capped by ragged shingles of slate.

Rudolph stood at the edge of the clearing, face knotted in contemplation. "The first temple," he murmured, as Brutus stepped up next to him.

"The what?" Brutus asked, obviously unimpressed with the mass of stone in front of him.

"The first—bloody hell, Brutus. We've been studying this for years!"

When Brutus failed to reply, Rudolph rubbed his eyes. "The first place man communed with the gods."

"Huh," Brutus snorted. "So...where's the rest of it?"

"Don't ruin this for me, Brutus."

The duke waved to his knights, who were waiting close behind. "Fan out, make sure we're not disturbed. I have some work to do."

CHAPTER TWENTY-FOUR

In the wee hours of the morning, despite his protests, Ivo was dragged from his straw mattress. Two soldiers, each bearing the arms and armour of the military police, shook him into wakefulness. It had taken hours for the conscript to finally drift off, fatigue doing little to drown out the sonorous snoring around him. Hobbling, he followed the two soldiers down the moonlit paths of the camp, worming their way to the core.

To Ivo's surprise, Roland stood outside Rook's tent. Judging by his ill-fitting shirt and long, dangling nightcap, he too was called from slumber. The quartermaster was talking with one of the soldiers who had had brought him, and was getting little more than dismissive grunts in return. Throwing his hands up in frustration, he wheeled about and spotted Ivo.

"Burn it all to cinder! They got you wrapped up in this, too."

"Wrapped up in what?" Ivo said through a yawn.

"Thought you knew. They haven't told me bugger all. Keep sayin' the commander'll have a word with us in a minute."

"I always took you for the patient type, Roland," Rook quipped as she emerged from the tent.

"Beggin' your pardon, sir," Roland half saluted, "but you did pull me out here in my jammies."

"You would think you've served with me long enough to know I don't call favours lightly."

Is it a favour if you have no choice? Ivo wondered.

"All righty then, what can we do for ya, sir?"

"It's about Sil."

The contempt dropped from Roland's visage in an instant. "Wait, is she okay? Where is she? This is why you should have put her bunk in my tent, I would have kept an eye on…"

Rook held up a gauntleted hand. "She's still here," she stated, nodding towards her own tent.

"Then what's the problem?" Ivo butted in, more out of annoyance than concern.

"She's…out. Completely unresponsive. Shaking, smelling salts, nothing's waking her up."

"By all that burns, is she still breathin'?" Roland asked, his face creased with worry.

"She's breathing," Rook assured the quartermaster. "Her eyes have been twitching, and she's been mumbling for close to an hour. Which is why we called you. She's asked for both of you by name."

"Well, let's stop gobbin' and help her! C'mon Ivo!" Roland grabbed the conscript by the arm, taking him by surprise and forcing him onto his bad foot.

Wincing and cursing, Ivo scrambled after Roland. Once in the candlelit interior, Roland dashed towards the cot at the far end. There, Sil lay wrapped in fur-lined blankets. Ivo was stunned by the relative luxury of Rook's quarters. Cushioned chairs, real pillows…

"Stop buggerin' around, Ivo!" the quartermaster called. Bumping and bumbling, he fell by Roland's side, almost planting his face against Sil's unconscious body. Roland's heavy hand caught him, taking the wind out of Ivo.

Layered under the pelt Sil lay still, her skin devoid of its usual exotic tone, pale and beaded with sweat. Her eyes darted behind closed lids, as though frantically watching a world seen only by her.

Roland bit his lips as he fished her hand from under the heavy blankets, gently slapping it to wake her. "C'mon Sil, you gotta snap out of it. You gotta…"

All Ivo could do was kneel there, as Roland grew more and more desperate in his attempts.

"Shit..." he mumbled, nervously glancing over his shoulder. Rook had left them. By the sounds of it, she was in conversation with a number of individuals outside the flap.

Ivo cocked an eyebrow in confusion, turning back to find Roland holding a small, shining piece of metal, what appeared to be brass. There was something peculiar about this long, pin-like thing with a latticework of lines covering its surface.

"You're not goin' to want to watch this," Roland said.

Roland slowly brought the needle towards Sil's hand, embedding the tip into her wrist.

What followed, Ivo couldn't say. No sooner did metal pierce flesh that a small, confined flash obscured his vision, leaving a solid white sphere in the middle of his eyes. His hands shot up in defense, and unsupported, he fell onto his side. This blindness was momentary, and no sooner did he pull his hands away than he saw Sil, stiff, and sitting upright. Roland stuffed the needle into a pocket under the edge of his collar. Afterwards, he waved a hand in front of Sil, whose eyes darted about the room uneasily.

As she caught sight of Roland her bouncing gaze steadied, and she dove towards him, wrapping him in a hug. Roland, though caught off guard, returned the embrace. "By all the gods, don't ever do that to me again," he choked out, swallowing back tears. "You're okay now." With a final pat, Roland pried Sil away and set her on the edge of the cot.

"What was that?" Ivo glanced from one to the other.

Sil jumped up and grabbed Ivo tightly, landing squarely on his bandaged wrapped foot. He yelped in agony.

"Roland...help?"

"She's just a bit panicked," Roland explained, wiping his tears. "Believe me, after the nightmares she's been having this is doin' her a world of good."

"Her hand just exploded!" Ivo exclaimed, pulling away from Sil.

"What's this about?" Rook passed through the flap of the tent and stopped in her tracks. Sil lay sprawled over Ivo.

"Don't worry, sir." Roland held a hand up. "She's right as rain, just needs a moment to collect herself."

"Clearly," Rook murmured. "You have ten minutes to…finish up." She wheeled about, hands behind her back, and strode out.

Satisfied the commander had gone, Roland whispered to Ivo. "Look, remember them marks on her arm. The sigils."

Ivo nodded dumbly, vaguely recalling something of the sort.

"Like I said, it's a conduit, a gateway for power. Well, people were never meant to channel that kinda stuff, messes with 'em in a lot o' ways."

"Roland," Ivo repeated, "her hand exploded."

"Nothin' exploded, don't need to worry about that," Roland responded. "She was having a reaction to the power, bit of an overcharge. Well, I vented it."

"You vented…What the fuck are you talking about?" Ivo glanced at Sil. "And why is she still stuck to me?"

Roland sighed, tapping the woman on the shoulder. Instinctively, her grip tightened, drawing a grunt from Ivo. His ribs compressed.

"It's okay, Sil. We got you." She looked at Roland with anxious eyes. "You can let him go, and we'll get you sat nice on the cot."

Like a child, she released Ivo, allowing him to fall back. Gently, Roland took her hand and guided her onto the cot. "Now, you see…" Roland stopped and scratched his beard. "Imagine a boiler."

"A what?" Ivo asked, heaving himself up.

"Okay, a bucket. Now, think of the power as water. It fills

and fills the bucket. If there's no holes, the bucket overflows." Patting his collar pocket, he added, "I just happened to have a way to put a hole in it."

Sil smiled. "I don't know what you did, but thank you. Thank you." She leaned in again, wrapping her arms around the bulk of the quartermaster. "The things I saw, Roland…fields burning, people dying…"

"Now now, it was just a bad dream. You'll be fine now."

"What happens if you don't…vent it in time?" Ivo asked.

Roland scowled. "Best not to talk about here. Besides, if it took this long to manifest, those symbols are either the weakest I've ever seen, or the subtlest."

Ivo nodded.

Sil gazed at Ivo. "It means so much that you came as well."

He shrugged. "Roland's the big hero here, with his fancy brass needle there."

"Rose gold," Roland interjected. "Takes the carving better than brass. Another little knickknack I picked up while working with Petyr."

"That needle made me well?" Sil asked, confused.

"It pulled the excess power from your body. Volatile stuff, dissipates without a proper conduit. Shame, it was the only needle we ever made. A failsafe, in case one of us were hit by side effects."

"But Roland," Sil asked, "why would you need a failsafe?"

"Well, you see…" he began.

Ivo cut in. "You have one of those marks on you."

"Yeah, I got a couple. Mostly healed over by now, can't really see them."

"For a quartermaster you seem to keep plenty of secrets," Ivo said.

Roland held up his hands. "It didn't seem pertinent. Besides, I doubt you'd believe me if I just told you everything at once."

Ivo supposed Roland had a point.

"What were the sigils for?" Sil asked.

"Oh, well, they were little things. One was to help me lose weight. That didn't work. One was to make me magnetic, that one kinda worked, ended up having it scratched out when I found my tools stuck to my hands."

"Seems a bit useless," Ivo sniffed.

"Well, you got to remember, Ivo, we had no idea what we were doing. I mean, Petyr hired a blind man to do most of the sigil work. Said he had steadier hands than anyone in the city. Must have died years ago…" Roland trailed off in thought. "Anyhow, I think it's about time we wrapped this up. Thanks for coming, Ivo."

"Yes, I thank you, Ivo," Sil agreed. "I will think of a way to repay your kindness."

Is it kindness if I didn't have a choice in the matter? Ivo wondered.

"Now Sil," Roland said as he stood, lifting the limping Ivo with him, "I'll talk to Rook, and see if we can get you set up in my tent so I can keep an eye on you."

"Well, why can I not go and sleep in Ivo's tent?" she inquired.

Ivo shot Roland a glance.

"Well, Ivo doesn't really have a tent."

"That seems rather unfair. Shouldn't he get a tent?"

Roland thought for a moment. "It's…complicated. As it stands, he's sharing a tent with the rest of the soldiers in his unit. And I don't think Rook'll be too keen on letting you mingle with 'em."

"Yes. I know of whom you speak." Sil's face scrunched in disgust. "The big, sharp faced one with the scar. She is always so rude."

"She's had a tough life," Roland explained. "You have to give her a break."

"Well, then can Ivo sleep in your tent as well? Keep him away from that awful woman?"

Ivo was about to agree when Rook cut him off, proudly stepping back into the tent.

"Out of the question. No special treatment for soldiers. He will bunk with his unit and that's the end of it."

"Don't worry, Sil," Roland assured her, "Ivo'll handle himself, one way or another. We'll see him in the morning."

"Now, if I may interrupt this happy little get-together," Rook said, "I have four hours to sleep, and I'd rather not waste them with idle chitchat."

Roland guided Ivo out of the tent. Sil followed closely, not allowing more than a foot of space between her and the quartermaster.

A soft sea breeze danced against Ivo's skin as he emerged into the night. That was the one upside to this whole damned venture. Ivo found himself falling in love with the sea. At once, he felt okay. Like happiness was just a wee bit closer than he had thought.

Ivo's fantasies of endless oceans and emerald horizons died with the breeze. The aroma of salt and clean air was overtaken by the musky, pungent odour of Roland.

Burn it all to cinder, he thought, *why does everyone have to stink?*

Although Ivo was certain at least some of the scent was wafting off of him, Sil didn't seem to notice, more concerned with remaining next to Roland.

Even with Roland's support, Ivo found it hard to move any faster than a shuffle, forcing him to spend time in proximity to the quartermaster's underarms. Once Roland had set him down, he took deep breaths to fill his lungs with fresh, untainted air.

"Well, I suppose this is your stop then," Roland said as he passed Ivo his walking stick. "Sorry we couldn't sort things out with Rook. You know how things are." His voice became faint, his gaze drifting off. "Used to be different, before all the weight of the world dropped on her shoulders. Tell ya, she was the happiest girl I'd ever met. By all that burns, I miss the old days..." Shaking his head, he added, "Enough of that, under the bridge as they say."

"Where is there a bridge? Who says?" Sil questioned softly.

"I'll explain later. For now, it's goodnight for us and goodnight for Mr. Ivo." He gave Ivo a meaty pat on the back, then headed down the path to his cozy tent, raised cot, and all the trappings of home.

Ivo glared at Roland as he strode through the camp. Lack of sleep deepened his envy. He nearly failed to notice a soft peck on his cheek. Taken aback, glanced at Sil wearing a sheepish grin.

"I was told that is how one shows appreciation," she said softly. Then she spun and ran after Roland.

Ivo's hand slowly rose to his face. This was perhaps the most affection Ivo had received from anyone in his entire life.

"Damn," Helena commented, appearing from the cover of the tent and clapping her hands. "She's got you right round her finger, doesn't she, hobbles? Me, I like my men a little less weedy."

Ivo stared at her, still reeling from the little kiss.

"Shit," Helena continued, "men so are easy to figure out. How long till she has you singing like a little bird?"

"What are you saying?"

Helena rolled her eyes. "I'm saying she's a spy! A two-timing agent working for Petyr. Or Borig. Or who knows? It's bad enough she's got Roland playing daddy, now she's got you by the balls!"

"You don't know what you're talking about," Ivo mumbled, limping towards his bed. Helena blocked his way.

"A strange woman shows up on the side of the road, covered in markings, with no recollection of her past. Next thing you know, shit goes belly-up at every opportunity. Sorry if I sound paranoid, but that's a wee bit suspicious."

Ivo snorted, stepping back and estimating whether he could get around the tent and sneak in through the back. "It's probably the curse," Ivo said, buying time as he gauged the distance.

Helena threw her hands up. "And now Roland's spreading rumours about a curse. Look, Igor, curses and magic are just smart people words to help them trick dumb scrubs like you. The only foul play is at the hands of that two timing bitch." Helena leaned close. "Look, for the sake of the unit, the army, and the whole damned city, watch yourself."

Come the dawn, Ivo found himself alone, all other beds having been vacated. He wasn't about to complain; most mornings the jostling and grunting that accompanied the waking soldiers forced him from slumber. Either they had been particularly quiet, or Ivo was dead tired. At least he had a good morning. Or noon, as the faint outline of the sun could be distinguished through the fabric overhead.

Strange. Not once since being dragged into this whole mess had Ivo been allowed to sleep in. Most times, he had been hoisted from where he lay and either slapped about or thrown into the nearest vessel of water large enough to hold him. Stranger still, the din of camp life seemed absent, eerily so. As soon as the light was bright enough to see by, cooks, fletchers and all manner of other staff were usually stomping back and forth, great bundles of goods clattering about.

Hunger finally roused Ivo from his bed. The broth they fed the soldiers was hardly filling, and Ivo hadn't eaten since the previous evening. Now, lunch was rolling around, and even the murky mystery soup sounded appealing. Aching, Ivo rose from his bedroll. He was already wearing his burgundy tunic, which had been washed once since departing home. At least it was comfortable, if a bit ripe.

As Ivo got to his feet, he noticed a peculiar aroma. Not the usual stink of military life, rather a smoky, acrid smell.

Definitely odd, but Ivo assumed it was an inattentive cook leaving a slab of bad meat over the fire. He paid it no mind. It was hardly his problem as long as it wasn't what they were serving him. Emerging into the noon sun, Ivo found himself alone, the tents and paths devoid of the usual hustle and bustle.

Ivo shrugged. Perhaps they all got called away to some project, or perhaps the mess carts were serving salt pork. Either would be sure to empty out much of the camp. Ivo could still pick up whiffs of something burning coming from the east side of camp. He picked out a plume of smoke, billowing up. The plume of black air was a fair way off, Ivo could tell. His eyes widened as it dawned on him that the smoke rose from a flame far, far more vast than he had first thought. And by the cloud of ash gathered above the camp, it was clear whatever was burning had been doing so for a while.

Something was wrong.

Ivo hobbled past empty tents and along clear paths, weaving through abandoned carts and dropped goods. All the while, the stink of cinder grew stronger and stronger, the air growing thicker and more acrid. The noon sun became a spectre, a faint outline behind the ever-growing cloud of soot.

Almost like home.

Rounding a bend in the road, Ivo caught the first glimpse of activity, a fellow hurrying with a bucket. No doubt attempting to douse the blaze. Ivo called out, asking what was going on but the man didn't stop.

Forced to keep pace, Ivo limped after the man, down a long stretch of straight road. The barked commands of Rook grew in volume and desperation. Ivo had the sudden urge to stop, turn around, and begin a mad hobble in the other direction. The camp was totally preoccupied. Few could stop him should he decide to…disappear.

But something forced him to maintain course. Partly it was curiosity, the desire to see what was causing a blaze of that magnitude. The other was…Ivo was unfamiliar with the new emotion. It was akin to his desire to save his own hide, only rather, he wished to seek out Roland and Sil.

"Lovely time to get attached," he grumbled.

Ivo rounded a corner, before the heat forced him to step back. Stumbling, he found his footing braced against a table set in front of the tent. Slowly, he stuck his head around the corner of the tent, attempting to take a look while exposing as little of himself as possible.

Indeed, there was a flame, but it was nowhere near the size he had envisioned. Bright orange tongues of fire danced about a pile no bigger than a large cart. And by the smell, Ivo assumed it was a cart of charcoal.

Fortunately, the fuel carts were kept isolated, a buffer of open ground between the inferno and any nearby inflammables. A circle of troops and supporting staff surrounded the blaze, none wishing to approach too close. Rook, who was stamping around the crowd, called for the blaze to be left alone and burn itself out and for the onlookers to return to their duties. Ivo was no kiln worker, but he knew that much charcoal would be burning for some time.

As she made another round of the crowd, Rook caught a glimpse of Ivo. "Hey! Gimp! Where's your charge?"

Ivo looked over his shoulder. Rook was indeed talking to him. Her visage darkened, the glow of the flame adding a demonic touch.

"I swear," she shrieked, nearly within striking distance, "if you lost her, I'll have you strung up by your bollocks."

Ivo feebly stepped backwards, then felt the bite of her gauntleted hands on his throat. Suddenly Roland, charging from behind, shouted, "Lay off, Rook! The boy didn't lose nothin'!"

The commander snarled, her wicked gaze shifting to Roland. "Step back, quartermaster, before I reprimand your outbursts myself. Too long have you stood by this hayseed layabout!"

Panting, Roland came to a stop next to Ivo. "Do what you want, sir, but I was watchin' her. Turned my head for two seconds, and she was gone." Ivo noticed the waiver in his voice. "I can't find her, Rook. I tried, burn it all, I tried." Roland began to break down, his cheeks flushing as he ran a hand through his greasy hair. "I looked around her usual haunts, askin' around. Then the fire started. I tell ya', I was here right quick. She weren't here, neither."

Rooks expression remained a stony combination of rage and contempt. "I'm beginning to regret leaving her charge up to you two…incompetents." Whirling, the commander watched the flickering flame reducing a ton of charcoal to soot. "It seems Helena had point. Our mysterious friend had us all played for fools."

"With all due respect sir, you're mistaken," Roland said, stepping towards her. "Sil's a sweet girl, wouldn't do nothin' to hurt nobody."

"Then how do you explain all this? It seems every day we have one mishap after another. Clearly the work of a saboteur. To make matters worse, our first army has suffered the same setbacks. Duke Rudolph himself was targeted by assassins." Roland started to speak, only to be cut off by Rook's raised hand. "Tell me it's a curse again and I'll see you demoted to latrine work." She inhaled, before continuing, "I've put out the order; if she's seen again around the camp, she is to be detained and taken to the noose. I won't let foreign agents run wild in my camp. Now, you're dismissed, both of you."

Defeated, Roland slumped, plodding away from the raging inferno. As he passed Ivo, he mumbled, "C'mon Ivo. I need help getting things sorted."

Wheeling on his crutch, Ivo limped behind the rotund quartermaster. "Sorted? Get what sorted?"

"I'll explain when we get to my tent. Just keep hobblin'!"

Fortunately, the hobble was a short one. Roland's tent near

the camp's centre, his position of quartermaster affording him some luxuries. By the time Ivo got there, Roland was busy throwing book after book through the flap. Dodging the flying tomes, Ivo ducked in, watching Roland frantically digging through a surprising number of books and documents.

"What are you doing?"

"Bakin' a cake, what does it look like!" the quartermaster snapped. No sooner did the words leave his lips that he shook his head, a semblance of his old self returning. "Sorry, Ivo. I don't mean to be nasty like, but the girl means a lot." He exhaled. "Between you and her, it's made a life stretched too long bearable." Wiping his eyes, he said, "No time to get sentimental. Gotta find the book." He pointed to a chest at the foot of his bed. "There. See if you can't find the book. Hard to miss, older than dust."

Wincing as he kneeled, Ivo flung the chest's lid open. Within, books were piled one upon another, each more crumbling than the last. "These all look pretty old!" Ivo called over his shoulder.

"Look for the one titled…" Roland paused. "Just look for one with gold squiggles on it, red cover!"

No sooner had Roland described the tome than Ivo spotted it.

"Got it!" He held the book triumphantly in the air, only to have it snatched from his hand.

Roland threw the book open, frantically thumbing through the pages. "It has to be in here…"

"What are you looking for?" Ivo inquired, trying to get to his feet.

"A sketch, one I made years ago," he replied, pages flying. "Looked an awful lot like the mark on Sil."

Ivo frowned. "Why didn't you think to check sooner?"

"After a century you start to forget things," Roland replied, still thumbing through pages. "Ah, there we go." Ivo took a look at the page Roland had stopped on. Sure enough, painstakingly sketched was a symbol; a double headed scythe on overlapping triangles.

"Usually somethin' this simple is a conduit, no power of its own..." Roland mumbled. "Oh, burn it all to cinder."

"What?" Ivo asked, stepping back as Roland got to his feet.

"Shite. Aw, shite! No wonder I didn't recognize it!" Roland pressed a meaty finger to the image. "It's no conduit. It's primal."

"What's that supposed to mean?"

"It's not manmade, that's what it means," Roland explained. "When I was workin' for Petyr, we kept coming across these legends. The first people to walk these lands all had different stories for how they got there. One thing that seemed consistent was talk of old, marked stones, each tribe bearing exactly one. A couple of scribblings passed down, but the mathematical perfection to recreate 'em was beyond our ability."

"So who made them?"

Roland shrugged. "Whatever made us. Don't matter though. All that matters is Sil has one of these on her arm, and now we got to go find her."

"Wait, we're just assuming these marks do anything. It could be nonsense."

"Oh no." Roland shook his head. "These have more meaning than a library of runes. This one in particular is...well," Roland paused, looking over the image once more. "I hope I'm mistaken, but it looks like...sower and reaper."

"Sow...like crops? That doesn't sound too bad."

Roland shook his head. "Goes beyond crops, I think. Primal runes are rarely so simple..." He closed the book. "To tell you the truth, I don't know what the mark is meant to do. My guess, Petyr or another madman thought to try and make sigils that have no right to be recreated. That much power could kill her, Ivo. Her and just about everything in a mile. We got to find her, and scratch the mark out."

Ivo held up his free hand. "Wait, I don't plan on dying here! If she's dangerous, isn't it for the best that she's gone?"

Roland looked at Ivo, visibly hurt by his words. "Ivo, this is Sil! If we have a chance at helpin' her, we should bloody well take it. She'd do no less for you, you know."

Ivo lowered his gaze, his sense of self-preservation at odds with the unfamiliar emotions brewing in his gut. Roland was right, Ivo knew that deep down. Even if it meant his untimely demise, he knew he couldn't just leave her.

He sighed, and went for the tent flap. "All right, I'll help. Let's find her before my brain kicks in."

Roland beamed. "I knew you had it in ya! Now c'mon, let's make for the gate right quick."

The two sneaked down the deserted streets of the camp, Ivo's limp setting a sluggish pace.

"You sure she's outside the camp?" he grumbled as they neared the camp's gate.

"She's a smart girl. I'm sure she sneaked out, caught wind of somethin' off and escaped." Roland assured him.

"Past the guards?" Ivo motioned to a number of squat, square towers set near the gates of the palisade wall. "And for that matter, how are we supposed to get out afterward?" Ivo stared at the hulking, brass geared ballistae visible over the palisade. From his brief time at the Charred Hill, Ivo knew these mechanical monsters packed enough push to throw a bolt near a mile, through metal, meat, and just about anything short of a fortress wall.

Roland noticed these as well. "Oh. Yeah, not too encouraging." He hummed in thought.

"I don't suppose you could ask them to just open the gate?" Ivo asked.

Roland shook his head. "'Fraid not. Not without a pass at least, gotta go through Rook for that. Doubtful she'd be game. We'd have to snatch one from one of the soldiers.

Probably one of the higher ups. Like…"

Ivo saw the look on Roland's face. "Oh no," the conscript said, horror crossing his face, "not her."

"What's wrong, hobbles?" Ivo winced.

Roland looked past him. "Helena! Just the person we're looking for."

Helena, clad in mail, held a hand up. "Don't bullshit me, Roland. You're looking for that Sil." Roland started to say something, but was cut off again. "She's gone. Saw her wandering off before the fire went up, outside the camp. Right for Dalwik."

"By all that burns, did you stop her?"

"And put myself in front of a wall crawling with archers?"

Roland went pale. "Oh no. Did she…"

"She was fine," Helena said. "They opened the gate for her, like fucking royalty."

Roland sighed.

"You seem awfully relieved," Helena said, putting her hands on her hips, "a saboteur just waltzing her way home."

"She's not herself, Helena! She has no idea what she's doing!"

Helena rolled her eyes. "Spare me, Roland. Point is, she's buggered off and I'm going after her."

Both Roland and Ivo raised their eyebrows.

"What, you don't think I have a dog in this fight? Say what you want, but when you start fucking with my brothers in arms, I take it personally."

"So how do you plan on gettin' into Dalwik by your lonesome?" Roland huffed.

"Get in? Sewer, found a bit of tunnel exposed by a cave-in. Lonesome; no. I got a smith to help me."

Roland cocked his head. "Wait, where did you find a smith?" Helena's face was blank as Roland's lit up. "Oh. Gotcha."

"Are you mad, Roland?" Ivo gasped, pulling the quartermaster to the side. "She'll kill Sil! That seems a bit counterproductive to me."

"First of all," Helena chimed in, "I have no intention of killing her. I'm bringing her back. She can have her trial or hearing or whatever, then it's off to the noose." Helena produced a rolled slip of paper from a pouch at her side. "Besides, you need me."

Ivo groaned, not much caring for an extended jaunt with Helena. The arbalaster snorted in return. "Quit bubbling, hobbles. It's not like you're coming with us anyway."

"Hang on," Roland stepped in, crushing Ivo's hope of returning to his tent.

"You're not convincing me to take him Roland," Helena sneered. "The prick can barely walk."

"He's comin'. Even if I have to carry him."

Helena crossed her arms, looking the quartermaster up and down. Seeing he wasn't about to budge, she grunted, "Well, better limber up."

Reaching for her belt, she unfastened the bindings on a large, old-fashioned arming sword—one that was familiar to Ivo.

"Here you go, Igor," she said, throwing the blade in the scabbard in a low arc, forcing Ivo to drop his makeshift crutch and catch it. As he stumbled, Helena added, "Figured you wouldn't be using it, so I took the liberty of using it myself. Besides, I'll just take it back once you're dead."

Ivo grumbled, fastening the heavy blade to his own belt. The weight nearly toppled him as he reached for his crutch, hopping on his one good foot. Propping himself up on his length of timber, he cleared his sinuses, hawking a blood flecked phlegm ball to the wilting grass below. Satisfied, he limped after Roland and Helena as the two headed towards the gates.

Despite the odd gathering of a soldier, a smith, and a cripple, the gate guards asked few questions. Between Helena's documentation and abrasive attitude, the soldiers at the gates wanted to spend as little time questioning her as possible. Apparently, Ivo wasn't the only one to be on the receiving end of her sour mood. After a curt conversation, the iron-braced gates drew open, and the three departed the camp.

The desolation wrought by the Rendheimers was immediately clear to Ivo. To his sides were strewn a graveyard of stumps, hundreds of trees being felled to feed the machine of war. Ahead stood the fruits of that labor; hulking siege constructs, towers and rams of leviathan bulk rose half-built in defiance of the walls. Upon their skeletal frames crawled dozens of engineers, driving massive nails into the wooden planks.

Great sheets of cast copper were drawn up from the huge stores of Rendsheim, hefted on buckling carts by broken, sad-eyed nags and placed on the latticework of war machines by brass braced cranes. There were also thousands of meters of rope, tons of timber, and more metal than all the forges of Dalwik. Par the course for the people of Rendsheim.

Ivo stumbled as he got caught up in marvels of industry, drawing an annoyed grumbled from Helena and a hasty correction by Roland. "No time for takin' in sights, boy," he instructed as he placed a hefty arm under Ivo's, taking a great deal of weight off. It allowed the conscript to take a faster, if forced pace, towards the vanishing tree line of the wood.

Ivo looked at Helena. "You said we were going through the sewer."

"I did." she affirmed.

"Then why are we going into the woods? You'd think they'd just flow their shit into the ocean."

"Wow, using your brain," Helena snorted. "I'm almost proud, Ivan."

"He's got a point," Roland added. "I worked on a couple sewage projects, and they all went straight to the sea."

"Right," Helena sighed. "Well, you got me. It's a tomb. Big old hole in the ground, caved in. I reckon there's still an open path to the city."

Ivo went pale, but nowhere near the white complexion Roland adopted. "Are you crazy girl?" he sputtered. "You want to go through the Ruthall?"

"That's what they call it? Catchy."

"Don't take it lightly, Helena. That place isn't meant for the living. We sealed it off for a reason, walls five feet thick."

"We? I thought they walled it off fifty years ago."

Roland cursed under his breath. "You know what I mean, we Dalwikers. But it's still a shite idea."

Helena chuckled. "What, worried about goblins and ghouls? I swear, you talk more and more like a five-year-old."

"Goblins, no. Been extinct for sixty years in these parts. Ghouls..."

"Come off it, Roland, you're scaring Hobbles."

Ivo did seem more faint than usual.

"I'm not jokin', Helena. There are things in that hole that ain't human. Too long forgotten, too long left alone."

"Then what do you suggest?" Helena asked, a glance of contempt shot over her shoulder. "Shall we walk up to the gate? Perhaps you have an old friend who can put in a good word. If we're lucky, they'll say hello before we get pin-cushioned."

Roland sighed.

"You want to find that Sil person, don't you?" Helena probed.

"Yes," he murmured.

"Good. My plan it is."

"A bloody tomb," Ivo grumbled, growing jumpy as the shadow of the trees loomed over them.

"No one's stopping you from running off," Helena said.

"By all means, bugger off."

"She's right, you know," Roland said, in a much kinder tone. "I can't ask ya to go into that place. Not for my sake, nor hers."

Ivo winced, his eyes darting from the forest to camp, the relative safety of his captors or the horrible, horrible freedom of the woods. And the woman who had so readily grabbed his attention.

"I, uh..." He shook his head. "Fuck it. Please, let's get this over with."

Roland smirked. "Good to hear Ivo." A shrill call rose from the depths of the forest. "Sure as shite hope you don't end up regretting it."

CHAPTER TWENTY-FIVE

"Suppose this is it then," Roland murmured, easing Ivo onto a mossy brick. It was one of many lining the edge of a shallow pit. Over twenty feet deep and fifty across, the hole had no earthly purpose amidst the narrow pines of the woods. Strewn about, signs of ancient stonework, chunks of aged mortar, and pale stone remained as though a structure once stood there.

Helena, at the very bottom of the pit, was tapping at an exposed patch of stonework. "Looks like a collapse," she called up, brushing aside the loose dirt. "Pretty recent too, no growth on the stones down here. Still, sturdy section of brick a few feet over, sounds like it's hollow. My guess, it's some kind of ceiling."

Roland sighed, placing his thumbs through the loops of his belt. "That'd be it. The far hall. Used to bury the foreigners here, farthest from the sea."

"Roland," Ivo said softly, "you know more than you're letting on."

The quartermaster slid him a glance. "Yes. I'm afraid that's no graveyard. 'Course, we didn't tell that to no-one."

"Then what is it?"

"That, my boy, is one of Petyr's laboratories. East wing, metalworking. Spent years of my life down there, before we sealed it up." His cheeks grew flushed, his eyes watering. "I tell ya, now that I'm here, I can't help get a bit sentimental."

"The other halls?" Ivo questioned.

"South hall was where they worked on sigils, mostly working on small animals and prisoners." His head swivelled away. "The north hall...I can't tell you nothing about that. All we heard was hearsay and rumour. None of it good, I'll tell ya. There's a reason we plugged the halls up as well as we did."

Helena began up the slope. "I don't suppose you brought a pickaxe. Pry bar, mattock, something heavy."

"Hammer'll do?" Roland replied, pulling a rusty hand sledge from his worn tool belt. The head was surprisingly large, clearly belonging to a much longer haft.

Helena frowned. "Burn it all to cinder, this'll barely make a dent. Old Dalwiker stonework, could hold up to a ballista. We need a longer haft."

Roland drummed his fingers along his stained leather apron, pondering. "A fresh branch would just bend, and any dried timber would be too brittle. We need something readymade, preferably ash or..."

Roland turned his head, spotting Ivo absentmindedly picking his nose. His ash spear haft turned crutch sat against his thigh.

"Ivo," the quartermaster began. Ivo jumped, hastily dropping his hand. Roland continued, "May I take a look at your cane?"

Ivo grumbled, leaning heavily on an old pine branch as he watched Roland work. *At least they took the time to snip off the twigs.*

His previous crutch now found a home slotted into the head of Roland's sledge. At the bottom of the pit, the quartermaster swung the ten-pound head in an arc of destruction. Ivo jumped as chips of stone showered him.

"Come on," Helena groaned, "it's not a Brennerburg whore. Really hit it."

"You want to give it a go?" Roland huffed, leaning on the haft of his sledge. "I've been smashin' stone longer than you've been alive, miss." Regaining his composure, the quartermaster wound up, and slammed the head into the stone once more.

On the second swing, the stone gave way with a gust of rank, stagnant air. The inertia of the sledge carried Roland forward and toppled him. Roland yelped as he collapsed onto the ceiling, and in turn the ceiling collapsed under him. In a cloud of dust, he disappeared.

Ivo and Helena peered into the newly formed hole, which had expanded greatly following Roland's tumble. Fortunately for Roland, the drop was a short one; ten feet down, he was sprawled across a pile of bricks.

"Hey, Roland! You still alive?" Helena called down.

He rolled over, blood dripping from his nose and staining his greasy beard a shade of crimson.

"Not a word," he spat, lifting himself onto his elbows. He looked from side to side, before slowly getting to his feet. Dusting himself off, he said, "All right, all clear. C'mon Ivo, I'll catch ya."

Before Ivo could object, he felt a heavy, armoured hand on his back. "You heard him, Hobbles," Helena said, giving Ivo a helping shove over the edge. He barely had time to yelp before finding himself in the smelly embrace of Roland.

"Ooph!" the quartermaster grunted, reeling back as he caught Ivo. "Little warnin' would be nice!" he called to Helena, setting Ivo onto his good foot and crutch.

As Roland helped Helena down, Ivo took in his new surroundings. Cyclopean stonework sprawled in either direction with the walls set eight feet apart. Sconces, rusted with neglect, were bolted to the bricks in even intervals. No doubt this was some kind of corridor, connecting larger subterranean rooms.

To his right, Ivo spotted the outline of a large, amorphous lump in the dark, beyond the feeble reach of light. It was the collapse Helena had hinted at earlier, blocking the corridor away from the city. This left their long, unlit path unobstructed, at least as far as Ivo could see.

Helena adjusted her mail coat, and peered down the hall ahead. "Shit," she muttered, "hope someone thought to bring a light." Helena turned to Ivo, who shrugged. The only thing he brought had been repurposed as a haft.

Roland, on the other hand, was fiddling with a brass cylinder that hung from his belt. "Got just the ticket," he murmured, slowly turning a large cog on the cylinder's side. Satisfied with his fiddling, the quartermaster depressed a large iron button along the flat top, next to the ring from which he held the device. A sharp, metallic grind could be heard, and the cylinder burst into flames. Ivo jumped back. Even Helena stepped aside, startled by the sudden blaze.

Roland cursed, rapidly adjusting the cog along the side as the flame licked his calloused hand. As he did, the flame retreated through a number of holes along the edge of the cylinder.

"Cheap piece of shit. I've seen better smith work on chastity belts," he grumbled. Once the flame was fully contained within the confines of the tube, Roland flipped a hook, dropping a squared off plate that shot a beam of light sixty feet down the corridor. Both Ivo and Helena looked at the device.

"What?" Roland said, holding the light up a bit higher. "It's a hand lantern. Standard issue to quartermasters. Bit finicky, but it beats a torch."

Ivo didn't fully trust the device. He had been burned one too many times by Rendsheim ingenuity.

Roland turned the beam of light down the long, unbending tunnel, leading towards the guts of Dalwik. Specks of dust danced in the flickering light, and long, wispy webs clung to every corner.

"I may have been mistaken," Helena hummed, a statement Ivo had been certain she would have never make. "I guess this isn't a crypt."

"No, but there's only one way out," Roland said, starting down the hall. "Unless you feel like climbing."

Not wanting to be left under the quickly fading light above, Helena and Ivo joined Roland. The sound of their footsteps rebounded off the tightly set bricks, followed by the thunk of Ivo's makeshift crutch. It wasn't long before the light behind them was nothing but a memory, the engulfing darkness kept at bay only by Roland's lamp. And the smell...It reminded Ivo of his grandmother—stale, cold, and dead.

Worse than the tang, however, was the monotonous uniformity of the walls. Each brick was like its neighbour, making any attempt to gauge progress dubious. It made Ivo wonder if the hall looped around on itself.

His worry was dispelled, only to be replaced moments later. The corridor abruptly opened up, the walls falling away into a room of monumental size. Roland's torch struggled to illuminate the far side of the room, instead picking up a number of moderately sized tables and strewn equipment, all in great disrepair.

"We're getting close," Roland muttered.

"Close to what?" Helena asked, peering into the dark. "What is this, Roland?"

"It's a workshop," he answered, stepping forward confidently.

"That's all you're going to tell me?" Helena questioned, looking over her shoulder.

"Yep."

The skeletal husks of furnaces sat cold in rows like stony teeth. Copper pipes once used to vent the acrid smoke now lay tumbled and oxidized. Rust coated anvils hunkered alongside their accompanying tools. And permeated throughout, a cloud of dust disturbed after many decades of stagnation. The flame of the lantern dimmed in the face of such a dense haze, barely picking out the fine details of a solid, wrought iron door at the far end of the room.

Chapter Twenty-Six

Brutus hastily dodged a piece of mortar, thrown in his direction by Rudolph. The duke was madly burrowing through stacks of debris within the tumbled confines of the temple. "Burn it all to cinder!" he bellowed, growing more and more desperate as he toppled the pile. "There's nothing! Nothing!"

"Calm down, sir," Brutus insisted, bringing his torch closer to the duke. The flame illuminated the hollowness of Rudolph's eyes, and the bloodshot madness bound within.

"How can I calm down? We were wrong, Brutus!" The duke wound up, hurling a brick at the wall of the minute structure. It shattered.

Rudolph slumped to the ground, resting on the pile he had created. "Years of work, thousands of lives," he muttered. "It was a goose chase. A dead end." His chest burned, the gash left by the vagrant having reopened during his frantic searching. Not that he paid it much heed. The physical agony was overshadowed by his mental anguish.

"Nothing, nothing," he chanted to himself quietly, pulling his knees up to his chest. "To tell you the truth," he murmured, "I didn't even know what we were looking for. A silver chest, a shelf of vials, an old sack." He motioned at the relative emptiness of the small room. "And nothing. Not an ounce of incanflagarat."

Rudolph produced a flask from his brigandine, flicking the lid open and downing the contents. "I wanted to stop Borig, and Petyr..." he mumbled as Brutus drew nearer. "But sometimes a shadow is just a shadow."

He took another deep swig. "I didn't see it, the truth. I was too busy trying to save the world for my own ends."

Brutus knelt down. A faint glimmer caught his eye, a crimson bead trickling down Rudolph's brigandine. Like hot ember, it glowed faintly, even in the light of the torch.

"Sir," Brutus stated, his good eye widening.

"Don't bother," Rudolph grumbled, taking another swig of spirits. "Don't try and make me feel better."

"Sir," Brutus said again, eyes focused on the droplet of incandescent crimson.

"You where right, this was a fool's errand. We should have stuck to our experiments, learned more before we set off o…"

Brutus grabbed the duke by the shoulder, snapping him out of his self-loathing. "Sir," he said again, pointing at Rudolph's chest.

Rudolph cocked an eyebrow, before looking at himself. His chest, now drenched in blood, sparked and flickered like hot coal, beads searing through the velvet of his brigandine and exposing tarnished steel plates. At once, the duke shot up, sending his flask flying, and spraying blood onto Brutus. Brutus gasped, reeling back as he wiped at his arming jacket. Small, blackened spots covered the red fabric, smoke rising from each.

"What the fuck is going on?" Rudolph cried, trying to maintain composure as drops of blood scorched the stone floor. "Brutus?"

The advisor, still fanning his torso, failed to reply.

Rudolph continued to watch as the blood burned its way through his armour, leaving his flesh intact. He felt little discomfort, save for the emotional trauma. It wasn't long before the blood ceased to trickle and dried, black and sooty on his armour. His brigandine was a mess, chewed through by the burning blood in multiple places. Where there weren't any holes, great patches of sooty scabs darkened the already black velvet.

"Did it stop?" Brutus asked, keeping well away from the duke.

"I…I think so," Rudolph replied, carefully bringing his hand to his chest.

The exposed metal was warm to the touch, and the dried blood powdery. Brutus watched with curiosity. "Did that…did that come from you?" he asked, stepping closer.

"I believe so." He was silent for a moment, engrossed in the dried blood. "The damn cripple kept talking about fire in my blood."

"Then why didn't it ever…do that?! Burn through steel, glow?"

"Perhaps I was too quick to dismiss this place. It would appear something strange is going on."

"No shit," Brutus muttered.

"Burning blood. Hardly worth the trip," Rudolph mused, curiosity bringing back his old self.

"That is where you are mistaken, oh lord." A thin, raspy voice, echoed from the crumbled doorway of the temple—one all too familiar to Rudolph. Both he and Brutus wheeled towards the faint light of the door. Illuminated by the flickering light of the torch stood the frail frame of the vagabond, clad in his tattered robe. Rotten, chipped teeth glowed sickly in the flame as he smiled cruelly.

"All your travels, all your struggles and sacrifices. It has all gone according to plan." Silently, the hooded man stepped into the temple.

"Oh, do not look so surprised, lord," he said. "It does not suit you."

"What surprises me, cripple," Rudolph replied, motioning for Brutus to ready his hammer, "is how you managed to track us down, and get past my guards."

"The guards? Simple, they posed a minor obstacle. Finding you proved even simpler." He inhaled deeply, his hood falling back and uncovering his bloodstained bandage. "You radiate power; you reek of it."

Rudolph put his hand on the grip of his blade, a thin, single-edged falchion with an intricate handle. "Get to the point, cripple. We have work to do."

"No," the vagabond stated bluntly. "Your work is done. You've made it here. Now the work falls to me."

Rudolph snorted. "What, this apotheosis you've been talking about."

"Indeed. Not for you, however." A long, wavy knife slid from the vagrant's loose robes. Rudolph heard the scraping of metal as Brutus hefted his hammer, taking on a defensive stance.

"I knew it," Rudolph glowered, "your machinations have always been towards your own end."

"And yet you followed of your own volition," the vagrant sneered in return. "Even the mention of godhood had you listening to every word." He held both his arms out, the dagger flashing in the torchlight. It was covered in fresh blood. "Besides," he continued, "it is not my end I work towards."

"Name the bastard. Borig?"

"It matters not," the vagabond stated. "All that matters now is the blood in your veins."

Rudolph cocked an eyebrow.

"Oh, you didn't know?" The vagrant grinned. "You feel it, don't know. The burning in your chest, the heat radiating from your heart."

Indeed, Rudolph's chest burned, akin to the smouldering pits of his forefather. "You..." Rudolph's eyes narrowed.

The vagrant bowed in an exaggerated manner. "Indeed. I must apologize, lord," he replied, pouring venom into the regal title, "for such a breach of trust. But we needed a vessel, for that which is bound here. And in you we found what we needed. Now, I need but extract your blood. Most of it, I'm afraid."

"Very well, freak." Brutus said, stepping forward and hefting his hammer. "Only fair that we spill some of yours in turn."

"So be it."

The vagabond lurched forward, curved blade flashing in the pale light. Rudolph barely had time to draw his own sword when the hooded figure was upon him. If it weren't for Brutus, the wickedly waved dagger would have found home in the duke's chest. The advisor deftly deflected the vagrant's blade downwards with a swing of his hammer. The head scraped against the stone floor, and Brutus followed up with the studded butt of the haft. The steel cap smashed into the vagrant's rotten teeth, sending yellow-stained enamel out in a spray. As the vagrant recoiled, the torch dropped by Brutus finally hit the ground.

Despite the staggering force behind the blow, the blade remained in the cloaked man's hand, and the vagrant remained on his feet. It took him but a moment to regain his composure, blood pouring from his shattered jaw. Still, the damned smile was plastered onto his face.

Brutus charged after the vagabond as Rudolph readied his blade. Stepping forward, he swung his hammer upwards, aimed squarely at the vagrant's jaw. Despite his great weight, Brutus was still capable of a rapid, accurate swing. Decades of training honed his work into an art, each arc of the hammer bearing enough force to topple a stone wall. But, for all his skill, all his experience, he simply could not land a blow on the hooded vagabond.

The vagrant, however, had less trouble. Despite the short reach of the blade, he landed a number of blows upon Brutus. Most were parried by the haft of the advisor's hammer. Several skimmed across the thick padding of his jacket, and a few sparked off his heavy gut plate. But enough found purchase in flesh to wear the advisor down, slowing him. Dark splotches began to form upon the surface of the padded jacket as blood flowed.

As Brutus slowed, Rudolph stepped in with a rapid lunge, flicking the narrow falchion towards the throat of vagabond. The blade missed its mark, slicing into the hood and cheek of the decrepit man as he ducked away, twisting from a shorthanded swing from Brutus' hammer. Flowing like a shadow, he flitted to the far end of the room. Rising to his full height, he sized up his two opponents. Thick, black blood flowed from the wicked gash on his face, the glint of rotted teeth and aged bone through the ichor.

Still, the vagrant stood, oblivious to his injuries. Rudolph didn't bother speculating as to how; it seemed this place had as much effect on the vagabond as on he. Behind the thick, bloodied bandage burned a sickly blue light over dead, useless eyes.

"You prove yourself a worthy opponent, lord," he gurgled. "A marked improvement from your guards. They fell far too quickly for my taste. No time to savour death." He ran the dagger over his fingers, and black blood oozed, dripping to the floor. It reeked of toxins, a sick acrid odour Rudolph equated to an alchemical lab.

"Sate my curiosity, freak," Rudolph glowered, adopting a low, defensive stance "What drugs have they been pumping into you? Tell me what flows in your veins?"

"There are more ways to attain power than your crude habits. I am surprised you have lasted this long." Sliding the blade under his bandage, the vagrant flicked the blade and freed his eyes.

The symbols seared into his eyes scorched a vibrant blue, the image of a thorny rose set upon overlapping triangles. Ebony ichor pooled at the corners of bloodshot eyes, running down in a morbid parody of tears. "Enough talk, I grow weary," the vagrant stated, picking his yellowed nails with the tip of his dagger. "Besides, there are events in motion elsewhere, and time is of the essence. Not that it matters much to you, you'll be bleeding to death shortly."

"Wouldn't bet on it," the duke responded. He lowered the blade of his falchion, feigning weakness in hopes of drawing the vagrant into an attack. It worked, too well.

No sooner had the blade lower than the vagabond was upon him, blade plunging towards Rudolph's heart. The plates of the brigandine, though scorched and eaten through, sent the dagger sliding off. As the blind man slid past, Rudolph brought the pommel of his sword up, cracking the vagrant in the ribs. This was followed by a wicked flick, sending the blade sliding through cloak and flesh. A long, deep gash ran up the vagrant's thigh, ending at his abdomen. A howl echoed in Rudolph's ear, the blind man losing his footing and sliding to the floor. Before Rudolph could follow up with a finishing blow, the vagrant had rolled away, and was back on his feet.

Brutus charged, readying his hammer for a short, precise strike to finish the wounded figure. His pace was greatly slowed, loss of blood taking a toll on the hefty warrior. Rudolph called out to him, ordering him to hold his ground and let the blind man bleed out. He was too late; halfway through the swing, the vagrant dove towards Brutus, flipping the blade in his hand and sweeping along the advisor's left hamstring. Brutus bellowed, falling to his knee and dropping his mighty hammer.

Smiling wickedly, the blind man rose to his full height. His bloody, flame-bladed dagger arced towards Brutus' thick neck. Arterial blood would soon flow. The smile, however, was warped into a bloody grimace, as Rudolph threw himself and the vagrant to the stone floor.

Twisting, contorting in ways no human was ever meant to, the vagrant caught Rudolph's falchion in a gnarled hand. Steel bit into bone as the blind man ripped the sword from Rudolph, throwing it aside as he positioned the tip of his own blade on Rudolph's neck.

As he fell, the duke felt a piercing sting, heard the hiss of steam, and then felt numbness. A cold lifelessness filled him, his body no longer under his control. His legs gave out, his arms refusing to reach out and catch him. His skull cracked on the floor, his vision blackening. In the dark, he heard blazing blood ooze onto his cloths and smelled burning fabric and charcoal.

As his vision returned to him, Rudolph could make out the gore drenched frame of the vagabond, and the glint of black steel in the dying light of the fallen torch. In his other hand was a leather flask ending in a thick, hollow spike. Upon the cured leather was branded a familiar symbol: a broken crown.

"Petyr," Rudolph wheezed through his ruined throat, struggling to get up on his elbows. His arms didn't budge.

"Quiet," the vagabond shushed in response, driving the hollow spike into the wound left by the blade. "Sit quiet and bleed to death. We have invested far too much in you, misguided lord of the ember. It's time we saw results."

The vagabond opened his mouth, readying another tirade of gloating. He never got the opportunity to, however. His head disappeared in a spray of gore and brain, shards of bone scattering many feet off. The force of the blow carried the rest of his body alongside with him, limbs stiffening as he fell like a board.

Standing over the fallen duke and slain vagrant stood the hulking form of Brutus. His hammer was held in both hands, set on the ground supporting his useless leg. Blood and brain covered the head and much the haft, a mark of its bloody work. Brutus too was drenched in blood, most his own. The advisor fell to his knees, tossing his hammer aside. Gritting his teeth, he crawled alongside the prone duke.

"Sir," Brutus whispered.

"Ah," Rudolph wheezed, "excellent timing as always."

Brutus cursed under his breath. "Shit." Rolling to his side, Brutus tore a piece of cloth off his perforated arming jacket.

Taking the makeshift bandage, he tore the leather pouch away from Rudolph's neck and pressed the cloth down. He held it for a moment, before the heat grew too intense, and he was forced to let go. The cloth was smouldering, flecks of burning blood still clinging to the fabric.

"Don't waste time on me," Rudolph said, trying to look at Brutus. "Get yourself patched up. I'm done."

"I'm not letting you die, sir," Brutus said, trying to rip a larger swath of fabric. "It's my duty to keep you alive, and I'll be damned if you die on me."

"Let's not bring business into it," Rudolph whispered with a grimace.

Brutus cursed again, examining the duke's still bleeding neck. "Sir, the blade went clean through your spine."

"I could tell," Rudolph stated, "I have an itch on my nose I've been trying to scratch for a good minute now."

"Sir, this is no time for joking."

"This is the perfect time. I doubt I'll have another opportunity, be a shame to waste this one."

"Don't say that, sir," Brutus placed a thicker cloth on Rudolph's neck. "We'll stop the bleeding. We'll do more research, find some way to fix..."

"No more drugs, Brutus," Rudolph murmured. "It did me no good in the first place. Besides, even if I get out, even if I can walk again, I'll just end up burning away. I like this way better."

"We'll get you more incanflagarat, research an alternative."

Rudolph chuckled. "I do believe that would be a terrible idea. You see what it's done to me. Worse, what it would do for Petyr. Burn it all to cinder, he outsmarted me. Once this is done, you'll need to report to Borig. Tell him of Petyr's treachery, and send my apologies for any unwarranted hostilities."

The duke looked at Brutus, who was still trying his best to stop the bleeding. "Burn the research, Brutus. Burn me. It would be better to wipe all this away, lest madmen like him, like me, get a hold of it."

"Sir, I…you shouldn't have done that. You should have let the freak end me, made a break for it."

"And leave Delilah a widow? Tell her that her child won't have a father, to save some drugged up noble? Would be a smudge on my good name. Besides, I like you too much. It'd take an eternity to find a replacement."

Smiling, he looked back at Brutus. "Let me go, Brutus. My story ends here. You still have yours, a life beyond this. Go back to Rendsheim, grow older and fatter. Live to see your children's children, see peace return to the warring cities, have your happy ending." His gaze grew distant. "This is mine."

Rudolph's breath went still. He lay there, a grin fixed on his noble face. Brutus sighed heavily, closed his eyes and bowed his head.

Rudolph Lug, Duke of Rendsheim, Master of the Pits and Lord of the Ember, passed into memory.

CHAPTER TWENTY-SEVEN

"Have you got it open yet?" Helena called, crossing her arms. She was pacing the shadowy walkways of the workshop, growing ever more impatient. Roland was hard at work with the door, having scrounged up a pitted iron crowbar. He was doing his best to pry the steel shod door open, sweat beading on his greasy brow. He had been at it for quite some time. It had some kind of lock sunk well into the stone walls, and no mechanism could be found on this side. Failing to find a way in, it was decided that they would improvise.

Ivo was thrilled with the delay. It allowed him a moment of peace. While Roland huffed and puffed the conscript enjoyed an uncomfortable seat on one of the many rotted workbenches. A more substantial individual would have caved such a structure in, but fortunately, Ivo was light. He occupied his time fiddling with a number of small, half finished knick-knacks he found on table. A spring loaded fire starter sans the flint, an unimaginably small gearbox, and other such interesting if useless marvels of past technology.

There was an odd similarity among the bric a brac. Ivo could faintly make out scratches in the steady light of Roland's lantern, placed over key points on the devices. Deep, deliberate scratches, dug in with awl and hammer. Try as he might, Ivo couldn't make out the shapes, so fine were the marks.

A loud crack pulled Ivo from his musing. Looking up, he caught Roland scrambling away from the falling steel door. The brick had given way, exposing three long channels dug into the stone and hefty, rusted bolts. In a cloud of dust, the door smashed into the ground, the cacophony of metal on rock echoing through the dead halls.

A moment of silence ensued, the whole party still as stone. No one dare move, ears straining for any sign of movement ahead or behind.

Nothing.

"Really bloody subtle." Stepping towards the door, Helena grabbed Ivo by the shoulder and hauled him to his feet. "Now that that's over and done with, may we kindly get on with it?"

"All righty," Roland huffed, lifting himself up with the iron bar. "Onwards."

Helena was the first through the door, Roland's light in her hand. She looked from side to side. "Roland," she called, looking over her shoulder, "didn't you say this place was abandoned?"

"Yep," Roland nodded.

"Well, you were mistaken."

Roland stepped through the door, followed by Ivo.

The room was in stark contrast to the one adjacent. The smooth stone floor was well travelled, free of dust and debris. Sconces on the walls were set with a number of torches, unlit and ready for use. Crates and barrels, freshly made and still smelling of pine lined the walls, and racks held a number of strange tools.

"I'll be damned," Roland murmured under his breath.

"Yeah," Helena agreed, "they got a whole bloody workshop down here." She turned to Roland, asking, "Any idea what it's for."

"Well, 'course not. Nope, before my time."

"Really," Helena said as she peered around the room, paying little attention to the quartermaster. Ivo, however, knew all too well Roland did have an idea. It didn't fill Ivo with confidence.

Four arching pathways branched from the sizeable room, no doubt a warehouse for the rest of the underground complex. To their left, the outline of ascending stairs could be made out. To their right, descending. And ahead, spilt mortar and brick from a cave-in some five feet down the tunnel.

"Do you reckon we're under Dalwik proper?" Helena asked, cautiously moving forward and scanning the room.

"Yes," Roland murmured, shouldering his sledge. "This'd be under the Marlin."

"The what?" Ivo asked, eyeing up a couple crates in search for a seat.

"Dalwik's royal quarter," Roland replied. "A platform set fifty feet above the rest of the city, sky scraping towers built on top. Goes as far down as it does up."

Helena looked back.

"Eh, I mean allegedly."

Helena placed her hands on her hips. "Awful lot of inside knowledge, Roland."

"Well, you live in a city long enough."

"About fifty years?" Helena asked.

Roland coughed. "Don't know what you mean. Can't say I've seen more than fifty years."

"Cut the bullshit, Roland. You're more transparent than a concubine's top. I know you're older than you let on."

Roland was about to interject, before Helena cut him off. "I know you worked for Petyr. I know you're as old as dirt. Spare me the details, and I won't dig."

"Well, eh...okay," Roland replied meekly. He turned to Ivo. "Better not to ask questions."

"So, Roland. Up or down?" Helena asked.

"Depends," Roland replied, stepping into the centre of the room. "Up, the most heavily guarded hall north of Merchant's Choke. Down, nothing good." He turned about. "If you ask me, I'd say she's down that way. That's were Petyr liked to do business."

"Outstanding," Helena mumbled, grabbing Ivo by the shoulder. "C'mon gimpy, into the bowels of Dalwik."

Chapter Twenty-Eight

Menace. The tunnel exuded menace. The cyclopean stone was stained many hues by mould, moisture and age, growing more decrepit by the foot. It appeared as though the bricks aged as they descended, each twenty feet adding another century to the structure. The spiralling staircase became rough, Ivo stumbling time and time again on his unfit crutch.

"Careful there, Ivo," Roland said, holding an arm out to catch Ivo. "Don't want to be trippin' here. Still a ways down, I reckon."

"How far down did they dig?" Ivo asked, craning his neck to peer around the bend in the stairs.

"Well," Roland glanced over his shoulder at Helena, "when we started digging, it was to expand the royal warehouse. Before I worked for Petyr in an official capacity, that is." He paused. "Then...poor Ingward, old friend of mine, came across a weak spot in the rocks. 'Course, Ingward was the curious type, started smackin' it with a pickaxe." Roland sighed. "Hole opened up under him. Screamed for a good long time before he hit the bottom."

"Dug into a cave? How far down?" Helena piped up.

"Don't know," Roland shrugged, "I never got to work on the stairwell. Got moved to, uh, other projects."

Roland nearly tumbled forward, his foot hitting heavily on a phantom step. Caught up in his storytelling, he failed to notice the stair's end. The stones beneath his feet shifted. Momentum forced the quartermaster to take more and more steps. He was far down the hall before he regained his footing, finding a number of solid stones. "Watch the flagstones. Mortar's breakin' apart."

"This is a dead end, Roland," Helena barked, looking down the hall. "No one's been down this way for decades."

Roland tapped the stonework with the haft of his hammer. It cracked.

"'Fraid not. This stonework is five years old; it's a new style of mortar, much brighter than old stuff." He sniffed. "It's somethin' in the air. Eatin' at the rock. Mind yourself not to breathe too deeply."

Ivo covered his mouth with his stained tunic in response.

Roland turned the dial on the lantern, the flame licking the lip of the opening. It did little to illuminate the rotten hall. Oxidized sconces held decayed timber, too damp to hold a flame. The stone was pitted and streaked with stains and mould, a faint dampness visible on the great bricks. Water had found its way deep down, or perhaps bubbled up from below. Either way, a noxious aroma oozed from the walls.

The tunnel exit came up far quicker than Ivo expected, and with much less pomp. The walls and ceiling just fell away, gradually disappearing into darkness. However, as the path was swallowed by blackness, a faint, pale light came into view up ahead. A weak, frail thing, much paler than the brass clad inferno Roland held in his hand.

And yet more, piercing the gloom of the hall and the glare of Roland's light. It hypnotized Ivo, the icy glow drawing his eyes in. Roland and Helena, too, were drawn in.

"Ready up, Helena," Roland murmured. "I can't tell you what's at the end."

What was at the end was a doorway, set in a solid stone wall. It was flat cut bedrock, many sharp edged tiers narrowed to an opening, a small portal. From the domed door shone the pale light, coldly illuminating the surrounding area. The rust streaks and mould were much greater here. The finer details carved into the wall had long since smoothed, fine lines crisscrossing the stone nearly imperceptible in the feeble light. Were it not for the solid construction the wall would have given out long ago.

"Solid bedrock," Roland murmured in astonishment, bringing his lamp up. He ran the beam of light down the length of the wall, both left and right. The sheer face disappeared into darkness.

"Looks like only one way to go," Helena snorted, shouldering past Ivo. "Unless someone fancies a bit of spelunking."

Ivo inhaled deeply, standing back as Roland and Helena moved towards the door. Roland had placed his lantern on his belt, leaving his hands free to heft his hammer. Helena produced a broad, tapering, short sword and an iron-rimmed buckler from her belt. Clearly, they both identified an immediate threat; one that Ivo wasn't keen on facing. He gripped the sword at his side, the weight doing little to quell the fluttering in the pit in his stomach. His sweaty palms rubbed against the leather bindings, and the blade felt unnatural in his hands.

He could feel a niggling in the back of his head, a voice demanding he turn tail and hobble away as fast as he could manage. A compelling argument, to be sure, but one with which Ivo simply could not comply. There was the enveloping dark, of course. Should he abandon the light odds were he would lose himself in the vastness of this cave. More importantly, for the first time in his life he felt he had something to strive for, a goal he wished more than anything to complete—a life he wished to save.

"Damn it," he mumbled, clumsily drawing the arming sword. Puffing out his chest, he started after his comrades, into the pallid light at the doorway.

All sureness failed Ivo as he passed beyond the door. Gilded pillars of marble lined the vast immensity of the hall, each a masterpiece in its own right. The rot present throughout the complex seemed absent here, leaving a grandeur usually reserved for royal libraries and banks. His mouth dropped open as he surveyed the understated elegance. Beautiful simplicity.

It was not the fine decor that caused Ivo to pause. Nor was it the strange, pale glow emanating from everywhere at once. Rather, it was the great pit set in the centre. While the hall covered nearly thirty thousand square feet, over half occupied by a cavernous depression. Granite tiles lined the edges of the drop, giving the impression of a straight edge when in truth it was as jagged as broken glass. The pit seemed flat, an illusion created by the vast expanse. Upon closer inspection, it dipped drastically, twenty feet down from the lip.

Within the centre, embedded in solid rock, was a bleached, skeletal frame of something. Humanoid to be sure, arms, and legs, and all. The dimensions weren't right, however; broad shoulders and long, noble limbs denoted something else entirely. And the scale…Compared with the hooded figures alongside, it was monstrous, perhaps ten feet tall in life.

One of the hooded figures turned to the intruders, arms crossed in front. "Some respect, if you would be so kind," an elderly male voice called. It boomed through the expanse of the hall. "You stand before divinity, new and old. Please, leave us."

Roland's eyes narrowed. "Petyr…"

The figure cocked his head slightly, before pulling back his hood. The pale light illuminated a bony, primeval face. Wispy white hair clung to a liver spotted skull, blowing in a breeze felt by none other. And a scar…Despite the great distance, it burned itself into Ivo's mind. A crown, shattered in two by a pick, set on overlapping triangles.

"Ah, Roland." A demoniac grin broke Petyr's face. "It's been too long, friend. You've weathered the years spectacularly." Petyr's gaze lowered. "I do believe that charm was mine, however."

"And have the world suffer your lunacy for another century?" Roland declared, his voice falling short.

A chuckle echoed about the room. Soft at first, though regal in bearing. The mannered laugh quickly broke down, as a rising, maniacal cackle bounced off the alabaster pillars. Ivo covered his ears.

"My lunacy will know no bounds, friend," Petyr boasted, holding his arms towards the great set of bones. "It will shape the face of the world. It will restore the order we disrupted. I will mantle godhood, and in my new form, impose my lunacy upon this mortal coil!"

"Speak sense, you prick!" Helena demanded, holding her sword towards Petyr. Roland quickly stopped her, forcing he to lower her arm.

"Just give us the girl," he said. "I know she came this way."

"Far too perceptive, as always," Petyr noted. "I'm afraid she's busy assisting me on my project." He waved to the second hooded figure.

Hesitantly, the second person brought hands up to a drooping hood. Shakily, they pulled it back to reveal exotic, brown skin and raven hair. Sil. Her eyes were glazed, distant.

"Don't take it personally," Petyr said. "I doubt she was fully aware of what she was doing. Most of my agents weren't. Save Sevejo, you remember Sevejo. Blind man, in charge of sigil work."

"Yes, he died years ago," Roland growled.

"You are not the only one pushing a century, friend. Although I must admit, other agents were of mortal stock. You were lucky to come across this one." He nodded to Sil. "I doubt Borig and Rudolph are having quite as good a time."

"Leave the girl out of this!" Roland shouted.

Petyr shrugged. "Perhaps. Indeed, she's served her purpose. I got my needle back."

"Bullshit!" Roland barked. "I got it right..." He reached for his neck, grabbing at something that wasn't there.

Petyr smirked, holding up a thin, gold needle. "Light hands, this one," he said, indicating the girl. "She was a convicted thief, I believe, from the far west. Strong willed girl, fiery. Well, until we had her mind...cleaned out."

"You fucking monster," Helena shrieked. "Can't do your own dirty work, prick?"

"'Tis not befitting," Petyr dismissed, waving Sil towards the group. "Go back to your friends, girl. Be free of my bonds. Your work here is done."

She lowered her head, silently marching towards them.

"I rarely bother with mortal affairs these days."

"Ivo, grab Sil," Roland murmured, stepping forward. Helena quickly overtook him, readying her sword and buckler.

"Enough of this shit, Roland. Let's just take his head off and end this whole damn siege." She broke off into a charge, passing the shuffling Sil and ignoring Roland's warning. The quartermaster grabbed Ivo, forcing him into a sprint after Helena.

Petyr chuckled audibly. Nonchalantly, he turned the pin over in his fingers, before pricking the tip of his index finger. Instantly, he pressed the finger to his bony forearm, the exposed skin crawling with a latticework of marks. Steam hissed from the point of contact, followed by a flash of light. Ivo pulled away from Roland as they both shielded themselves. His eyes stung, and his flesh burned. For a brief moment, it was as if the sun sat not but a few feet away. Then, cold nothingness.

Ivo's vision cleared, and the vista of the sunken pit lay before him. Petyr still stood by the bones of the long dead being, faintly smoking. Helena was sprawled half way between Ivo and the mad duke. Her skin was scorched, burnt black by the heat Petyr had given off, and her sword was thrown clear of the pit. The metal of her mail coat shone brighter than silver in the pale light, fire cleaning the black finish off. What lining and padding was left now smouldered.

Roland was by Helena's side in an instant, followed by Sil. She had done away with her ceremonial robes, and now wore her usual doublet and striped pants. "Helena," she said, tears rolling down her cheeks. "I'm so sorry, Helena."

"Time for sorries later, Sil," Roland barked, throwing Helena over his shoulder. "We can talk about this after we've gone."

Ivo used the broad blade of his sword as a cane, pushing himself up and backing away from the still smouldering Petyr. He appeared immensely smug.

"By all means," he chortled, dusting off his robe, "make your escape. Flee to your city, fortify your walls." He turned the pin over in his hands. "Truly, it matters little to me. The gods left many things with their passing." He indicated the bones. "And I have mastered them." The lines on his skin began to glow, each sigil oozing power. "Now, I think it's time I took their place. It will start here. And you have the good fortune to witness it personally."

Petyr turned the needle over in his fingers once again, looking it over with a mix of reverence and nostalgia. He smirked, before plunging the point into his wrist. A sharp, high-pitched sizzle echoed through the marbled halls, as glowing crimson mist pouring from his aged veins. The light emanating from the sigils on the duke darkened. Still, Petyr drove the needle further into his skin, gritting his teeth. He did not stop until flesh had completely enveloped metal.

The spray of power-tainted blood ceased, the wound closing as the needle entered his veins. The glow returned to his marked flesh. Petyr flexed his fingers, examining his hand. Light crept through the duke's veins, running up his arms and into his neck. The glow seeped into his eyes, a sickly crimson emanating from the duke.

Ivo prepared to turn and flee, but paused noticing Roland. The quartermaster was doing his damnedest to haul the charred body of Helena away, struggling to move the bulk of the soldier and her gear. Her head lolled to the side, a soft wheeze escaping her scarred lips. She was still alive, if barely. Ivo decided, then and there, that he would keep it that way.

Petyr snorted, amused by Roland's efforts to save Helena. "You haven't changed a bit," he mused, slowly striding forward. "Always one to try and save a corpse. Shame, you had such potential."

Ivo overheard Helena groan, "Fuck...off..."

Petyr's brow furrowed. "Insolent to the end." He raised his hand, his veins burning brighter.

Sil charged towards the duke, planting herself between the two and Petyr. She stood defiantly, one arm held firmly to her chest and the other at her side.

"I have no quarrel with you, girl!" Petyr spat. "Leave before my good nature runs thin."

"You enslaved me against my will, and stripped me of my old life." Sil bared her teeth. "If that is not reason for a quarrel, I know not what is."

Petyr smirked, straightening and lowering his hand. "You would stand before a god in the making in defense of a cripple, a corpse, and a traitor. Admirable, truly. A far cry from the little shrike at my doorstep not a year ago."

While the two barked back and forth, Ivo limped to Roland. The quartermaster was making a slow go of it, the dead weight of Helena and her gear greatly hindering his timely escape. Despite this, he waved Ivo off when he attempted to assist.

"I've got this!" he assured Ivo, redoubling his efforts. "Get Sil out of here! She's playin' with fire!"

Ivo turned back to Sil and Petyr. The two had their eyes locked, Petyr adopting a much more aggressive pose. It was clear he was preparing another strike.

"Now," Roland said, "before she's a pile of ash!"

Gritting his teeth, Ivo broke into a limping scuttle. His brain begged him to stop, to turn about and bolt through the door. Muscles stiffened, and his blood ran thick. And yet he pushed on, towards Sil. Even as tongues of flame surged from Petyr's outstretched palm, Ivo pushed on. He shielded his face from the encroaching heat, seeing his time run out. At any moment, he expected to be consumed by the flame, to be reduced to cinder.

But the flame did non consume him. The heat did not envelope him. Cracking his eye open, Ivo found himself surrounded by flowing fire. But it was still unpleasantly cool, the damp frigid deep, pulling heat through Ivo's tunic.

Her hand outstretched, Sil parted the pouring flame. A fine, rimy dusting ran up her arm, her dark skin turning pale under a layer of frost. Sweat dripping from her forehead froze on her skin, falling off as small, crystalline shards. Ivo wondered how Sil managed to cool the air around her. Or perhaps absorb the flame. Ivo swore he could see the swirling frost pulling from her splayed fingers to the mark on her arm, twisting and flowing into a maelstrom of ice.

The flame abated, Sil falling forward onto her knees as the force pushing her ceased. She breathed deeply, exhaling mist. Petyr seemed no better, leaning heavily on the bones next to him.

"Heresy…" he gasped. "You channel the power of gods, wretch. Power that I must mantle. You have no right." He pushed himself up, shakily moving towards Sil. The burning light once again flowed up his wrist, igniting his eyes with a sickly aura. "Of all my servants, of all my investments," he rasped, "you've been the most disappointing."

Petyr's scowl deepened once he spotted Ivo, who despite his better judgment had pulled himself next to Sil. "The vermin act in unison." His eyebrows shot up. "You seek to displace me! You would take my throne! Undo my work." He raised his hand, embers trailing from his fingertips as he gesticulated an intricate symbol.

Petyr was unable to complete his spell. Steam fizzed from the charred stump of his wrist, his gnarled hand dropping to the stoney ground. Ivo's sword, passed to him from Roland, was burnt black along the cutting edge. He had lunged forward, severing the mad duke's hand.

Petyr looked on in disbelief, burning blood oozing from his new stump. Not in pain, but disbelief.

"You've harmed me. Impossible. I am a god. I am a god. I am..." he whispered. Ivo, paying little heed to his cryptic murmurings, was pushing himself upwards to take another wicked hack when he spotted a small, burning symbol on the floor.

Petyr's hand, brass needle still poking through blackened flesh, bore a sigil of familiar design. Overlapping triangles, a circle binding the middle. Ivo had little time to react, as Sil pulled him back onto the cold floor. She said nothing, but it became apparent to Ivo that something was wrong. The stink of cinder, the growing heat upon his flesh. Finally, the bloating, burning form of Petyr. His blood ran as molten steel, veins of white-hot power coursing through him. Then, Sil obstructed Ivo's view.

A blast of scorching ember. Then blackness.

CHAPTER TWENTY-NINE

"This...Sil," Brutus asked, turning from the window, "what of her?" The steel bindings around his lame leg grated harshly as he marched to the table of the Charred Hill's war room. Grunting, he sat down across from Ivo. "The guild masters would like to know of any loose ends to this whole mess."

Ivo exhaled, scratching the burns running up and down his sword arm. "She...didn't make it. She died saving me from Petyr. We couldn't find any of her remains." His head lowered.

"I am at liberty to disclose that she was not the only agent of her kind. Petyr had planted three such individuals. One made herself known shortly after our...tactical withdrawal from Stahlsheim. She attempted to take Borig's life, but ultimately fell short. Her head was sent to us, as a rare sign of good will against a new, common foe." He sighed. "The third...well, it would appear that this Sil acted with no ill intent. And she did contribute to the fall of a growing menace. She will have a ceremonial burial, along with those who fell at Dalwik and Stahlsheim."

"I see," Ivo replied.

"One last thing," Brutus stated, "the council and Duke Borig both agreed that Roland and yourself be given estates in the newly established Dalwik protectorate, in honour of your service to the city." Brutus leaned in, speaking in a low, harsh voice, "On the grounds that nothing more is mentioned of Petyr or his witchcraft. Understood?"

"Understood."

"Good," Brutus folded his hands. "We're done here. Now

if you excuse me, I have important business to attend to."

As if on cue, a soft mewling echoed through the far door of the room, sending Brutus shooting up in his chair. He scrambled to his feet, and rushed to the door, before settling back into his usual curmudgeon demeanour. "You may show yourself out," he told Ivo, then disappeared into the next room.

Ivo had taken a long, nostalgic stroll through the guts of the Charred Hill, as the aromas of sweat and blood, the many rotting boards, and innumerable stains met his senses. Even the old barracks, where Rook could be heard chewing out a number of new recruits made him feel wistful. No doubt his old bunk was now occupied, and his ill-fitting helmet nestled upon the brow of a bright-eyed youth. Ivo was almost sad to see it all go.

Wait, what the hell am I talking about?

Ivo stepped into the grey, faded light of Rendsheim. The smell of cinder wafted over the hulking stone walls from the great pits. Plumes of smoke flowed upwards, joining the pale mass above. The grounds of the Charred Hill teamed with activity, a swell of recruits joining the city's armies in a patriotic upwelling, having heard of Petyr's depravity.

A familiar, rotund individual could be picked from the crowd, plodding towards Ivo. At his side was a tall, bandaged figure.

"Ivo!" Roland called, waving as he approached. "They're done with grillin' ya, eh?" A hefty pat on his back nearly knocked Ivo over. His foot was still sore, making balance a tricky task.

Helena was quick to catch the wavering conscript.

"So, you got the same song and dance?" Roland asked.

Ivo grinned. "And a new house in Dalwik."

Helena snorted, her disdain muffled by heavy cloth. "You get singed and get a new house. I'm more char than human, and I got bugger all."

Roland frowned. "Come on, Helena. You know you're free to visit." He shot a glance at Ivo. "At my home at any rate. Speaking of which…" Roland looked over his shoulder.

A hooded form stood a few feet behind. "She insisted on coming to see you in person, so you two can make your way to Dalwik together."

"Are you coming along?" Ivo asked.

Roland shook his head. "Not right away, at any rate. Got to keep an eye on the old dog." He put a hand on Helena's shoulder.

Ivo smirked, looking past the two. Helena grunted.

"What are you waiting for, Hobbles? Get going."